─────────────── ★ ───────────────

Shari Baird lay on her back, her arms and legs outspread.

Anna rushed over to her and her breath caught in her throat. Shari's mouth was open wide in a grimace of pain, her pale blue eyes immense and staring. There were dark bruises on her neck. Now Anna noticed that Shari's green Sanitation shirt had been ripped open and that blood had seeped into the fabric in dark splotches. Seeing something on Shari's chest but unable to make it out, she turned her head and brought her hand to her mouth.

An ankh had been deeply carved into Shari's flesh, just above her left breast. Though crudely rendered, it was unmistakable—the loop atop the cross.

"Don't touch anything." Allen was at her side. Hal and Gerry stood a few feet away, staring in horror.

Anna had no intention of touching anything. "Call the police—fast," she said, but Gerry was shaking his head.

"No hurry. She's dead, wouldn't you say?"

She stared at him in amazement. Then she turned to Brianna, who was peeking in at the door. "Call the cops!"

─────────────── ★ ───────────────

EVIL JUSTICE

EVAN MARSHALL

W✦RLDWIDE®

TORONTO • NEW YORK • LONDON
AMSTERDAM • PARIS • SYDNEY • HAMBURG
STOCKHOLM • ATHENS • TOKYO • MILAN
MADRID • WARSAW • BUDAPEST • AUCKLAND

To my brother,
Howard Marshall,
with love

Recycling programs
for this product may
not exist in your area.

EVIL JUSTICE

A Worldwide Mystery/September 2012

First published by Severn House

ISBN-13: 978-0-373-26815-3

Printed in U.S.A.

Acknowledgments

As always, my love and thanks to my wife, Martha Jewett, my sons, Justin and Warren, and all my dear friends for their support.

I would also like to thank my agent, Maureen Walters at Curtis Brown, for always being there for me; and Edwin Buckhalter, Amanda Stewart, Megan Roberts, Piers Tilbury, Anna Telfer, and the entire staff at Severn House for being such a complete pleasure to work with.

ONE

'PAPER, LADY? Ankh Killer strikes again!'

Anna Winthrop stopped short. The young man standing with an armload of *New York Posts* at the corner of West Forty-Third Street and Ninth Avenue held a paper out to her. She fished in her pocket and, gaze fixed on the front page, absently handed him some change.

ANKH KILLER STRIKES AGAIN! screamed the headline. Anna stepped out of pedestrian traffic to read the story. The fourth victim of the serial killer who had been terrorizing Manhattan for the past three months was a twenty-seven-year-old divorcée named Paulette Edwards, owner of a nail salon called Nailed, on Eighth Avenue. Like the three previous victims, she had been strangled. Then the killer had carved his trademark ankh symbol into her chest. A homeless man rummaging in a Dumpster on West Forty-Ninth Street had found the body. Anna shuddered.

There was a photograph of Paulette, a sweet-looking young woman with big dark eyes. She had posed for the picture with her arms folded on a table in front of her, her slender fingers with their long, elaborately painted nails visible. Also visible was an ornate gold ring, which had been missing when her body was discovered. According to the police, the homeless man who found her body had not taken it, which meant her murderer had.

Stuffing the newspaper under her arm, Anna continued east on Forty-Third Street, weaving her way through the growing number of people filling the sidewalk even at

5 a.m. on a Saturday. Though her shift as a section supervisor of the New York Sanitation Department's Manhattan
Central 13 garage didn't start until six, she liked to be at
her desk early, get a jump on things.

Spotting at least a dozen men and women walking with
newspapers open before them, engrossed in the news of
the serial killer's latest victim, Anna reached the middle
of the block and passed through a gate in the chain-link
fence that surrounded the garage. Crossing the drive, she
entered the nondescript two-story tan brick building. As
she stepped into the coolly cavernous space, the door to
the stairway to the break room upstairs opened, and Kelly
Moore and Brianna Devlin emerged in their spruce-green
uniforms. Kelly was holding a newspaper open in front
of her, her intense blue eyes huge, her blonde hair hanging down as she read. Husky, dark-haired Brianna read
over her shoulder.

'Have you seen this, Anna?' Brianna asked in her deep
voice.

Anna nodded and held up her folded *Post*.

Kelly closed the newspaper with an angry rustle. 'Try
explaining that to your mother who's been begging you
to move back home to Brewster.'

Brianna frowned. 'She doesn't really think you're next,
does she?'

'Why not? Do you think this poor Paulette thought
she would be next? It could be any of us, you know that.'

'That's right,' Anna said, passing them and heading
down a corridor formed by cinder-block columns on the
left and a wall of offices on the right. 'Which is why we
have to be even more careful. No walking alone at night…
keep away from strange men—'

Behind her, Kelly laughed. 'You mean all of them?
I'll start by staying away from all the guys on our crew.'

Suppressing a chuckle, Anna entered her office and switched on the fluorescent light. On her desk sat a box of Stella D'oro cookies and three Styrofoam coffee cups. Kelly was smiling. 'It was my turn, right?'

Brianna snorted. 'Your turn! I hate to clue you, sweetheart, but you've missed about fifty turns.'

Kelly and Brianna often joined Anna for coffee in her office at the start of the day, before heading out on their collection route.

Anna sat down behind her desk as Kelly and Brianna fell into the lemon-yellow love seat—a piece of 'mongo', something good that someone's thrown out—that stood against the far wall. When Anna looked up, Kelly was poring over the newspaper again. 'There's a piece here about all the victims so far,' she said, laying the newspaper on the desk so Anna and Brianna could see.

It was a splashy double-page spread. Along the top were photographs of the four women whose lives had been taken by the Ankh Killer, their profiles underneath.

'The first,' Kelly said, reading, 'was in January. Lauri Shepard—do you remember her?' She pointed to a photo of a strong-boned woman with shoulder-length blonde hair. 'She was a firefighter with Engine Company Fifty-Four, at the corner of Forty-Eighth Street and Eighth Avenue. She was twenty-seven years old, single. She was found on Twelfth Avenue, dead in her own car, early on the morning of January twenty-sixth. She'd been strangled, her blouse torn open, an ankh carved into her chest.'

Brianna frowned. 'Just what is an *ankh*, anyway?'

'It says right here.' Anna pointed to a boxed feature in the lower right corner of the spread. '"The ankh",' Anna read, '"is an Egyptian hieroglyphic character interpreted to mean *life*".' She snorted. 'Not in this case. "It is sometimes also called the Egyptian Cross, key of the Nile, or key of life… It has been found in tomb paintings… In modern times it has been adopted by various cultural groups such as Hippie and Goth; Neopagans revere it as a symbol of life and immortality".'

The three women sat silently for a moment, sipping coffee and eating cookies. Then Anna took the newspaper and read aloud about the second victim. 'Carmela Santiago,' she said, and they all gazed down at a photo of a heavyish woman with dark hair and Hispanic features. 'She was thirty-eight and engaged to be married. She worked at the Bronx Zoo. She was found in an alley off Arthur Avenue in the Bronx, not far from her home, on February twenty-sixth. She was strangled, an ankh carved into her chest.'

Anna moved on to the third victim, pointing to a photo of a beautiful dark-haired young woman with fair, patrician features. 'Her name was Crista Sherrod. She was thirty-three, unmarried. She spoke several languages and worked as an interpreter at the United Nations. Her body was found on March twenty-sixth in a Dumpster behind One Hundred United Nations Plaza, the fifty-two-story luxury residential tower where she owned a condominium. She was from an influential family—her father is Harrington Sherrod, son of one of the founders of Sherrod Sprain, the big advertising agency. The family has been well known for generations in Darien, Connecticut.'

'And now this Paulette,' Brianna said, peering down into the woman's large, soulful eyes. 'Nice nails.'

'She owned a nail salon,' Kelly said. 'What do you expect?'

With a sudden movement, Anna closed the newspaper, giving her head a little shake so that her ash-blonde hair moved back and forth across her face. 'Let's talk about something else.'

At that moment Allen Schiff, Anna's district superintendent, popped his head into the room. "Morning, ladies. Anna, we've got an official start date for Caitlin Whitelaw. This Monday, seven to two. She'll be doing all one hundred hours of her community service here—that's a little over two weeks. And you're in charge!' he said, smiling broadly, and was gone.

When Anna turned back to Kelly and Brianna, they were practically salivating. 'Monday?' they said in unison.

Anna nodded in weary resignation. 'I'm afraid so.'

'Remind me—what was it she did?' Brianna asked.

'I know all about it,' Kelly said. 'She was at Kennedy Airport for a flight to Italy to see one of her many boyfriends. When she went through security they found a false bottom in her handbag. In it was one of those collapsible batons. She said it was a gift for the boyfriend.'

'Yeah, right,' Brianna said.

Kelly nodded. 'Everyone knows the girl is violent. Remember she beat up her maid? She had to do community service for that, too—though not here, unfortunately— and attend anger management classes. Obviously she had plans for that baton, and they didn't include gift-giving.

'Anyway,' Kelly went on, 'the airport security people arrested her. She pleaded guilty to felony possession of a dangerous weapon. Imagine…Caitlin Whitelaw, here in our garage mopping floors and cleaning toilets.'

For a moment they sat and tried to imagine this. Finally Anna shook her head. 'It does seem hard to believe.'

Caitlin Whitelaw, daughter of the Manhattan real estate tycoon Hamilton Whitelaw, was a member of what the papers were calling the Girlzillas—spoiled socialites, daughters of movie stars, minor royalty, or plain old million- and billionaires. They were the new young breed of female jet-setters, famous for being famous, rich enough to do anything they pleased…until they went afoul of the law, which seemed to be happening more and more frequently lately. Caitlin alone had been arrested several times, some of the arrests abroad, such as when she climbed naked into the Trevi Fountain in Rome and sang 'Volare', or when she dumped a pot of scalding-hot paella over the head of a waiter in Seville because the mussels were gritty.

'This is going to be such fun,' Brianna said.

Anna's brows lowered over her vivid green eyes. 'You'd better behave yourselves. Don't bother her. Treat her as you would any person who works here in the garage.'

'Yeah,' Kelly said with a smirk, 'any person who works here in the garage and is set to inherit—what?—half a billion dollars?'

Anna ignored her, reflecting that she herself, the daughter of billionaire Jeffrey Winthrop, might actually fit that category, or almost. 'As I said, no funny business.'

There was another knock and they turned. Shari Baird stood in the doorway, a big smile on her pretty face. 'Is it true, Anna?'

Anna forced herself to smile politely back. 'Is what true?'

'Caitlin Whitelaw's going to be working here? This Monday?'

Anna sighed. 'Yes, it's true. How did you know?'

'Allen told me.' Shari worked her fingers back through her dark, luxuriant curls. 'Who would ever have thought this job would be so glamorous!' she said and departed, an excited little giggle floating back to them from the corridor.

Anna knew what was coming. When Shari was safely out of earshot, Brianna ran her hands through her own dark shoulder-length hair as Shari had done and mimicked in a high voice, 'Who would ever have thought this job would be so glamorous!' Then she stuck her finger down her throat as if to gag herself.

'Brianna, stop it,' Anna scolded, barely able to keep the laughter out of her voice. 'It's not right.'

'Yeah, it's not right,' Kelly said, also laughing. 'Her voice is much higher than that.' Abruptly she scowled. 'I can't stand that woman.'

Brianna seconded the feeling. Anna, remembering to be professional, said nothing.

Shari Baird and her partner, Rob Cahill, were the newest sanitation workers on Anna's crew, having started at the garage only about a month earlier. Oddly, though twenty-five-year-old Shari was invariably sweet and little-girl-like, everyone seemed to dislike her.

'What is it, exactly,' Anna began, 'that you—all right, *we*—don't like about her? I can't quite put my finger on it.'

'Oh, I can,' Kelly said. 'She's a complete phoney. That little-girl act works wonders on the men, poor fools. It doesn't hurt that she's beautiful, with that cute little figure, that pug nose...' She narrowed her eyes to slits. 'But I'd love to see the *real* her.'

Brianna let out a loud meow. 'I've seen the real her, and it wasn't pretty.'

'What do you mean?' Kelly asked excitedly.

'I told you about it—when she was fighting with Gerry, remember?'

'Oh, right. Tell Anna about it; let's see what she thinks.'

Anna frowned. Gerry Licari was a fellow section supervisor. She had always found him easy-going and couldn't remember ever having seen him lose his temper. 'Gerry and Shari were fighting?'

'Were they ever!' Brianna said. 'It was only three days ago, on Wednesday. I was heading out to the courtyard for a cigarette. Before I got to the door, I heard a man and

a woman arguing. I could tell they were trying to keep
their voices down, but they weren't doing a very good job
of it. I stopped—'

'And eavesdropped,' Kelly said.

'Yeah, there's no law against it. After a minute I knew
the man was Gerry, but I couldn't figure out who the
woman was. She didn't sound like anyone here. Gerry
sounded furious. I had never heard him like that. He said,
"It's enough. Now it's got to stop." And the woman said,
"It will stop when I say so." And he said, "Listen, Shari,"
and I was surprised, because she didn't have her usual
little-girl voice. At that point I dropped my cigarettes.
Gerry must have heard it, because he suddenly stopped
talking. That's when I got out of there.'

Anna looked at her watch. 'And you two had better get
out of *here*,' she said good-naturedly.

Glancing at their own watches, Kelly and Brianna
jumped up and hurried out to their collection truck. Anna
tidied her desk, tucking the half-empty cookie bag into a
drawer and tossing the coffee cups. Suddenly a shadow
passed across her desk and she looked up. Gerry Licari
stared down at her, his usually pleasant face dark.

'Gerry, you scared me,' she said with a laugh.

'Was Brianna talking about me?'

'Uh—'

'I know she was. What was she saying?'

'She heard you and Shari arguing in the courtyard on
Wednesday. Is everything all right, Gerry? Shari's on my
crew. Is there anything you need me to say to her?'

He thought for a moment, staring down at the desk,
and then shook his head. 'Did Brianna hear what we were
talking about? I *thought* I heard someone.'

'No. She only heard you say something had to stop.'

His gaze met hers and he nodded abstractedly. Then

he turned and left her office. Anna followed, intending to inspect the trucks as they rolled out. Stepping into the corridor, she saw Gerry crossing the garage floor toward the break room stairs.

Far at the back corner of the garage, a movement caught Anna's eye. Deep in the shadow of a tall pile of discarded tires stood Shari. She clearly hadn't seen Anna. She was too intent on watching Gerry, her eyes as cold as stones in her little-girl face.

TWO

At lunchtime on Monday, Anna was in the break room finishing the chicken salad she'd picked up on her way to work when two members of her crew, Fred Fox and Bill Hogan, sat down and began to discuss the Ankh Killer.

'I'm telling you, my wife's afraid to go out any more,' Bill said. 'Sometimes she has to work late, and just walking from her building down to the subway scares her to death.'

He seemed pretty nervous himself, though Anna had never seen him look better. He was doing well at AA. Since she had sent him to the Sanitation Department's Medical Division for alcohol counseling, she hadn't once detected alcohol on his breath. His once-pasty skin was rosy. Was he truly nervous about the Ankh Killer, Anna wondered, or did he have on-the-wagon jitters?

Fred, small and wiry, snapped his blue eyes to Anna and gave her a frown that made him look even more like a small ferret than usual. 'What about you, Anna? Are you scared of this guy?'

Anna rose, tossing her trash into the wastebasket. She thought about it. 'Not really. You know how it is. These things always happen to someone else.' Remembering what Kelly had said—*Do you think this poor Paulette woman thought she'd be next?*—she left the break room and headed down the corridor toward the stairway.

As she put her foot on the top step, a sound came from behind her and she turned. The door to a walk-in supply closet less than a foot from the stairs had opened just enough for a man's head to poke around it. The head belonged to young Tommy Mulligan, another member of Anna's crew. He hadn't seen Anna. His expression stormy, he looked up the corridor, then down; when he saw Anna, his eyes grew immense.

'Tommy,' Anna said, frowning, 'what are you doing?'

He stepped quickly out of the closet and shut the door behind him, then gave her a big smile. 'Oh, hey, Anna, how's it goin'? I was just looking for a package of paper towels for my truck.' Holding up a pack of paper rolls, he fell into step beside her and they started down the stairs together.

They had gone only a few steps when another sound—a thump—came from behind them. As Anna turned to see what it was, she saw Tommy's face turn ashen.

'So!' he said suddenly, continuing down the stairs and crowding her a little, as if to keep her from turning around. 'What's the word on this crazy guy who's killing all these women?'

He was trying to distract her, she was sure of it. 'Tommy, what's going on?'

'Going on? What do you mean?'

'That sound came from the supply closet.' Her eyes grew wide. 'Is…someone else in there?' Could it be what she thought it was? A closet tryst wasn't like straight-shooting, third-generation-Sanitation Tommy; besides which, he'd recently become engaged to his girlfriend, Colleen, a lovely young nurse.

'I guess I should have taken one from the top,' he said, holding up the package again. 'It sounds like they fell.' He gave an easy laugh. 'I'll pick them up later.'

Now there came another, much louder sound behind them, and as they both spun around and gazed up the

stairs, the closet door flew open. It was Shari. Neaten-
ing her mussed hair, she flashed Tommy a cold look of
warning, much like the look Anna had seen on her as she
had watched Gerry from the shadows. As Shari turned to
Anna, her sweet-little-girl smile appeared. 'Oh, hi,' she
said, and turned and headed in the opposite direction,
toward the women's locker room and showers.

Tommy let out a sigh as he and Anna descended the
rest of the stairs and emerged into the vast space of the
garage. Suddenly he turned to face her. 'It's not what you
think, Anna.'

'I wasn't—'

'Yes, you were. You were thinking Shari and I were
doing something in that closet.'

'Well,' she said with a laugh she couldn't help, 'you
must have been doing *something* in that closet.'

But he didn't laugh along with her, only shook his head
and repeated solemnly, 'Not what you think,' and left her,
heading for his truck.

The stairway door opened and Shari emerged. 'I'm
sorry,' she said, approaching Anna. 'I know that kind of
thing is totally against the rules. I want you to know it
will never happen again.' She fanned her hand in front of
her face, blew out some air. 'I don't know what came over
me.' She headed for her own truck, where her partner, Rob
Cahill, was already sitting in the cab, waiting.

LATE IN THE MORNING of the following day, Anna was at her
desk catching up on some tonnage reports when Tommy
knocked on her door. He looked troubled.

Anna gave him a kind smile. She had decided to say
nothing more about the supply closet incident. 'What's
up, Tommy?'

'Can I sit down?' he asked, and when Anna nodded he

dropped on to the yellow love seat. 'Anna, you know my job means a lot to me, right?'

She frowned, puzzled. 'Yes, of course.'

'And you know I try hard to follow the rules, do things right?'

'Yes…'

'Then I'm going to ask you to please believe me when I say what happened yesterday wasn't what it looked like. I can't tell you what it *was*, but I want you to take it on faith that I would never do anything improper on the job.'

She laughed. 'Tommy, I doubt you'd do anything improper *off* the job. I do believe you. But if something's wrong—if you're in any kind of trouble—you know you can come to me, right?'

He nodded seriously. 'Thanks, Anna. I do know that.' He cast his gaze around her office, as if unsure what to say next.

'How are the wedding plans coming along?' she said, rescuing him.

He gave her a wide smile. 'Really well. We've decided to get married in September. Colleen's dad knows a guy who owns one of those fancy function halls and he's gonna give us a good deal.'

'That's wonderful, Tommy. I'm happy for you both. Now let's agree we're not going to talk any more about what happened. I do believe you, and I appreciate your coming to me like this.'

He slapped his hands on his knees and rose, clearly relieved. At the door he turned to her. 'I love Colleen, Anna. More than I thought I could ever love anybody.'

And then he was gone. The closet incident was soon forgotten as Anna became more deeply involved in her work. It wasn't until late that afternoon, as the dying sun sent long golden fingers across the garage floor, that she remembered it again.

Shari and her partner, Rob Cahill, had just pulled in and were parking their truck slantwise against the far wall. Anna watched as Shari hopped happily down from the passenger side, in sharp contrast to Rob, who climbed down and slammed his door so hard the clang echoed through the warm air. Looking furious, he saw Anna and started toward her.

Then Shari did an interesting thing. When she saw where Rob was heading, she cut him off, hurrying over to Anna and planting herself in front of her. Rob stopped suddenly, took this in, and stormed off.

'Anna,' Shari said breathlessly, 'can we talk for a minute?'

Anna watched Rob go through the door to the break room stairs. 'Uh, sure.'

In Anna's office, Shari forewent the love seat in favor of a chair beside Anna's desk. Before she sat, she scooted the chair forward a good twelve inches, so that her face was now close to Anna's.

'What's up?' Anna asked, uncomfortable.

Shari lowered her head, on her face an expression of pure shame. Slowly, without raising her head, she looked up at Anna from under smoky lids. 'I'm sorry about what happened yesterday, Anna. I wanted to say something sooner but…well, I guess I just didn't know what to say. I'm so embarrassed.'

'Embarrassed? Why?'

Shari flushed a dark red. 'Why do you think, Anna? That's no way to behave on the job. I don't know what came over me. Well, actually,' she amended with a tiny smile, 'I do. Tommy can be a lion. When he gets like that, he's impossible to say no to.'

Anna frowned. 'Whoa, hold it, Shari. Are you telling me you and Tommy—'

Before Anna could finish, Shari nodded quickly. 'Of course. I could tell you knew as soon as you saw us. Anyway, I wanted to tell you I'm sorry and that it will never happen again. I'm going to speak to Tommy and tell him it's over.'

'"It" being your affair?'

'Yes.'

'What would you say if I told you Tommy said nothing improper happened in that closet?'

Shari tossed back her head and laughed—a pretty, tinkling laugh. 'What would I say? I'd say he's engaged, that's what I'd say.' She rose. 'Thanks so much, Anna. Like I said…never again.' She turned to leave.

'Shari—' Anna said, and Shari spun around. 'I understand you were having some trouble with Gerry last week.'

Shari's expression grew cold. 'Is that what he was telling you on Saturday?'

Anna, saying nothing, simply stared.

Finally Shari said, 'Who heard us?'

'That doesn't matter. Shari, part of my job as section supervisor is to make sure everyone on my crew gets along. I don't know what you and Tommy were doing in that closet—'

'But I just told you—'

Anna cut her off with a raised hand. 'I know what you told me. Tommy told me otherwise. He didn't, however, say what *was* going on. But whatever it was, I'll bet it shouldn't have been happening. Then I find out you and Gerry were arguing in the courtyard. That makes two people with whom you've interacted inappropriately. A few minutes ago, your partner slammed the door of your collection truck and stomped off. That's three.'

Shari made a dismissive noise and rolled her eyes. 'Rob is such a priss. I made a joke he said was "off color", and not appropriate coming from a woman. Sexist pig.'

'All right,' Anna said, accepting that explanation for now. 'And what was the problem between you and Gerry?'

The cold look returned. 'Didn't Gerry tell you?'

'No,' Anna answered truthfully, 'he didn't. But he's not on my crew; you are.' She waited.

'It was nothing. He's another hypersensitive one. I had been teasing him. He wanted me to stop. So I stopped.'

'Teasing him about what?'

Shari shrugged. 'I…It's embarrassing to say it. I told him he had a great backside.'

'You *what*?'

The younger woman nodded. 'It was meant in fun. But Gerry said he's a happily married man and that I had to stop. So, like I said, I stopped.'

Anna scrutinized Shari's face. Shari was waiting, clearly to see if Anna would buy her explanation.

'I don't believe you,' Anna said at last.

Shari looked hurt. 'I have no reason to lie. And I'm sorry if it looks like I'm not getting along with people here.'

'Looks like! You're not.'

Shari seemed to ignore this. 'Anna, I really need this job. The last thing I would do is jeopardize it. You have no idea what my life was like before this.'

Much as she disliked Shari, Anna found herself interested in what she would say. She gave a small nod of encouragement.

'This job has done wonders for my self-assurance,' Shari said. 'I guess my lack of confidence is the reason I haven't been able to land good jobs before this one.'

A lack of confidence? Anna almost burst out laughing. She let Shari go on.

'I'm sure my confidence problem is because of my childhood. We were really poor. We lived in a trailer park in a little town in Kentucky.' Shari hung her head in shame. After a moment she looked up again. 'I'll tell you the truth. My father abused me from an early age. I was an only child, you see, and my mother died when I was an infant. She was killed when a train hit her car.'

'How horrible,' Anna said.

Shari nodded sadly. 'That left me alone with Dad. He was a hopeless alcoholic. I can't remember a time when I wasn't fighting him off. It was horrible. I got out of there as soon as I could.'

'How old were you?'

'Seventeen. I'd planned it carefully. I'd been saving what money I could from the jobs I'd had—waitress, cashier, that kind of thing. When I felt I had enough to get away, I waited until Dad passed out one night and slipped away. I had enough to get to New York. I've had all kinds of jobs here, but they weren't any better than the ones I'd had in Kentucky. Then I found out about the Sanitation Department.'

'How?' Anna asked.

'Actually,' Shari replied, 'it was because of you.'

'Me?'

Shari nodded. 'I read a story in the newspaper about how you solved the murder of that homeless man. There was some information about you—how you'd worked your way up from sanitation worker to supervisor. I thought, "That's what I want to do." So I found out what I needed to do. I took the Civil Service exam, applied for the job… and got it. I was so happy. The best part is that I love this work as much as I thought I would.

'So you see, I would never do anything to put my job in jeopardy. I want to get along with everyone. If I've made a few mistakes in judgment, I'm sorry. I'll work hard to do better in the future.'

Shari rose and gave Anna a grateful smile. 'I appreciate your listening, Anna. I want to be the best I can be at my job. I'm always interested in any advice you might have. Like I said, you're a role model to me.'

AT THE END OF her shift, Anna went up to the women's locker room and changed from her uniform into jeans, a silk top, and sandals. She had a drinks date with her sister Gloria at a café near New York Presbyterian Hospital, where Gloria was doing her residency. Anna intended to walk to the Upper East Side and enjoy the warm April air.

Leaving the locker room, she found Rob Cahill leaning against the wall of the corridor. He looked up sharply, his eyes troubled.

'Sorry, Anna, I didn't mean to ambush you.' He took in her street clothes. 'I guess you gotta get goin'.'

She didn't have to walk. 'No, Rob,' she said kindly, 'I've got some time. It seems like you need to talk.'

He nodded eagerly, like a little boy—though he was anything but: tall, muscular, with a sandy-colored moustache that matched his hair, and eyes even greener than her own in a rugged, masculine face.

'Let's have a drink,' she said, and together they left the garage and headed over to Hurley's, a bar a couple of blocks from the garage.

'Drinks are on me,' Rob said when they were seated, and Anna wondered if he had ever let a woman buy him a drink.

'All right,' she said amiably. 'I'll have a gin and tonic.'

'Coming right up,' he said, and ordered that along with

a beer for himself. As the waitress walked away, his gaze was on her bottom, but Anna could tell he wasn't really looking.

'What's on your mind, Rob?'

Nervously he grabbed a handful of bar mix, then started picking out the peanuts and popping them into his mouth. 'I never thought I'd be having this conversation. You know me, Anna, I get along with everybody...'

'Rob,' she said, not unkindly, 'let's cut to the chase. Let me guess. You want a new partner.'

He looked at her in amazement. 'How did you know?'

She started to reply, then just shook her head. 'Call me psychic. So what's the problem?' She smiled. 'Shari's off-color jokes?'

He wrinkled his brows, puzzled. 'Huh?'

'Shari said she told you a joke you felt was unsuitable coming from a woman.'

He slowly shook his head in wonder. 'She told you that? She's unbelievable. That's not what happened at all.'

'Then tell me what did happen.'

He finished the bar mix in his hand and looked away.

'OK,' he said at last, turning back to her. 'She came on to me.' At Anna's look of surprise, he nodded. 'It was right in the middle of our route. I'm dumpin' a trash can into the hopper. When I turn around, she's watching me with a funny look on her face. She says, "You're so strong. I need a strong man to help me with something at my apartment." When I ask her what the trouble is, she wiggles her eyebrows and says it's "her pipes".'

Anna nearly choked on her water. 'Her pipes?'

'Yep. I told her what she could do with her pipes.'

She could see why Rob wanted a new partner, and said as much.

'That ain't the half of it,' he said. 'Listen to what she

pulled last week. We were on Broadway, servicing the litter baskets. One minute Shari's heading around the truck, I figured to empty a basket. The next minute, she's gone.'

'Gone?'

'Yeah. She just disappears. I didn't know what to do. I waited a little bit, thinking she'd be back, but after about five minutes I realized I better get goin', so I went on without her.'

'Did she come back?'

'Yeah,' he said, shaking his head in wonder. 'Three blocks up Broadway I see her comin' outta this alley next to one of those electronics shops. She doesn't look at me, doesn't say nothin', just hops up into the truck like nothin' happened.'

'Did you say anything?'

'You bet I did.' The waitress set down their drinks. Rob took a long sip of his beer. 'I asked her where she disappeared to. And you know what she told me? "I needed a cigarette".'

'A cigarette?'

'Mm-hm, calm as you like. Well, you know me, Anna—or maybe you don't know me so well. I let her have it. I told her no partner o' mine was going to disappear like that. I told her this was a joint operation and I wasn't gonna put up with somebody who didn't carry her share o' the weight. She's poison. I can't work with her. I hate her. We never even speak. And she's givin' me a bad name.'

'What do you mean?'

'People who live on our route are starting to give us *both* dirty looks, and that ain't fair, not when I don't do nothin' I shouldn't. She's the one who doesn't know how to treat people.'

'How, exactly, has she not treated people properly?'

'She's got a wicked temper. For instance, a couple o'

weeks ago, we were servicing this apartment building on Fifty-Fourth Street and the superintendent comes out and tells us to stop leavin' the trash cans all over the sidewalk. I apologize to the guy, tell him it won't happen again, and he nods and starts walkin' back into the building. Meanwhile, Shari grabs one of the trash cans and throws it at his back.'

Anna sat up in surprise. 'Was he hurt?'

'No, but he was furious. He said he was going to file a complaint. I figured that would take care of her, so I didn't say nothin' to you about it. But I guess the guy didn't complain after all, 'cause you didn't know about it.'

'No, I didn't,' Anna said, already thinking about what she would say in her report recommending that Shari Baird be suspended.

THREE

By THE TIME Anna left Hurley's it was nearly four o'clock.
She and Gloria had agreed to meet at four thirty. She hailed
a cab at Forty-Third and Sixth.

Traffic was heavy. When she got out of the cab at East
Sixty-Eighth and York Avenue it was nearly a quarter to
five. She hurried along the hospital drive and was nearly
to the entrance when Gloria came out in her white doctor's coat.

She looked awful. The straight blonde hair she was so
vain about hung to each side of her face like ragged curtains. Her pretty face was devoid of make-up—unusual
for Gloria—and her shoulders were hunched. As Anna
got closer, she could see that her sister had been crying.

'Gloria,' Anna said, concern in her voice. She put an
arm around her sister's shoulders, leaned toward her.
'What's the matter?'

Gloria brought out a wad of tissues from the pocket of
her coat and blew her nose. 'I need to talk to you.'

'Yes, of course. We're having drinks, remember?'

Gloria shook her head vehemently. 'No, I can't go out
like this. I want to go to your place.'

Anna didn't argue. She stepped up to the edge of the
hospital's circular drive and grabbed a cab someone had
just left. Once they were seated inside and heading down
York, Anna said, 'Can you tell me now?'

'It's Donald.' Gloria had been married to Donald Stone,
a plastic surgeon, for ten months.

'Is he all right?'

'Oh, he's fine!' Gloria shouted, and both Anna and the cab driver jumped.

Suddenly Anna suspected what this was about. Donald was perhaps the most handsome man Anna had ever met—short on personality, long on handsome. Anna imagined that women threw themselves at him all the time. Had Donald caught one of them? 'What has he done?'

Gloria looked up and frowned, as if only now aware that there was another person in the car with them. 'I'll tell you when we get to your place.'

The driver's shoulders fell. Gloria said nothing until they were pulling up in front of Anna's apartment building on West Forty-Third between Ninth and Tenth avenues.

As they entered the building's vestibule, a door opened on the right. Anna drew in her breath. She and her downstairs neighbor, Iris Dovner, were in a constant state of war. Past battles had involved Anna making too much noise in her high heels (Mrs Dovner banged her ceiling with a broomstick) and Anna giving her empty cans and bottles to homeless people (Mrs Dovner called the police). It was anyone's guess what the cause of the next skirmish would be.

From around the door came the elderly woman's head—a ball of flyaway white hair around a deeply wrinkled face. Her body followed, enveloped in one of her immense muumuus, this one a vivid turquoise with stylized fish all over it. On her feet she wore sparkly gold mules adorned with fluffy pink feathers.

Gloria stopped and stared at her, as if unsure what she was. Anna realized they had never met.

'Hello, Mrs Dovner,' Anna said, making an effort to be pleasant. This was no time for a fight. 'I'd like you to meet my sister, Gloria.'

'Hi,' Gloria said through her stuffed-up nose.

Mrs Dovner gave one begrudging nod. Then she appeared to notice that Gloria had been crying. 'You all right? We don't need any trouble here.'

Anna stiffened.

'Trouble?' Gloria looked baffled. 'What kind—?'

'Never mind, Gloria,' Anna said, and faced the older woman. 'There won't be any trouble, Mrs Dovner…unless you make it! Come on,' she said to her sister, and practically dragged her up the stairs. From below came the slamming of Mrs Dovner's door.

'What on earth—?' Gloria said as she entered Anna's apartment.

'She's not worth explaining,' Anna said with a wave of her hand. 'Sit. I'll make some tea.'

Gloria sat on the sofa like a mouse until Anna appeared with the tray. It wasn't until she had taken a sip that she composed herself and announced, 'Donald's having an affair.'

So Anna was right. 'Oh, Gloria.'

'With one of his nurses. Isn't that a cliché?'

'Yes, but that doesn't make it any less painful. How could he, that rat!'

Gloria nodded quickly in agreement. 'We haven't even been married a year, Anna. What am I going to do?'

'Hold it. Back up. What exactly is going on? How did you find out?'

Gloria set down her cup. 'It wasn't hard. Donald may be a great surgeon, but when it comes to everyday things he's pretty dumb. I was taking his clothes to the cleaners and found a credit card receipt in the pocket of one of his blazers. Another cliché. It was from Bar Americain. Anna, that's *our* place. How could he?'

'Maybe it was for business,' Anna offered hopefully.

'Oh, it was business all right. Funny business. When he got home last night, I asked him about it. His face turned snow white and his eyes got huge, like a deer in the headlights. He didn't even deny it; he just started saying he was sorry.'

'Who is she?' Anna asked.

'I told you, a nurse. Her name is Helene. I even know her! And I swear, Anna, she's not nearly as pretty as I am.'

Anna had no response to this. 'So what did you say when he apologized?'

'I told him to leave, but he wouldn't. He said the apartment was as much his as mine, and that if I didn't want to be with him, I could leave.'

'And did you?'

'No. It was late. I slept in our bedroom and he slept in the guest room. When I got up this morning he was already gone. I can't go back there, Anna.'

'Then where will you go?' Anna asked, but a dark foreboding had crept into the pit of her stomach.

'I want to stay here with you.'

Anna opened her mouth to speak but Gloria rushed on. 'I can't go all the way home to Mom and Dad in Greenwich. It's forty-five minutes away.'

'But what about Beth and Will?' Anna asked, referring to their youngest sister and older brother, who both lived in Manhattan.

'No. Beth warned me not to marry Donald. I can't take her *told-you-so*s. And Will and Lisa have their hands full with little Nina.'

'And I don't have my hands full?' Anna asked before she realized she shouldn't have.

'Don't you want me here? Oh, excuse me,' Gloria said, a nasty tone coming into her voice, 'I forgot how busy you are with all of your garbage.'

Anna's occupation was practically an obsession for Gloria, who periodically tried to steer Anna to professions she deemed more suitable for the daughter of billionaire Jeffrey Winthrop of Greenwich, Connecticut.

'Don't start,' Anna warned. 'It isn't that I don't want you here, it's…' That Gloria was a pushy, opinionated know-it-all and that she had a difficult time spending more than half an hour at a time with her? No, she couldn't say that. Her shoulders dropped in resignation. 'Of course you can stay with me.'

Gloria gave her a pouty smile. 'Thanks. I promise I won't be any trouble. Just until I figure out what I'm going to do.' She brightened. 'It'll be fun! Just us girls.'

'Mm,' Anna said absently, already wondering whether it would be Mrs Dovner or Gloria who would drive her insane first.

THAT NIGHT, Anna's boyfriend, Santos, called. 'Want to catch a movie or something? Maybe get a bite to eat?'

'I wish I could,' Anna whispered, 'but Gloria's here and I think I'd better stay with her.'

'Is she all right?'

'Physically, yes. Mentally, she's a mess. I'll explain when I see you.'

'OK. Miss you,' he said, and hung up. When Anna turned around, Gloria was standing only a few feet away. She wore one of Anna's robes. It was obvious she had heard what her older sister said.

'It's OK,' Gloria said. 'You're right. I'm a total mess. I've got to get ahold of myself. Come sit down, Anna. Tell me what's going on in your life.'

It was, Anna realized, the first time Gloria had ever asked her that. They sat down on the sofa in Anna's living room and Anna told her what was going on at work—specifically, what Shari Baird had been up to.

'Oh, she's trouble, Anna. You'd better get rid of her.'

'I intend to. Though I certainly can't deal with it on Monday. That's when Caitlin starts.'

No sooner were the words out of her mouth than Anna realized what she had said. She stared wide-eyed at Gloria.

'Caitlin? Caitlin who?'

'Never mind.'

'Anna…' Years ago, when they were little girls, if Gloria said Anna's name in that tone, she usually followed it with a tackle.

Anna sighed. What did it matter? It would be world news. 'Caitlin Whitelaw.'

Gloria, ever the gossip-monger, gasped. 'You mean community service? At your garbage garage?'

'I've told you, Gloria, there's almost never any garbage in the garage. Only when the trucks return partly filled—'

'Yeah, whatever. And you're in charge of her? Unbelievable. When would be the best time for me to stop by?'

'Stop by!' Anna faltered. '*No* time would be the best time. It will already be a circus. You stay away, Gloria, I'm warning you.'

Gloria pushed out her lower lip. 'All right. I just thought it would be fun. I think she's divine.'

'Divine?'

'Absolutely. Beauty, wealth…and such style. Have you ever been to one of her parties?'

Anna laughed. 'No, I think I was accidentally left off the guest list.'

'No, no, not that kind of party. She hosts parties at clubs. She's sort of a party promoter. I hear they pay her millions.'

'Like she needs millions.'

'That's irrelevant, Anna. We should know that. You and I and Beth and Will have big fat trust funds, thanks to Daddy. If we didn't want to, we wouldn't have to work a day in our lives, but we all do. Just like Caitlin.'

Anna hated talking about this. Ever since their father and his partner had sold their company, Winthrop and Carnes Medical Products, to Johnson & Johnson, making themselves instant millionaires, Anna had, for some reason she couldn't quite explain, been a little embarrassed by her family. She never spoke about her parents at the garage. How would Kelly and Brianna react? she sometimes wondered. Santos knew, of course—had even met her family—but that was different.

'Anyway,' she said, 'you are not to come by. I'll be happy to tell you anything you want to know.'

'All right,' Gloria said, despondent. 'Pay attention to what she's wearing.'

'What she's wearing? I hope that to sweep the floors and brush the toilets she'll be wearing old jeans and a T-shirt.'

Gloria shrugged.

The phone rang. Anna leaned over to the end table and grabbed it. It was Donald. She pointed meaningfully to the phone.

'Don't you dare tell him I'm here!' Gloria whispered.

'No, Donald,' Anna said pleasantly, 'I'm afraid she's not. Is everything all right?'

'Uh…yes, fine,' he replied in an unconvincing tone. 'Listen, if you hear from her, tell her to call me, OK?'

'Of course,' she said, and replaced the receiver. 'Don't you think it's cruel to make him worry like this?'

'No more cruel than what he did to me. If he's lonely

he can call Helene. Now,' she said, changing the subject, 'let's go online and see what else we can find out about Caitlin Whitelaw.'

FOUR

At ROLL CALL on Monday morning, Anna broke the news
to the few who didn't already know.

'We're going to have a special guest with us over the
next two weeks. Caitlin Whitelaw will be doing community service here in the depot, and I expect each and every
one of you to be on your best behavior. You are to show
her courtesy and respect. You are to treat her as you would
treat anyone else here at the garage. You are not to stare
at her or try to engage her in conversation. You are not to
take pictures of her with your cell phone; if you do, your
phone will be confiscated and you will be subject to suspension. Is that clear?'

She looked at each of the sanitation workers before her,
gauging reactions.

Kelly and Brianna each wore a little smirk. Ferret-like
Fred Fox shifted his glance about, as if trying to figure out
what everyone else was thinking. Beside him, his partner,
Bill Hogan, looked blank.

Seventy-five-year-old Art Lederer, with his gray buzz
cut and gentle blue eyes, looked puzzled. Anna was sure
he had no idea who Caitlin Whitelaw was. His partner,
Terrence King, of short stature and in his early fifties, was
as unreadable as ever.

Tommy Mulligan looked vaguely troubled. His partner,
Pierre Bontecou—like Tommy, in his twenties—was looking at Anna, a big smile on his good-looking dark face.

Pablo Rodriguez and Ernesto Balcazar, both in their

early thirties and with similar stocky builds, appeared uninterested and eager to get to work, shifting from foot to foot and gazing about.

At the end of the line, Rob Cahill stood as far from his partner, Shari Baird, as possible, his gaze trained straight ahead. Shari wore her usual darling-little-girl expression, beaming happily. Anna half expected her to take out a lollipop.

'That's it,' Anna said. 'I hope you all have a great day.'

On the way to her office she checked her watch: it was 6:20, forty minutes before Caitlin was due to arrive. When she entered her office, Allen Schiff was sitting on the yellow love seat.

'I hate to add to your workload,' he said, consulting a clipboard overflowing with disheveled papers, 'but I've got a new person coming for you today.' He held up the clipboard and on the top sheet Anna saw the letters *WEP*. She knew what was coming. The city's Work Experience Program gave Welfare recipients work assignments in exchange for their benefits. Since Anna had been promoted to supervisor nearly three years ago, only a few WEP participants had been assigned to Manhattan Central 13. For the most part they had been good workers, providing cleaning and maintenance help the garage always needed. The problem was supervising these people, which Anna found far too time-consuming to be worth the extra help.

But she had no choice. 'You don't mean today, Allen?'

''Fraid so.' He flipped back the top sheet, scanned the page underneath. 'Woman by the name of Lorraine Canady. Fifty-two, lives not far from here, on West Forty-Sixth Street.'

'And she'll be doing...?'

'You know, the usual. Sweeping, cleaning the bathrooms and showers...'

'In other words, exactly what Caitlin Whitelaw will be doing.'

He looked at her. 'Yeah, I suppose it is. I'm sure they'll make a great team.'

'Funny, Allen, very funny,' she said, and watched him go.

At her door he turned back. 'She'll be here at seven.'

The same time that Caitlin was arriving. She checked her watch again. Ten minutes to go. When Anna had arrived at the garage at 5:30, she had found none of the paparazzi she had expected at the gate. She decided to take a look now.

As she left the building, the chain-link fence came into view and, behind it, a solid mass of people that filled the street. At the left of the crowd, toward Broadway, three police cruisers sat with lights flashing. She scanned the people, looking for the cops themselves, but saw none.

'Looking for someone?'

She spun around. 'Santos! What are you doing here?'

His tanned face burst into a dazzling white smile. 'What do you think? Somebody's got to make sure this circus doesn't get out of hand.'

She glanced over at the crowd and now spotted two news vans. Then she turned to look back at Santos, tall, slim, and so handsome in his dark-blue uniform. Another cop approached him; Anna recognized him as Margolin, a buddy of Santos who had gone through the Academy with him. He nodded a hello to Anna, then turned to Santos. 'Party time. Dark SUV on its way,' he said, and pointed east. A forest-green Ford Explorer was indeed heading their way, moving slowly to negotiate the crowd. The vehicle pulled up to the chain-link gate.

'Later, Anna,' Santos said, and hopped over to where several other cops were waiting for the SUV. Now another man appeared—Anna couldn't tell from where—and she recognized him as Sanitation Police Lieutenant Mark Edwards. Allen Schiff appeared beside Anna, and Edwards approached them both and greeted them.

'I take it you're in charge of our special guest,' Allen said to Edwards.

Edwards smiled. 'Lucky me. Maybe she'll give me her autograph.' He turned suddenly because the SUV had come to a stop at the gate, which the other police officers were now opening.

The vehicle's door began to slide slowly open. The crowd surged in from each side, necks craning to get a look at Manhattan's bad girl.

From out of the SUV stepped an overweight, middle-aged African American woman in worn, too-tight jeans and a faded red T-shirt.

Collectively the crowd groaned in disappointment.

'Who's that?' Anna said.

Allen raised the clipboard he was still carrying. 'I told you. Lorraine Canady, Work Experience Program.'

Lorraine heard her name and looked up uncertainly. Allen, ever chivalrous, stepped forward. Anna heard him introduce himself. Then Lorraine looked back into the SUV and told whoever was driving, 'It's OK. I'll see you later.' She slid the door shut and the vehicle drove off.

'Anna,' Allen said, leading Lorraine over. Anna noticed that she limped slightly. 'I'd like you to meet Lorraine Canady, who'll be working here as part of the Work Experience Program. Lorraine—Anna Winthrop.'

As Anna took Lorraine's hand, the older woman gave her a kind smile. 'It's nice to meet you, Ms Winthrop.'

'Please—call me Anna.'

'Anna.'

Lorraine turned back to the street and laughed. 'I guess they knew I was coming.'

'Well, actually, they're here for Caitlin Whitelaw,' Anna began, then saw the twinkle in Lorraine's deep brown eyes.

'Everybody knows that,' Lorraine said. 'It looks like she and I will be doing pretty much the same job.'

'True,' Allen said with a laugh, then turned to Anna. 'I'll get started on the paperwork with Lorraine while you're out here.' He and Lorraine entered the garage.

Anna turned back to the street. A murmur rose from the crowd: another car was making its way slowly down the street, but this one was no SUV. It was a silver Rolls-Royce, not unlike one Anna's father had once owned.

Edwards hurried forward as the beautiful car slid to a stop. A black-uniformed chauffeur hopped out and came around to open the door. When he did, nothing happened at first. Now the crowd held its collective breath, waiting for Caitlin to emerge. At last they were rewarded.

A very pointy silver Manolo Blahnik pump appeared, followed by a slim ankle, a long, shapely leg, then the other leg, and at last the shoes touched the pavement and Caitlin herself emerged, an angelic vision with her silky blonde hair blown perfectly by an obliging breeze. Edwards stepped forward, said a few words to her, and she smiled and nodded. The chauffeur reached into the car, brought out an orange crocodile Hermès Birkin, and started to follow. Edwards stopped him, said something, then looked embarrassed when the chauffeur nodded coolly and plopped the bag into his arms.

'Cait! Caitlin!' the reporters screamed, and like a compass finding due north the young woman swiveled around and smiled her trademark gummy smile. A thousand cameras flashed.

'Hey, Caitlin!' a reporter cried. 'How do you think it will feel to have to work like the rest of the world?'

'I don't know!' Caitlin replied without missing a beat. 'I've never done it!'

The crowd laughed, loving her. She squealed with delight.

'That's enough of that,' Anna heard Edwards mutter, and he stepped purposefully forward, handing Caitlin her bag. In her heels she was slightly taller than he was. As she listened to him, she turned her head slightly, a look of intense concentration on her face. Finally she gave one nod.

'I'm here to work!' Anna heard her squeal, and then Edwards was leading the socialite into the building.

'Caitlin! Caitlin!' the crowd hollered after her, but Caitlin had disappeared with Edwards into the darkness of the depot.

Inside, Anna found Kelly and Brianna standing not far from Allen's office, waiting.

'Scat!' she told them.

'Aw, Anna...' Kelly groaned.

'Remember what I told you,' Anna warned them.

'Come on, Kelly,' Brianna said, leading her partner away. 'She'll be here for two weeks. We'll have our chance.'

Anna opened her mouth to respond to that, but at that moment Allen poked his head out of his office door. 'Anna, could you come in here for a moment, please?'

Arriving in Allen's doorway, Anna was met with a strange sight. Allen had in his office a love seat similar to Anna's, except that it was tan with brown and gold stripes. On its right side sat Caitlin, cool and slim and beautiful in her gossamer pale-violet dress, her posture perfect, those amazing legs tucked modestly to one side. On the left sat Lorraine. Her jeans, which Anna now saw were covered

in white cat hair, strained at the waist. On her feet were
heavy brown paratrooper boots, definitely not Manolos.

Anna stared, transfixed. 'Anna,' Allen said, breaking the spell, 'you've met Lorraine but not Caitlin. Anna
Winthrop—Caitlin Whitelaw.'

Anna leaned forward politely and shook the socialite's
soft hand, at the same time getting a whiff of some exotic,
no doubt insanely expensive fragrance. 'A pleasure,' Anna
said. Caitlin beamed. She looked, it occurred to Anna,
as if she'd arrived here to attend some wonderful party.

'Now,' Allen said, clearing his throat, and addressed
the two women. 'You're both here to do pretty much the
same kind of work, so let's go over it.' And he proceeded
to outline their duties—mopping and sweeping the garage
floors, vacuuming offices, and cleaning the bathrooms,
locker rooms, and showers upstairs. Anna excused herself and returned to her office. As she sat down, her phone
rang.

'Is she there?' It was Gloria.

Anna let out an exasperated sigh. 'Yes, she's here, Gloria. Are you going to call and ask me that every day?'

'Don't be so grouchy, Anna. You haven't just lost the
love of your life.'

That was Gloria, always so dramatic. And Anna sincerely doubted that Donald was the love of Gloria's life;
she had made comments in the past that made it clear she
saw him simply as a highly appropriate husband. She was
fond of him, of course, but Anna was pretty certain that
was about as far as it went.

'She's very pretty, isn't she?' Anna said, taking pity
on her sister.

'What is she wearing?'

'A beautiful dress of some wispy violet-colored mate-
rial—very spring-y.'

'Yeah…?' Gloria encouraged her.

'And these amazing strappy silver shoes. Manolos, I'm sure of it, because I've seen them somewhere on Fifth Avenue. Oh, and a Birkin. Orange croc!'

'Wow…' Gloria breathed, then Anna heard her speaking to someone in the background. 'Anna, I've gotta go. What are we doing about dinner tonight?'

Anna paused, taken aback. Gloria sounded as if they'd always lived together and always would—a terrifying thought.

'I…really hadn't thought about it. I don't usually do anything fancy—maybe a salad, some fruit from Mr Carlucci's,' she said, referring to her favorite produce stand.

'We'll go out,' Gloria said. 'My treat. Well, I better run.'

'Wait a minute,' Anna said. 'What about Donald?'

'What about him?'

'Have you spoken to him? What's going on?'

'Nothing's going on, Anna. Has he called again since that one time? No. I guess he's not much interested, now that he's got Helene.'

'Gloria, I promised him I would call him if I heard from you; that's how we left it.'

'He still should have called again.'

Anna shook her head impatiently. 'But how do *you* feel? Don't you want to speak with him?'

'About what?'

'About the two of you. Your marriage. You can't avoid him forever.'

'Anna, darling,' Gloria said slowly, 'I'm not avoiding him. Avoiding someone suggests that you're together. Donald and I are finished. I don't want a man who would cheat on me before our first anniversary. The next thing I'm doing is calling my lawyer. I'll see you tonight.'

With a sigh, Anna replaced the receiver. That was

Gloria's pain talking, she was sure of it. There had to be a way Gloria and Donald could work things out, a way she could forgive him. Amazingly handsome, successful surgeon Donald had looked past Gloria's pushiness and lack of self-knowledge to the truly kind, well-meaning person inside. How many men would be willing to do that?

Anna heard voices in the corridor outside her office and lifted the blind on the window to peer out. Allen Schiff walked by, followed by Lorraine and Caitlin, who were chatting amiably. Lorraine wore an orange safety vest over her jeans and T-shirt. Caitlin had traded her wood nymph dress for crisp dark trouser jeans and a T-shirt in a pink and white faux camouflage pattern that clashed with the Day-Glo orange of her vest. She, too, wore heavy boots, except that unlike Lorraine's, these were brand new, no doubt purchased for this occasion.

'I've never done anything like this,' Anna heard Caitlin tell Lorraine. 'Is it very hard?'

Lorraine shot Caitlin a dark look but said nothing. This should be interesting, Anna thought, and started to let the window blind drop when something caught her eye and she stopped. Far across the garage, in the shadow of the stack of discarded tires, stood Shari, watching the two women—no, watching Caitlin, Anna amended. Shari had that inscrutable look on her face again, her eyes narrowed slightly, her expression anything but darling.

If there were any chance that Shari would be staying on Anna's crew, Anna would have gone out to speak to her. But Anna's next item of work was to write up a report recommending Shari's suspension. If she had her way, the troublesome young woman would be gone by the end of the week. She swiveled to her computer monitor and started typing.

MUCH TO ANNA'S SURPRISE, Caitlin did quite well her first day, not only performing her duties cheerfully and efficiently but also becoming positively chummy with Lorraine. At lunchtime the two women sat together in the break room, Lorraine eating a turkey sandwich she had brought from home, Caitlin picking at a duck breast salad her father had had delivered from Dean & Deluca. Anna had stationed herself at the table to ward off any possible interlopers.

A little before two o'clock, Anna was crossing the garage toward the break room stairs when the door opened and Caitlin and Lorraine came out. They were laughing, their rapport so easy that they might have been friends for years.

Seeing Anna, Caitlin smiled and hurried over. 'I think it's the end of my…shift, huh, Anna?' She giggled. Lorraine was smiling, clearly amused by the younger woman.

'That's right,' Anna replied. 'How did the afternoon go?' she asked both women.

Lorraine shrugged as if to say 'fine'.

Caitlin giggled. 'I had no idea work could be such fun.'

'No problems?' Anna asked.

'Nope,' Caitlin answered, but Lorraine stepped forward. 'There was something upstairs…'

Anna frowned. 'Upstairs?'

'Oh, that was nothing,' Caitlin said to Lorraine.

'What was it?' Anna persisted.

Since Caitlin clearly didn't want to talk about it, Lorraine took over. 'It was right after lunch. We were working in the women's rest room, cleaning the floor. We put this big bottle of disinfectant on the floor against the wall under one of the sinks while we were cleaning. A woman came in and used the bathroom, and while she was washing her hands she kicked over the bottle. The stuff went everywhere. Even though the woman did it herself, she got all mad and told Caitlin she was careless. Caitlin told the woman she was sorry, but the woman said, "What did you just say to me? What did you call me?" And she claimed Caitlin called her something bad. Then she walked over to Caitlin and said, "Give me those silver pumps you had on when you got here and we'll make believe this never happened." That was when I went up to this chick and told her to take a hike before I put her lights out.'

Anna looked at Caitlin in amazement. 'Is that true?'

Caitlin, looking reluctant, finally admitted, 'Yes.'

'What was the woman's name?' Though Anna had a pretty good idea.

'She said it was Brianna,' Lorraine said.

'Brianna?'

The two women nodded.

'What did she look like?'

'Petite,' Lorraine began. Definitely not Brianna. 'Dark, curly, hair. A very pretty face, like a little girl.'

As Anna had thought. 'I'm sorry this happened. I appreciate your telling me about it. I'll see that it doesn't happen again.'

At that moment Mark Edwards appeared to help Caitlin negotiate the paparazzi mob that had gathered again outside. He and Caitlin left the garage together. Lorraine nodded a goodbye to Anna and headed back upstairs to the women's locker room. Anna went in search of Shari.

She found her stepping down from the passenger side of her and Rob's collection truck. Rob was already gone.

'Oh, hey, Anna,' Shari said. She was carrying a motorcycle helmet.

Anna planted herself in front of the younger woman. 'What's that?'

Shari laughed. 'Haven't you ever seen a motorcycle helmet before?'

'I understand you caused some trouble upstairs this afternoon.'

'Trouble?' Shari said innocently, pale-blue eyes wide.

'Cut the little-girl act. I know what you did and I'm adding it to my list of reasons why you should be suspended.'

Shari's face grew dark and angry. 'Suspended! What have I done?'

Anna didn't bother answering. 'Until I can get you out of here, watch your step, Shari. I've got my eye on you.'

Suddenly the loud roar of an engine filled the air of the garage and, to Anna's amazement, a man on a motorcycle rode in from the front drive. He jerked to a stop a few feet from where Anna and Shari stood and pulled off his helmet.

'Hey, babe,' he said to Shari. He looked to be in his early thirties and was good-looking in a rough, unkempt sort of way, with heavy-lidded brown eyes, an unshaved face, and a lot of dirty-blond hair pushed every which way by the helmet.

'Who are you?' Anna demanded.

Shari was climbing on to the back of the beat-up old Yamaha. Anna noticed a sticker on the bike's front fender bearing an odd symbol, the letter *A* within a *U*. 'He's my boyfriend,' she said, menace in her voice.

'Dennis Ostrow at your service,' the man said with an arrogant bow.

'How did you get in here?'

He laughed. 'Yeah, it was a surprise to me, too. I guess in all the confusion the cops thought my sticker here meant I was official.'

Anna would speak to Santos about this. 'Get out of here, both of you.'

Ostrow looked surprised. He put his helmet back on and gunned the engine. 'Let's go, babe, looks like we're not welcome.'

Shari put on the helmet she had been carrying, wrapped her arms tightly around Ostrow's middle, and gave Anna a sneer. 'Let's go,' she said, and Ostrow hit the gas, turned the bike around, and zoomed out of the garage.

When she turned to go back to her office, Allen Schiff was standing in the corridor, eyes wide in surprise.

'Don't ask, Allen,' Anna said with a weary sigh. 'Don't ask.'

FIVE

ANNA TWIRLED SPAGHETTI on her spoon, then popped it into her mouth. 'Your cooking is getting better and better,' she told Santos, who was crossing his tiny dining area carrying a fresh bottle of red wine. Sitting down, he poured Anna a glass, then stared down at his plate for a moment as if lost in thought.

'What is it?' she asked.

He looked up. 'I feel guilty that we didn't ask Gloria to join us. You said she's pretty down.'

'I know,' Anna said, rolling her eyes, 'I'm a terrible sister. But I'm sorry, Santos, there's a limit. We would have to hear about Donald throughout the entire meal. He's all she ever talks about.'

'Can you blame her?'

'No…I just don't want to be the one who always has to hear it.'

He frowned, thinking about that.

'Besides,' Anna added, 'she's always had the hots for you. Now that she's single, or soon to be, she's especially dangerous around you. The last thing I need is competition from my own sister.'

He laughed. 'So what's she doing tonight? For dinner, I mean.'

'She's watching *Law and Order* reruns and eating Lean Cuisine. She thinks one of the reasons Donald had an affair is that she's not thin enough. Plus, she says if she's going to be on the market again, she's got to look her very best.'

'I see.' He took a sip of wine, then grabbed the stereo remote and changed the CD to some jazz they both loved. 'Let's talk about something else. How did Caitlin do today?'

'Surprisingly well. For all the stories you hear about her, her behavior was completely appropriate. I really don't anticipate any problems.' Santos nodded in approval. 'Shari pulled a good one, though.'

She had been keeping him up to date about Shari. Now she described the young woman's encounter with Lorraine and Caitlin in the women's rest room.

He blinked in amazement. 'Why does this woman still have her job?'

'Because I've only just sent in my report recommending that she be suspended. I don't think it will be long now.'

He nodded. 'Who was that guy she rode off with at the end of the day?'

'Her boyfriend, Dennis Ostrow. Speaking of whom, how on earth did he get past you guys?'

He gave a helpless shrug. 'I wasn't at the gate, so I'm not exactly sure, but from what I've put together, when the gate was opened for Caitlin to go through, Ostrow saw his chance and drove right on in.'

'Why didn't someone go after him?'

'Under normal circumstances, someone would have. But it seems as if every cop in Midtown North Precinct is dedicated to keeping the paparazzi away from Caitlin. She hadn't even reached her car when Ostrow did that. We had to make sure she reached that car without any trouble from the press. In other words, we had bigger fish to fry.'

'Yeah, a big, very rich fish. Oh,' she said, remembering. 'I wanted to ask you something. Ostrow had a sticker with a weird symbol on his bike. An *A* inside a *U*. Have you ever seen that before?'

He was nodding. 'That figures. Yeah, I've seen it. I'm surprised you haven't, given your line of work. Have you ever heard of Urban Access?'

'No.'

'How about urban exploration?'

Unsure, she gave a little shrug.

'That's not its only name,' he said, eating a meatball. 'They also call it draining, urban spelunking, urban caving, vadding, trolling, building hacking, reality hacking, roof and tunnel hacking...or just plain UE.'

'But what is it?' she asked impatiently.

'It's the exploration of places that are usually unseen and more often off limits. For instance, these people like to get into abandoned buildings. One night a couple of months ago a cop friend of mine in the Bronx got a call about a break-in at a warehouse that hasn't been used in at least twenty years. A resident in a building nearby saw a light inside. The building is slated for demolition so a highrise can go up, which explains why these jokers picked it. Last chance, and all that. Anyway, when my friend got there he found seven people inside, all of them wearing helmets and carrying flashlights. Know how they got in? They crawled through a drainage tunnel.'

'Eew.'

'Oh, nothing grosses these people out. In fact, the grosser the better.'

'But *why*? What's the point of it?'

'Why? To say you've done it, seen these places no one else has seen. The point? Because it's forbidden! You wouldn't believe the calls we've gotten. Factories, hospitals, mental asylums—they love those—sewers, storm drains, subway tunnels...you get the idea.' He shook his head in disapproval. 'In a place like New York City, the last thing the police need is to have their time wasted by these nuts.'

'So this Dennis character is an urban explorer,' Anna said thoughtfully. 'Have you ever met anyone from this particular group?'

He shook his head.

She said, 'I wonder if Shari does this urban exploring, too.'

'Probably. From what you've told me about her, it sounds as if she makes a point of making a nuisance of herself.'

'True,' Anna said, and took a sip of wine. 'Very true.'

They were quiet for a moment. When Anna looked up, Santos's gaze was troubled.

'What is it?' Anna asked.

'Oh, it's my niece, Libby. She's my younger brother Hector's daughter.'

'Isn't Hector the one who lost his wife?'

'Yeah, Carla. She died of breast cancer a year ago. Libby—Elizabeth—is their only kid.'

Anna shook her head sadly. 'So what's going on with her?'

'You mean aside from being fifteen years old? She's giving Hector a lot of trouble. Last week she went on a date and didn't come home until two in the morning. When Hector confronted her, she told him to mind his own business. Her grades are dropping at school and she's skipping a lot of classes.'

'Has Hector gotten any help?'

He nodded. 'You name it, he's gotten it. First he spoke with some people at Libby's school. The school psychologist had tried to speak with her, but she wouldn't open up; she just kept nodding, but she wasn't really listening. So the psychologist recommended that Hector take her to an outside psychologist. No luck there, either; she gave him the same treatment.'

'So now what?'

'Actually,' he said, looking up to meet her gaze, 'I was thinking maybe you could help.'

She blinked in surprise. 'Me?'

'Anna, the kid has no mother. Fifteen years old and no woman to talk to. Hector does his best but it's not the same, you know that. I was thinking maybe you could talk to her. I think she might listen to you. You're the kind of woman a girl would admire—intelligent, hard-working, ethical, kind.'

She put her hand over his. 'Why, thank you, Santos, that's really sweet.'

'I'm not saying anything that's not true.'

'What, exactly, would you like me to say to her?'

'That she's got to make school her top priority. That if she doesn't get good grades in high school, she won't get into a good college. That this is not the time to be so involved with boys.'

'Ha! You think a fifteen-year-old girl is going to listen to that?'

He shrugged, nodding in concession. 'All right, so you tell her she needs to cool it a little bit with the boys. You would be a perfect role model for her, someone to look up to. A success. We don't have any women quite like you in our family.'

She smiled kindly. 'Of course I'll talk to her.'

'Thanks, Anna,' he said, and gave her hand a squeeze.

'Now, how do we set this up?' she asked.

'I was thinking I could invite Hector and Libby to join you and me for a movie and dinner. That way you could get to know Libby, maybe ask her some questions…I don't really know the best way.'

'That way will work fine,' she said. 'Let me know where and when. I'll be there.'

THE NEXT MORNING, Shari remained true to form.

A little after seven o'clock, long after all the sanitation workers should have left for their rounds, the sounds of a man and a woman shouting echoed through the garage. Before Anna could even get out of her chair, Allen Schiff was in her doorway. 'Anna, those are your people. Take care of it.'

She hurried out. Near the stack of tires—Shari's favorite spot, it seemed—stood Shari and Tommy. Tommy, his face a deep red, shouted, 'It's enough! It's over!'

Shari, her head tilted back so that she could meet his gaze, hollered back, 'I'll tell you when it's over!'

'I could kill you,' Tommy said.

Anna ran over to them. Seeing her, they pulled apart.

'Hey! What's going on?' she asked them.

Tommy stared at the floor. Shari was watching Tommy. 'Nothing,' she said.

'That was a loud nothing,' Anna said. 'Why aren't you on your routes?'

Neither had an answer to that.

'Tommy,' Anna said, 'where's Pierre?'

'He's already out.'

'Why? Why aren't you with him?'

Again, no answer; he kept his gaze fixed on the floor. Anna turned to Shari. 'What about you? Is Rob already out?'

She nodded.

'I'm writing you both up,' Anna told them. 'Now get

out of here. Catch up with your partners. And don't let me catch you two together again.'

Tommy opened his mouth to protest, as if he were about to remind Anna that nothing was going on between him and Shari, but Anna silenced him with a stony look. Both he and Shari slouched away. She watched them—keeping their distance from each other, heading out to the street through the chain-link gate.

'So what were they fighting about?' Allen said, suddenly beside her.

'They wouldn't tell me.'

'Anna, get rid of that woman. It's not a suggestion anymore; it's an order.' He walked away before she could reply.

She returned to her office. She would follow up on her report about Shari, see where it stood. She made a mental note to speak to Tommy again.

Around eleven thirty, Gloria called. 'What are you doing?' she asked.

'What do you mean, what am I doing? I'm working. Aren't you?'

'Of course.' In the background could be heard a woman's voice over the hospital's paging system. 'Donald came to see me.'

'He did? Where?'

'Here at the hospital.'

'What did you do?'

'I wouldn't see him.'

Anna sighed. 'Don't you think he deserved at least that?'

'No,' Gloria said lightly. 'Let's try that new café on Broadway for dinner tonight. My treat.'

A feeling of sad foreboding overcame Anna. How long

would this go on? 'Gloria,' Anna said politely, 'you haven't even asked me if I have dinner plans.'

'Do you?'

'No,' she said, unable to lie.

'All right, then. See you tonight. Oh, and Anna—'

'Hold it, Gloria,' Anna said, because Caitlin Whitelaw and Lorraine Canady had just appeared in her doorway. They both had red faces and angry expressions and were breathing hard. 'I gotta go,' she said, and hung up.

'Anna—' both women began at once.

'Hold it!' Anna said. 'Lorraine, you start. What's going on?'

'It's the princess here,' Lorraine said, tossing her head in Caitlin's direction. 'She thinks she's got special privileges, doesn't have to work.'

'That's not true,' Caitlin said. 'I just get really tired.'

Lorraine made a sound of disgust. 'I do twice as much work as you do and I've got a bum knee. You're lazy, that's all.'

'I expect you both to do your best,' Anna said, and Caitlin flounced off.

Lorraine turned to Anna with a snort and a triumphant smile. 'I don't care if she's the queen of England. Nobody's going to take advantage of me. I got it rough enough without having to put up with the likes of her. Thinks she's better than everyone else, slacking off.

'I don't have anybody taking care of me the way she does,' the older woman went on. 'It's just me and Jordan, and Jordan's got his problems; he can't always work.'

Anna gave her a quizzical look.

'Jordan is my son. He's…sensitive. I don't expect him to hold down a job like everybody else. So it's up to me since I lost my Bradley.'

So she was a widow. 'Don't ever hesitate to come to me if there are more problems, Lorraine.'

'Oh, I won't,' Lorraine said, suddenly haughty, and gave one curt nod before turning and walking away.

It was then that the warm, still air of Manhattan Central 13 garage was shattered by a woman's throaty scream.

SIX

ANNA JUMPED UP, emerging from her office as Allen Schiff, Hal Redmond, and Gerry Licari emerged from theirs.

'It came from over there,' Gerry said, pointing to the right.

At that moment Brianna Devlin came into view, a look of horror on her face. 'Hurry,' she called to them, and headed back in the direction from which she had come. Anna and the three men followed.

Brianna led them to the right. In the far wall of the garage was the door to the small courtyard where Brianna had overheard Gerry and Shari arguing. Brianna stopped short of going through the doorway, instead pointing and stepping aside so that the others could pass through. Anna went first.

The small courtyard—no more than fifteen feet square—was protected from the alley that surrounded it on three sides by a twelve-foot wall of tan-painted cinder blocks. The doorway was situated at the courtyard's extreme right end. Anna stepped through the doorway, saw nothing at first, then looked to her left. Against the courtyard's far outside corner stood a tall stack of large, empty wooden crates that had been placed there for temporary storage. At the foot of this stack, Shari Baird lay on her back, her arms and legs outspread.

Anna rushed over to her and her breath caught in her throat. Shari's mouth was open wide in a grimace of pain, her pale-blue eyes immense and staring. There were dark bruises on her neck. Now Anna noticed that Shari's green Sanitation shirt had been ripped open and that blood had seeped into the fabric in dark splotches. Seeing something on Shari's chest but unable to make it out, she turned her head and brought her hand to her mouth.

An ankh had been carved deeply into Shari's flesh, just above her left breast. Though crudely rendered, it was unmistakable—the loop atop the cross.

'Don't touch anything.' Allen was at her side. Hal and Gerry stood a few feet away, staring in horror.

Anna had no intention of touching anything. 'Call the police—fast,' she said, but Gerry was shaking his head.

'No hurry. She's dead, wouldn't you say?'

She stared at him in amazement. Then she turned to Brianna, who was peeking in at the door. 'Call the cops!'

IT DIDN'T HELP that the paparazzi who maintained their constant Caitlin vigil were already in place. As soon as the police began to arrive they got wind of what had happened and surged at the garage entrance, hungry for information to send back to their newspapers or TV or radio stations.

Ten minutes later, Allen spoke quietly in the corridor with two homicide detectives. Anna had met them nearly a year ago, in connection with the homeless man she had found murdered behind her apartment building.

Homicide Detective Rinaldi was a petite, olive-skinned woman in her early thirties. She was exotically attractive but clearly made every effort to hide it; she wore no make-up on her large, almond-shaped eyes and kept her mass of dark hair pinned tightly to the top of her head. Watching her speak with Allen, Anna remembered her brusque, no-nonsense, often rude manner.

Her partner, Homicide Detective Roche, though nearly a foot taller than she, was nevertheless in Rinaldi's shadow—Anna remembered that, too. Lanky, his movements slow and deliberate, the red-haired man seldom spoke and almost always deferred to Rinaldi. Today was no exception. Rinaldi, her hands on her slim hips, was clearly giving Allen orders, while Roche quietly observed.

Allen turned and came toward Anna, the detectives in tow. 'Anna,' he said, 'these are—'

'We've met,' Rinaldi interrupted. 'We need to speak to everyone who was in the garage when this woman was found. Where can we do that?'

'How about my office?' Anna said, and Rinaldi nodded. 'I'll get my stuff and clear out.'

'No, I want you there,' Rinaldi said. She turned to Allen. 'The first one I want to talk to is the woman who found the body.'

Allen nodded and went off to find Brianna. When she appeared in Anna's doorway, she looked even worse than before, her face blotchy, her hair disheveled, her eyes crazed. 'Anna, I need to go home.'

'After we speak with you,' Rinaldi said before Anna could reply. 'Sit here,' the detective said, pointing to the other end of the love seat on which she was already sitting. Anna sat behind her desk, and Roche took the chair next to it.

'OK,' Roche said, suddenly finding his voice, 'tell us what happened.'

Brianna turned to him as if surprised that he had spoken. She took a deep breath, her hefty shoulders rising and falling. 'Well...I was done with my route. I wanted a cigarette before I went up and showered. We're allowed to smoke in the courtyard, so I went out there, and Shari was lying there.'

'There was no one else there, obviously.'

'No.'

'Did you see anyone near the door? Inside the garage, I mean.'

Brianna hesitated, her gaze darting to Anna, who knit her brows, wondering what Brianna didn't want to say.

'Near the door?' Brianna said. 'No.'

Rinaldi had caught it, too. 'Ms Devlin, if there's something you should tell us and you don't, I'll have you charged with hampering an investigation.'

Distressed, Brianna looked from Anna to Roche and back to Rinaldi. Finally she said, 'I—I passed someone as I was going in.'

'Oh?' Rinaldi prompted, sitting up straighter.

Brianna nodded. 'He—he was running in from the courtyard.'

'Well,' Rinaldi said, dropping her notepad into her lap, 'then let's have it.'

They all waited. Finally Brianna spoke.

'It was Tommy. Tommy Mulligan.'

Anna gasped. 'Brianna!'

'Quiet!' Rinaldi snapped. 'Ms Devlin, remember what I just said.'

Brianna nodded meekly. 'It was, Anna; it was Tommy. He ran in from the courtyard, went right past me.'

'Did he say anything?' Roche asked.

'No, he just ran past me.'

'And how did he look?' Rinaldi asked.

'Upset.'

'How so?'

'His face was all red and he was breathing hard. When he glanced at me, he looked…scared.'

'Scared?' Anna said.

'Ms Winthrop,' Rinaldi said, 'if you say one more word you're out of here.'

Anna snapped her mouth shut.

Brianna was nodding quickly. 'He looked like…well, like he'd done something wrong. And like he was upset that I'd seen him.'

Anna felt her heart sink. She closed her eyes and put a hand to her forehead. When she removed her hand, Rinaldi was looking at her. 'Where is this Mulligan?'

'He—he shouldn't have been in the garage. He should have been out on his route. So should Shari.'

'Well,' Roche said with disdain, 'obviously neither one of them was "out". So where is this Mulligan guy now?'

Anna shrugged, shook her head. 'He must be here. I don't know—maybe upstairs.'

'Upstairs?' Rinaldi said.

'The break room is there. Also the locker rooms, showers, rest rooms…'

'What else can you tell us?' Rinaldi asked Brianna.

Brianna looked helplessly around the office. 'Nothing. That's all I saw, until I found Shari.' Her eyes grew huge. 'She had that mark on her. That ankh symbol. That's what that murderer does…'

'That will be all, Ms Devlin,' Rinaldi said. When Brianna was gone, Rinaldi turned to Anna. 'You have Caitlin Whitelaw doing her community service here, yes?'

'Yes.'

'And where is she now?'

Anna couldn't help laughing. 'Do you think she's the Ankh Killer?'

Neither Rinaldi nor Roche even cracked a smile.

'Do you think this is funny?' Rinaldi said.

Anna felt as if she were back in grade school. 'No,' she said, and gave her head a defiant toss, 'of course not. This woman was on my crew. Tommy Mulligan is on my crew.'

'Then why are you cracking jokes?'

'Because I don't see what Caitlin could possibly have to do with any of this.'

'Where is Caitlin now?' Rinaldi asked, undeterred.

'I have her cleaning the garage floor with Lorraine—Lorraine Canady; she's working here on the Work Exchange Program. They should both be right out there in the garage.'

'Get her,' Rinaldi said.

'Who—Caitlin or Lorraine?'

'Who do you think? Caitlin.'

'I'll get her,' Anna said, boldly meeting Rinaldi's gaze, '...after you tell me why.'

Rinaldi considered Anna for a long moment. At last she said, 'You know who her father is. I'm surprised he's not already here, screaming that we're putting his daughter's life in danger by exposing her to a murderer.'

Rinaldi was right; Anna hadn't thought of that. She rose. 'I'll get her.'

'Wait,' Rinaldi said. 'Before you do that, get Mulligan.'

Anna felt sick to her stomach as she left her office and started down the corridor. She glanced toward the courtyard door and saw members of the crime scene unit going in and out. Then she went upstairs, looking first in the break room. It was empty, pieces of crumpled wax paper and aluminum foil strewn across one of the long tables. She called into the men's showers and locker room. There was no answer. Back downstairs, she quickly checked the garage's perimeter, but Tommy was nowhere to be found.

Giving up on him for the moment, Anna went in search of Caitlin and found her alone in the corner of the garage farthest from the entrance, sluggishly mopping the floor. As Anna approached her she looked up, fear in her eyes.

'Where's Lorraine?' Anna asked her.

Caitlin shrugged. 'How should I know?'

It appeared Caitlin and Lorraine had gone their separate ways after their contretemps that morning. 'The police want to talk to you,' Anna told her.

'The police! Why?'

Anna didn't respond to that. 'Come with me, please.'

With an exasperated sigh, Caitlin fell into step behind Anna and followed her to her office. As the two women entered the room, Rinaldi looked up expectantly. 'Where's Mulligan?'

'I can't find him.'

Rinaldi shot Roche a meaningful look; he nodded, removing his cell phone from his pocket. 'What does he look like?' he asked Anna.

'Twenty years old, short dark hair…hazel eyes, I think. Medium height.'

Roche went out to the corridor and they heard him speaking into his phone.

'This doesn't look good for him,' Rinaldi said to Anna, who had no response. Rinaldi turned to Caitlin with an ingratiating smile and gestured for her to sit in the chair Roche had just vacated. 'Miss Whitelaw,' she said, 'I'm Detective Rinaldi, and out there is my partner, Detective Roche. I just want to ask you a few questions.'

Caitlin scowled, waiting.

'Where were you when Ms Devlin found Ms Baird's body?'

'I was at the corner of the garage—at this end, not the courtyard end—cleaning.'

'What did you do when you heard Ms Devlin scream?'

'Do? Nothing. What should I have done?'

Rinaldi gave a polite smile and gave her head a shake, almost as if she were apologizing for the impertinence of her question.

'Did you know Ms Baird?' Rinaldi asked.

'No, not really.' Caitlin made no mention of Shari kicking over the bottle of disinfectant; Anna saw no reason to do so either.

Caitlin turned to Anna. 'I called my father. He's on his way over here,' she said, and Rinaldi's smile vanished. 'This is a dangerous place. I can't stay here.'

This should be interesting, Anna thought, inwardly rolling her eyes. With any luck, Allen Schiff or perhaps even Mark Edwards would deal with Hamilton Whitelaw.

'Miss Whitelaw,' Rinaldi said, 'what did you tell your father about what's happened here today?'

'What do you think I told him? That a woman was strangled and carved up in the courtyard.'

Rinaldi made a face. 'You realize the press is going to be all over you about this.'

Caitlin nodded as if resigned to this fact.

'You must give us your word that you will not speak to them about any aspect of this case.'

'Why would I?'

'Because as I just said, they're going to ask you about it. You must say "No comment" or "That's a matter for the police" or even "I'm not at liberty to discuss that". Do you understand?'

'Yes.'

'Because if you do speak to the press about this, the judge who sent you here will find out about it.'

Anger rose in Anna. 'That's a bit harsh, don't you think?' Anna asked angrily. 'She has just assured you that she won't talk about it. Can't you leave it at that?'

Rinaldi spun on her, fire in her eyes. 'Keep out of police business. How dare you question what I say? That goes for you, too, by the way—and for everyone who works here. In fact, I'm going to ask Allen Schiff to make an announcement to that effect to everyone on the staff.'

'Suit yourself,' Anna said. Rinaldi looked at her in irritation but said nothing. 'All right, Miss Whitelaw, you may go now. Thank you for your time.'

Caitlin jumped up and hurried out. Roche returned and reclaimed his chair.

'Ms Winthrop,' Rinaldi said, 'who else was here in the garage when Ms Baird's body was discovered?'

'None of my crew except Brianna, of course, and Tommy. Allen was here. Also Hal Redmond—he's supervisor of section 1302—and Gerry Licari—he supervises 1303. I don't know about the people on their crews; you'll have to ask them.'

Rinaldi wrote all this down and told Roche to make sure the three men remained on the premises for questioning. Roche nodded.

Meanwhile, Anna cast her gaze about the office, her thoughts crazed. Where was Tommy? If he hadn't killed Shari, which of course he hadn't, why had he run from the courtyard, alerting no one, and then fled the garage—which it appeared he'd done.

'OK,' Rinaldi said, shifting on the love seat and flipping to a fresh page in her notepad. 'Now I need you to tell me about this woman, Shari…'

'Baird. What about her?'

'What was she like? Did she have any enemies that you knew of? Anybody she didn't get along with?'

Inwardly Anna laughed. Where to begin? She decided Tommy himself was a good place to start—best to get that over with. Much as she hated to implicate him further, she would have to tell the police eventually about his encounters with Shari, and it might as well be now. She told Rinaldi and Roche about catching Tommy and Shari in the supply closet upstairs; about how Tommy said it wasn't the way it looked. Then she told them about breaking up the fight between Shari and Tommy that morning, and how neither of them would tell her what they had been fighting about. (She neglected to mention that Tommy had said he could kill Shari.) Finally, she told Rinaldi about the argument Brianna had overheard between Shari and Gerry, figuring it would come out anyway. Rinaldi nodded slowly as she wrote down what Anna said.

'Her collection partner is Rob Cahill,' Anna went on. 'He's still out.' She told them what Rob had said about Shari—how she had come on to him, how she had vanished unaccountably while servicing the litter baskets, how she had grown furious and thrown a trash can at a resident.

'I want to see Cahill as soon as he's back,' Rinaldi told Anna, who nodded. The two detectives stood. 'Here's my number,' Rinaldi said, handing Anna a card. 'When Cahill comes back, call me. Ditto for Mulligan—though I doubt that will happen. Now, there's one more thing you can do for us: open Baird's locker. She had one here, right?'

'Yes, of course. The locker rooms are upstairs. I'll get the master key.'

Anna took the key from her desk and led the two detectives upstairs to the women's locker room. As they watched, she opened Shari's locker.

There wasn't much inside—a pair of jeans, a T-shirt, a pair of Adidas running shoes, a toothbrush, a tube of toothpaste, a can of Right Guard deodorant, a pack of Camel cigarettes.

'Wait,' Roche said, pointing. 'What's that at the bottom?'

Anna lifted the running shoes. There was, indeed, something there, a folded sheet of paper. Anna picked it up. Before she could unfold it, Rinaldi snatched it from her and opened it. It was a note, written in ballpoint pen in bold script.

Shari—
Why are you doing this to me? You know how much
I love you. Please don't hurt me this way. I promise
I won't ask any questions. Just come back.
All my love,
Dante

'Who's Dante?' Rinaldi asked.

Anna shrugged. 'I have no idea.'

'There's no one here at the garage by that name?'

'No.'

'Go through the clothes,' Rinaldi ordered Roche, and she and Anna watched as he looked inside the shoes, checked the pockets of the jeans and the T-shirt.

'Nada,' he said.

Rinaldi shot him a surprised look, then turned to Anna. 'We'll hold on to this note. If you think of who this Dante might be, call me.'

AFTER THEY'D GONE, Anna returned to her office and sat very still, thinking.

Tommy, what were you doing in the courtyard? Why did you run? Where are *you?*

Her phone rang. It was Allen Schiff. 'Anna, you're not gonna believe who's here.'

'Let me guess. Hamilton Whitelaw.'

Allen laughed. 'I guess it was bound to happen. Like we need him here now. Talk to him and get rid of him fast.'

'Me?'

'Of course, you. Who else? You're Caitlin's direct supervisor.'

'With all due respect, Allen, you're the district superintendent. And then there's Mark Edwards, who I thought was supposed to be responsible for Caitlin.'

'Edwards isn't here—obviously—and the cops want to talk to me about Shari.'

Anna blew out her breath. 'All right. Where is he?'

'His limo pulled up a minute ago. The reporters went nuts. One of the cops is bringing him in.'

Replacing the receiver, Anna jumped up in time to greet Hamilton Whitelaw in the corridor. The bigger-than-life figure looked odd in the narrow space. Taller than he appeared on television and in photographs, he wore an impeccably tailored dark-blue suit, a crisp white shirt, and a maroon-and-navy paisley tie. His famous bald head shone in the office's fluorescent light. His thick features were scrunched into a nasty scowl, his dark eyes barely visible under his prominent brow.

'Hello, Mr Whitelaw. I'm Anna Winthrop, Caitlin's direct supervisor.'

They shook hands.

'Winthrop…' He frowned. 'No relation to Jeff Winthrop, I assume.'

'He's my father.'

'Your father!' he faltered. 'What on earth is a billionaire's daughter doing working for the Sanitation Department?'

It wasn't the first time Anna had been asked this question, and she was sure it wouldn't be the last. 'Do you know my father?' she asked.

'Sure. Haven't seen him in ages. How is he doing?'

'Very well, thank you. I'll give him your regards. Now, what can I do for you, Mr Whitelaw?'

'What can you do for me? You can let me take my daughter home. I'm not leaving her in this dangerous place so she can get murdered.'

Now Anna was aware of a blue-uniformed figure standing behind Whitelaw. When Whitelaw shifted slightly, she realized it was Santos. Instinctively she opened her mouth to greet him, but he shook his head and gave her a warning look. She returned her attention to Whitelaw.

'Your daughter is working here on the judge's orders, sir. None of us here has the authority to release her, and neither do you.'

His eyes bulged in apparent amazement at her bluntness. Behind him, Santos's brows rose.

'I want to see her,' Whitelaw said.

'I suppose that's all right,' Anna said. 'Come with me, please.'

Both Whitelaw and Santos followed her to where Caitlin was working.

'Daddy!' Caitlin threw her mop aside, water splashing everywhere, and rushed into her father's arms.

'Are you OK, sweetie?'

'No, Daddy, I want to go home,' she said in a pouty voice. 'It's scary here.'

Anna shot Santos a look.

'Honey,' Whitelaw said gently, 'I'm afraid you're not allowed to leave. But I'll tell you what. When you're finished for today, I'll pick you up and we'll go out for steaks. How's that?'

She pushed out her lower lip. A tear appeared in one of her green cat's eyes and ran down her cheek. 'All right, but I don't want to be out here all alone anymore.'

'That's not a problem,' Anna said. 'You can clean right outside my office.'

Whitelaw looked to his daughter to see if that was acceptable. 'All right,' the young woman said, then picked up her mop and grabbed the handle of her rolling bucket. Anna led her, Whitelaw, and Santos back to the corridor where the offices were located.

'Stay strong, baby,' Whitelaw murmured to her, taking her in his arms and kissing her on top of her blonde head.

'OK, Daddy,' she said, and sloshed some gray soapy water on the floor.

When he was out of sight, Santos motioned for Anna to come into her office. 'Anna, they've found Tommy Mulligan.'

Her eyes grew wide. 'Where?'

'In the Bronx, on a number six train, dressed in jeans and a T-shirt and a baseball cap pulled down low over his face.'

'Santos, Tommy is innocent, I know he is. He is simply incapable of doing something like this.'

'Then why was he running?'

'Why do you think? Because he knew he would be blamed.'

'That doesn't make sense, Anna. Why would he think that?'

'Because he and Shari had been fighting; everyone saw it. He was so angry he said he could kill her.'

'People say all kinds of things. Just because Tommy said that doesn't mean he would think anyone took it seriously.'

'Where is he?' she asked.

'Central Booking.'

She shut her eyes, lowered her head. 'Poor Tommy. Running away wasn't smart, but I'm sure this will all be cleared up soon. The police will see that he couldn't have killed Shari.'

'Then who did?' Santos said, and when Anna looked up, he was shaking his head.

'I'm sorry, Anna,' he said, 'but it doesn't look good for him. It really doesn't.'

SEVEN

It was four-thirty when Anna left her office, started across the garage toward the gate to the street, and stopped in the middle of the floor. Turning her head to the right, she saw the open door to the courtyard, a rectangle of bright sunlight against the grimy wall of the garage.

Like metal drawn to a magnet, she found herself changing course and walking to the courtyard door. Approaching it, she looked in each direction and, satisfied that no one was around, went out.

Why had Shari come out here? For a cigarette...or to meet Tommy again? Poor Tommy, running from the blame he knew would be placed on him. Anna knew he could never have done something like this, could never hurt someone. Yet how well did she really know him? She knew he came from a long, proud line of sanitation workers, that he was recently engaged, and—from what she could tell—that he was an honorable, truthful young man. That he could have hurt Shari, let alone be the Ankh Killer, was simply too preposterous to consider.

She walked slowly across the enclosed space. At the far end, she stopped to examine the pile of wooden crates stacked against the wall. Four crates formed the stack's base. Atop those sat three crates, atop these two more, and at the very top, like a child's building blocks, one crate formed the peak. Anna guessed the distance between this top crate and the top of the wall to be about a foot. If someone on the other side were able to reach the top of the wall, it would be a simple matter to climb down the stack of crates, a virtual staircase.

She took a last look around, then left the garage. Once out on Forty-Third Street, instead of turning west toward home, she turned east and entered the alley in which the courtyard stood.

It was quiet here, secluded. With a stepladder it would be easy to get to the top of the wall. Which meant that, theoretically, anyone—not just someone in the garage—could have killed Shari. Eager to tell Santos, she headed home.

'Paper, lady?' a newsboy called as she approached Ninth Avenue. He held it out for her. ANKH KILLER CAPTURED; MADMAN IS ONE OF NEW YORK'S STRONGEST.

Distressed, Anna shook her head and walked on.

'FACE IT, ANNA,' Gloria said, spearing a lettuce leaf, 'you're not going to believe it until the police put the proof right in front of your nose. You can't accept that one of your precious sanitation workers might be a murderer.'

She, Anna, and Santos were sitting in the dining area of Anna's apartment. Santos held his tongue—something Anna had no intention of doing.

'One more strike against the Department of Sanitation, right, Gloria? Add it to the list of reasons why I should get out of there, find that more "suitable" job...whatever that is.'

'That's not what I said,' Gloria retorted, putting down her fork.

Santos came to the rescue. 'Anna, it's not that what you're saying about someone climbing over the wall isn't possible. Sure it's possible. But the police aren't going to take it seriously, because it doesn't go anywhere. Yes, Shari's killer could be just some stranger from over the wall, but who? The fact is, most murders are committed by people the victims know, more often know *intimately*, and that's the tack the police are going to take. Clearly Tommy and Shari were having an affair. They were also seen arguing violently.' He shrugged, reached for a slice of bread. 'Seems pretty clear to me.'

'But I told you, Tommy said he and Shari *weren't* having an affair, that it wasn't what it looked like.'

'Oh, for Pete's sake, Anna.' Gloria flung out her hand, nearly impaling Santos with her fork. He inched his chair away. 'If it wasn't what it looked like, what was it? What do you think he's going to say? He's engaged! He's ashamed. Not to mention he could be suspended for that kind of behavior. Grow up.'

Anna gazed down at her untouched salad. 'It's more than that. I know Tommy. He couldn't do this. It's as simple as that.'

There was nothing Gloria and Santos could say to this. They all ate in silence for several moments. Then Gloria looked up, an arch look in her eye. 'I understand you had an interesting visitor at the garage today.'

'Oh?' Anna said, her tone aloof.

'Don't "oh" me, dear sister. Hamilton Whitelaw came to rescue his little girl. It was on TV. Did you speak to him? What's he like?'

Anna shrugged. 'As bossy and pompous as he seems on TV. He demanded that we release Caitlin from such a dangerous place.'

'Dangerous?' Gloria said.

'Mm-hm. A murderer in the garage equals dangerous, don't you think?'

'Ah.'

'What did you tell him?' Gloria asked.

'That I don't have the authority to release her. She's there on the judge's orders.'

The buzzer sounded. Anna frowned. 'Who could that be?'

'Probably Mrs Dovner,' Santos said with a laugh. 'She wants to tell us we're talking too loud.'

Anna went to the intercom. 'Who is it?'

'Anna, it's Donald.'

Gloria gasped, jumped out of her chair, and ran over to Anna, gesticulating wildly. 'I'm not here! I'm not here!' she mouthed.

Anna hesitated a moment, not happy at having to lie, before answering. 'Donald, Gloria's not here.'

'I know she's staying with you, Anna.'

'How does he know that?' Gloria whispered hoarsely.

Donald went on, 'Please tell her I want to talk to her. That I'm sorry. And…that I love her.'

Gloria's face froze. Then she started to cry, putting her face in her hands.

'Are you sure?' Anna asked her.

Gloria nodded quickly.

'OK,' Anna said, regret in her voice, and pressed the button. 'I'll tell her, Donald.'

There was a long silence. Then, 'Thanks, Anna,' and the sound of the building's front door opening and closing.

'What am I going to do?' Gloria said through her tears.

'Why can't you just talk to him?'

'I—I can't, Anna. Don't you see? Not after what he's done to me.'

'He's hurt you; I understand that. But doesn't he deserve a chance to say he's sorry?'

'He just did.'

'I mean in person. Don't you love him? Usually we forgive people we love.'

'Come on, Anna,' Gloria said, removing her hands from her face. 'You sound like a Hallmark card. Yes, I love him. Or I thought I did, before— Oh, I don't know!' she blurted out, bursting into fresh tears, and ran into the bedroom. Anna looked across the room at Santos and shrugged. Then he motioned that they should get going. They would be meeting Hector and Libby for a movie tonight.

THE MOVIE LIBBY wanted to see—to Anna's surprise, a small independent film about a woman artist in Paris in the late 1800s—was playing at the Paris Theatre, on West Fifty-Eighth Street across from the Plaza Hotel. Anna and Santos had agreed to meet outside. As she approached the theater, she saw Santos, in jeans and a short-sleeve shirt, standing not far from the box office. He gave her a kiss. 'Thanks for doing this, Anna. Oh, here they are.'

Anna had met Hector at a Reyes family birthday party. He was a little taller than Santos, but not, in her opinion, as handsome, though he had kind brown eyes and a sweet smile. He looked exhausted. Ten steps behind him was Libby, talking animatedly on her cell phone.

'Hi, Anna,' Hector said, and kissed her on the cheek. 'Thanks for meeting us.'

'Of course.' She laughed. 'It looks like she's kind of busy.'

He gave a humorless chuckle. 'If she had her way, she would talk on the phone all the way through the movie.'

'I thought she wanted to see this film.'

'She did. But it seems she can't be out of touch with her friends for more than ten minutes. Also, she wouldn't want to give us the satisfaction of seeing her enjoy the movie. But don't worry,' he said, 'the cell goes off in the theater. Libby, come on.'

Libby was a beautiful girl, with pale creamy skin, startling pale-gold eyes, and full, naturally red lips. Her thick, lustrous hair cascaded down over one shoulder. Anna had never met her before—she hadn't been at the party where Anna met Hector. Carla must have been a knockout. Still on the phone, Libby walked up to her father.

'Off,' he ordered. She ignored him. 'Off!' he repeated.

She rolled her eyes. 'I gotta go,' she said into the phone. 'My dad's being a pill.' She clicked off the phone and looked at him with a sullen expression.

'Libby, this is Anna. I've talked about her before.'

'Hi,' Libby said, extending a languid hand.

Anna shook it warmly. 'It's nice to meet you, Libby.'

'You had that murder at your garage, right?'

'Yes,' Anna admitted, uncomfortable.

'That is so totally cool.'

'Libby, say hello to your Uncle Santos,' Hector said as Santos approached them with tickets.

'Hey, Uncle Santos,' Libby said in a dead voice.

Santos leaned over to plant a kiss on her cheek. 'How are you, Libby?'

She rolled her eyes. 'I'd be better if my dad would stop making me come to stupid things like this.'

At this, Hector grabbed her shoulder and pulled her to one side. 'Now listen, young lady,' Anna and Santos heard him say, 'I won't have you behaving so rudely. I've spoken to you about this before. This is your uncle, who loves you very much, and his girlfriend. They both deserve your respect and your best manners.'

For a moment Libby glared at him, hostility in her eyes; then suddenly she pasted on a garish fake smile. 'Better?' she said with false ladylike cheerfulness. 'Shall we go in?'

She led the way. Hector gave Anna and Santos a look that said, 'Do you see what I have to deal with?' and followed her in. Anna and Santos took up the rear.

In the theater, Anna made a point of sitting next to Libby. The film turned out to be quite lovely and moving, but Anna spent as much time covertly watching Libby as she did watching the movie. Anna could tell that Libby was enthralled; clearly this was a story that spoke to her in some way. She kept clenching and unclenching her fist, as if stirred by some emotion; at one point Anna heard a sniff and looked over to see that Libby was crying.

Outside on the street after the film, Anna blew out her breath. 'Wow. I feel exhausted. That was a beautiful story. Did you like it, Libby?'

Libby shrugged. 'It was OK.'

Anna, Santos, and Hector exchanged looks. 'Let's get something to eat,' Hector said, and he and Santos led the way down Fifth Avenue; Hector wanted to take them to a Lebanese restaurant he loved on West Forty-Ninth Street. Beside Libby, Anna walked slowly so that they would lag behind the men.

'I'm surprised you didn't like the movie more,' Anna said easily.

'Why?' Libby asked, though she looked as if she couldn't care less what Anna thought.

'Well, you picked it, after all. And it was about a painter—your dad tells me you're quite an artist.'

Libby rolled her eyes—one of her favorite gestures, apparently. 'All parents say stuff like that about their kids.'

Anna laughed. 'Maybe, but he says you've won a number of awards at school. Isn't that true?'

'Yeah. So?'

'So it means you have talent. What are your plans?'

Libby looked at her, her brows wrinkled. 'Plans for what?'

'Plans for after high school,' Anna replied matter-of-factly. 'Are you thinking about art schools?'

'Art schools! My dad says at the rate I'm going I'll be lucky if I get into college at all.'

'What do you mean, the rate you're going?'

'He says I spend too much time with boys and not enough time on my homework.'

'Do you think that's true?'

'I do spend a lot of time with boys, 'cause you know what? They like me. They make me feel special.'

'Your father likes you. In fact, he loves you. Your whole family loves you. That should make you feel special.'

'Family,' she said with disgust, and kicked at a Burger King wrapper on the sidewalk.

'What about your homework?'

'What about it?'

'Do you spend much time on it?'

'No, because I hate it. Well, most of it. I do like art,' she admitted.

'Yeah, it's always like that,' Anna said.

'Like what?'

'Stuff you don't like always comes along with the stuff you do like. But you gotta get the bad stuff done, too.'

'Why?' Libby asked, looking Anna in the eye.

'Because that's the way the world works,' Anna replied. 'In your case, you love art, but you hate having to do your homework in the subjects you don't like. Let's say your goal is to make your living as an artist one day. To do that, you'll probably want to go to art school. To do *that*, you're going to need good enough grades to get in. So getting the bad stuff done is actually necessary if you're going to reach your goals.'

'What about *your* goals?' Libby said with a superior smirk. 'My dad says you work in a Sanitation garage.'

'That's right, I do. My goal was to be a supervisor with the Sanitation Department. I'm doing that job now, and I hope to rise higher in the ranks. But to get to this point, do you know what I had to do?'

Libby shook her head.

'I had to collect garbage. I did it for more than two years. All different times of day, in the heat of summer and the cold of winter, I grabbed trash cans outside apartment buildings and emptied them into collection trucks.'

'And you liked that?'

'No,' Anna said with a laugh, 'not at all. My muscles ached, I got scratched, sometimes bags opened up and garbage spilled all over me...it was awful.'

'Then why did you do it?'

'Because, as I just told you, I wanted the good stuff that was at the other side of the bad stuff. And I got it.'

Hector stopped in front of a restaurant with a sign that said AL-AMIR and turned to Santos, Anna, and Libby. 'Here it is.' He held the door.

Libby went in first, her gaze unfocused as if she were deep in thought.

EARLY THE NEXT MORNING, as Anna and Gloria hurried to get ready for work, the phone rang. Anna grabbed it as she struggled with an earring.

'Is this Anna Winthrop?' It was a man's voice, slightly raspy—an older man, Anna thought.

Gloria had appeared in Anna's doorway. 'I don't want to speak to him!' she whispered.

'It's not Donald,' Anna told her, and got back on the phone. 'Who is this?'

'It's George Mulligan. I'm Tommy Mulligan's father. Is this Ms Winthrop?'

'Yes, Mr Mulligan. What's wrong. Did something happen to Tommy?' She realized how dumb that sounded.

'No, no, he's fine,' George Mulligan said; 'as fine as you can be at Rikers Island. Ms Winthrop, I'd like to see you.'

Anna considered. There was no law against her talking with Tommy's father. In fact, she might learn something useful from him. 'Can you meet me at noon at the Akropolis Coffee Shop at Forty-Seventh and Eighth?'

'I'll be there, don't you worry. And thanks.'

'Wait,' she said before he could hang up. 'How did you get my number?'

He gave a little laugh. 'It wasn't easy, I'll tell you that. But I was a reporter back in the day. Things like getting phone numbers were a cinch…and we didn't even have the Internet then.'

SHE SPOTTED HIM immediately, a man in his early sixties, sitting in a booth near the door. He was considerably overweight, but his hair was deep black like Tommy's and he was still a handsome man. When she approached his booth he glanced up, then quickly took her hands firmly in his own. 'I can't thank you enough. Forgive me for not getting up,' he said, and indicated a cane leaning against the wall nearby.

She slid into the booth. A waitress came over and poured them coffee. 'You said Tommy was at Rikers,' Anna began when the waitress had gone.

He nodded. 'I'm going crazy thinking about him there. You gotta help me.'

'How?'

'Listen,' he said, laying his thick hands on the table. 'Believe it or not, besides me and now maybe his fiancée, you know Tommy better than anybody. You know he couldn't have done the things the police think he did, right?'

'Of course.'

'Then help me prove it.'

'But how?'

'I don't know… Maybe there's something you're not thinking of—something that proves Tommy couldn't have done it. Maybe there's something you saw or heard but you forgot, something that points to the person who did do it. Because it's somebody in your garage, Anna—you don't mind if I call you Anna?'

'Of course not.'

'You know it's someone in there. Someone who set it up to look like my Tommy did it, or maybe didn't plan it that way but is only too happy to let him take the fall.'

'It may not have been someone in the garage,' she said. 'Someone could have climbed over the courtyard wall and down a stack of crates that are on the inside. And this person could have escaped the same way.'

But he was shaking his head. 'I told you last night I was a reporter. I had to retire a few years ago because of my MS, but my mind is as sharp as ever. I know and you know that the answer is there in that garage. You just haven't seen it yet.' His dark eyes looked deeply into hers. 'Please. Will you help me? My Evelyn's dead eleven years now. Tommy was our change-of-life baby, a miracle we'd prayed for. Now he's all I have. I can't lose him.'

Looking into this man's eyes, feeling his pain, Anna knew there was only one answer. 'Of course,' she said. 'I'll help in any way I can, try to find out who really did this.'

She took his phone number and gave him her cell phone number. Standing up was a long, painful process for George, though he politely refused help. 'I will let you bring me my cane,' he said with a smile. It didn't seem to help much. Stooping, he took a step, then another, heading for the cashier.

'No, no, my treat,' Anna said hastily, but he put up a gentlemanly hand.

'I wouldn't think of it,' he said, and reached for his wallet.

EIGHT

AFTER ROLL CALL the following morning, Anna returned to her office and stopped short. In the center of her love seat sat Santos, looking solemn.

'What's wrong?' she said.

'There's been another Ankh killing.'

Wide-eyed, she stepped into the room and fell into her chair. 'When?'

'She was found about half an hour ago.'

She leaned forward on the desk. 'Then this proves it. Tommy's not the Ankh Killer.'

He gave her a pitying look. 'Anna, no one really thought Tommy was the Ankh Killer—except the *Post*, maybe, and they probably didn't really believe it, either. What people do think—including the police—is that whoever killed Shari was copycatting the Ankh Killer. Which leads us—'

'Not necessarily to Tommy.'

He cleared his throat. 'If Tommy is as innocent as you say he is, then why did he run?'

'I told you. Because he knew he would be blamed. Everyone here knew he was having some kind of trouble with Shari. Then he found her dead. He knew what people would think.'

Santos drew up one corner of his mouth in an expression of concession. 'That's pretty much what he's told the police.'

'You haven't told me about the new murder.'

'It was an older woman this time—quite a bit older, in

fact. Sixty-seven. Her name is Ruth Wolf. She was an affluent society type, worked part-time as a docent at the Museum of Natural History. From what we can tell, she went to the museum this morning to do some work on an upcoming exhibit. Her husband says preparations for the exhibit were behind schedule, so Ruth went in early. She parked in the back and walked up to a rear door she usually used…except this time she didn't make it to the door. We think the killer was waiting for her behind some bushes near the door. Another docent found her.'

'What…did he do to her?'

He drew in a sad sigh. 'The same as he's done to the others. Strangled her…carved an ankh into her chest. The woman's husband is a basket case. He's a big executive with some cosmetics company on Park Avenue. He's probably best friends with the mayor. You can bet this victim's going to get a lot of press.'

It was nearing seven. 'I'd better get outside before Caitlin gets here,' Anna said.

Later, she sat at her desk, trying to concentrate on her work, but it was no use. She couldn't rid her mind of the image of poor Ruth Wolf approaching the museum door and being grabbed and strangled.

Her cell phone rang. Impatiently she flipped it open. 'Gloria, stop calling me at work.'

'What did you say, darling?' came Tildy Winthrop's birdlike tones.

'Oh, Mother, I'm sorry, I thought you were Gloria.'

'Obviously. That's one of the reasons I'm calling. I understand she's staying with you while she and Donald sort things out.'

'They're not sorting anything out, Mother. Gloria won't even speak to him. She says it's over. She's very hurt.'

'Of course she's hurt. Do you think I don't know what that feels like?'

'Mother! Too much information.'

'It was a very long time ago, dear. Before any of you were born. I forgave your father, because I love him. And Gloria loves Donald. You've got to talk some sense into her.'

'You do realize it's Gloria we're talking about.'

'Don't be smart, dear. Gloria may seem opinionated and pushy, but in reality she's insecure. And she looks up to you, do you know that?'

'Hah! Then why is she constantly trying to find me a new career, steer me into a more appropriate life?'

'That has nothing to do with it. She admires you as a person, respects your judgment. Tell her she's got to at least try to work things out with Donald. She can't do that unless she speaks to him.'

'Do you think I haven't tried?'

'Not hard enough, obviously. Your father and I are counting on you, Anna. Make her see reason.'

'Fine, Mother.' This was usually the most expedient response.

'Good. But that wasn't even the main reason why I was calling. Now let's see… Oh, yes. I want you to move out of Manhattan.'

'*What?*'

'You can't stay in that city with this madman running around strangling women and carving symbols into them. And now you've had that murder right in your garage!'

'But that wasn't the Ankh Killer.'

'Does it matter? Murder is murder. The point is that your father and I want you to come and live here for a while. Until the police catch these killers.'

The thought of commuting between Manhattan Central

13 garage and the 15,000 square-foot, ivy-covered field-stone mansion in Greenwich, Connecticut, in which she'd grown up made Anna laugh out loud. That wasn't her life anymore. 'Thank you, Mother, but no. Manhattan is my home. I promise I'm being careful. Besides, you know I start work at six a.m. I'd have to get up at…three! No, it's just ridiculous.'

Tildy was silent.

'Are you there, Mother?'

'Yes, I'm here,' Tildy said sadly. 'Here wasting my time. You refuse to help your sister and you refuse to protect yourself.' She sniffed. 'When all is said and done, I don't suppose what I think matters much at all.'

'Mother, what's wrong?'

'What? I told you what's wrong.'

'No, it's something else, I can tell. Is it Daddy? Is his vision worse?' Ten months earlier, Jeff Winthrop had revealed to his children that he was suffering from glaucoma.

'Yes,' Tildy admitted. 'His vision is getting worse. Anna, I'm so afraid. I can't lose him.'

'You're not losing him, Mother. People don't die from glaucoma.'

'It's not that. Your father is different lately.'

'Different in what way?'

'He's forgetful. He doesn't remember things he himself said a day earlier. Sometimes I find him just sitting and staring. And his drinking is getting worse and worse. He's having his first drink of the day earlier and earlier. Anna, I don't know what to do.'

'That's simple. You take him to his doctor for a complete work-up. Can you do that, Mother?'

'Yes, of course. He'll fight me, you know that, but I've got to do it.'

'Is this why you're so upset? Why you asked me to live with you?'

'Partly, I suppose,' Tildy admitted. 'But your father and I do worry about this ankh maniac. You must promise me you'll be extremely careful. Don't walk alone at night—take cabs. For that matter, don't walk alone in that garage of yours, which apparently isn't safe, either. Make sure you have lots of locks on your apartment door. Don't let in any strangers.'

'I promise, Mother. Now please, call Daddy's doctor and make an appointment. He'll send you to specialists, I'm sure, but start with him.'

'All right, dear. Thank you. Oh, and Anna?'

'Yes?'

'I love you very much.'

Anna looked at the phone in surprise. In her WASPy family, saying 'I love you'—or expressing any emotion, for that matter—didn't happen very often. 'I love you, too, Mother. You know I do.'

'Yes, I do know, dear. Goodbye.'

As Anna closed her cell phone, her desk phone rang.

'Anna, it's George Mulligan. I've hired an attorney—a man named Farrell—but at the arraignment the judge refused bail and Farrell couldn't talk him out of it.

'Tommy called me. I told him you said you would try to help him. Anna, he wants to tell us what happened at the garage the day that woman was killed.'

'Isn't that something he should be telling Farrell?'

'He already has. Farrell said he would do what he could, but he didn't seem to think what Tommy said made any difference. In other words, I don't think he believes Tommy. Never mind that the entire case against Tommy is circumstantial.' George made a sound of disgust. 'Anna, I'm going to see Tommy tomorrow. Will you come with me?'

The following day was Sunday. 'Of course I will.'

'Good. I'll come by for you at seven thirty, if that's OK. The earlier the better with these prison visits, I'm told.'

'All right. I'll give you my address.'

'I already have it.'

'How?'

He laughed. 'Like I told you, I used to be a reporter.'

As she hung up, a shadow passed across her open door and she looked up to see Gerry Licari. His usually cheerful face was somber, his brows drawn together.

'Have you got a minute?'

'Sure, Gerry. What's up?'

He shut her door and sat down in the chair beside her desk. 'Anna, why did you tell the cops I'd been arguing with Shari?'

She swallowed. 'Gerry, I had to. If I hadn't, Brianna would have. She heard the two of you.'

'What did you tell them?'

'Only what Brianna told me—that she'd heard you and Shari arguing in the courtyard.'

He looked down, wet his lips. 'I don't know what to do,' he muttered.

'About what?' She laughed weakly. 'Gerry, the police aren't going to think you killed Shari just because you'd been arguing. Other people here have far more incriminating stories to tell, believe me.'

This did little to comfort him. He met her gaze. 'I need your advice, Anna. You're always so calm and sensible. I—I don't know who else to talk to.'

'What is it?' she asked, concern in her voice.

'I'm ashamed, but I'm going to tell you anyway.' He shook his head, his eyes wandering. 'Where to begin…? About a month ago, I was leaving the garage and Shari happened to be leaving at the same time—or so I thought.

I was headed for the subway station and she walked with me for a little while. We chatted—about nothing in particular—and for some reason we got on to the subject of her apartment. She said she lived in a dump and wanted to make some improvements but had no one to help her. Specifically, she asked me if I would help her put up some towel racks in her bathroom.'

Anna frowned. 'Towel racks?' She remembered what Rob Cahill had told her about Shari and her 'pipes'.

'That's right. She said she was all thumbs when it came to tools and fixing things, and that she'd be grateful if I could come up sometime and help her.'

He drew a deep breath. 'I don't have to tell you that I knew she wasn't talking about towel racks. I don't know what came over me. She was so gorgeous, so young. I was flattered.'

'And what did you do?' As if she didn't know.

He dropped his gaze in shame. 'I went up to her apartment with her right then and there.'

'Gerry,' she said, 'do you think you're the first guy ever to have an affair?'

'It wasn't an affair!' he broke in. 'It was one time. One terrible time.'

'Terrible? I don't—'

'I can't believe I was so gullible. We were…in bed, when all of a sudden the bedroom door flew open and there was this guy with a camera. It was the same guy who came for Shari on the motorcycle on Wednesday— Dennis Ostrow is his name. Anyway, he started flashing away before I could even get out of the bed and pull my clothes on. I was furious. I called Shari a terrible name and she just looked at me with this cold, hard look in her eye.

'I got out of there fast, hoping that was the end of it, but

I knew it wasn't. And the very next day when I walked into my office there were prints of the photos spread out on my desk, right out in the open. Anyone could have seen them. I was horrified. I grabbed them up and stuffed them in my pocket. When I looked up, Shari was standing there. She had that same dead look in her eyes. She said she wanted two thousand dollars or she would show the photos to Vera. She knew my wife's *name*. Anna, this woman was a monster. She'd researched my life, my family, knew where I live.'

'What did you tell her?'

He wiped his hand across his damp forehead. 'What do you think I told her? I couldn't let Vera see those pictures. It was a mistake! A single mistake! I couldn't let it ruin what we have. I *love* her. I know, I know—if I loved her, why did I go up to her apartment?'

'Because you're a man,' she said drily.

He didn't disagree.

'So what happens now?' she said. 'Shari's gone, but Dennis isn't. Do you think he would show the pictures to Vera?'

'Oh, I know he would. He called me this morning.'

Anna stared in surprise. 'What did he say?'

'That just because Shari was dead didn't mean I didn't have to pay up. And he asked for *four* thousand. Anna, I don't have that kind of money. At least, not so Vera wouldn't notice.'

She gave him a pitying look. 'Gerry, isn't it time to stop the lying? The only way to disarm this creep is to confess to Vera. If she loves you as much as you love her, she'll understand; she'll forgive you. Then you can go to the police and file blackmail charges against Ostrow.'

He chewed his lip thoughtfully. 'I suppose you're right.

Vera would understand. She might not forgive me right away, but she would understand. But I would never go to the police.'

'Why not?'

'Because this guy is dangerous. If he knew I'd told the police about him, I'm sure he would come after me. He's like that, Anna; I could tell. Violent. Cold, like Shari.'

'All right, then. Confess to Vera but don't go to the police.'

He rose. 'I knew you would know what to do. Deep down I suppose I knew that was the answer. I guess I was hoping there was some other way.'

'You mean to keep Vera from learning the truth?'

'Sure. What she doesn't know can't hurt her.'

Her gaze slid to his face. What an odd thing to say, she thought. She paused, processing all of this. 'What are you going to say to Ostrow the next time he calls?'

'That it doesn't matter if he shows the pictures to Vera, because I'm going to tell her everything.' He opened the door. 'Thank you, Anna.'

'Anytime,' she said, giving him a supportive smile, and watched him walk down the corridor into his own office and close the door. A movement to her right made her turn her head. Brianna stood just outside Anna's office, her gaze fixed on Gerry's door. She gave Anna an inquiring look.

But Anna wouldn't betray Gerry. She checked her watch, then gave Brianna a chipper little grin. 'Don't you need to get started on your route?'

'Mm,' Brianna said, preoccupied. 'Anna,' she said softly, 'does Gerry know you told the cops I overheard him arguing with Shari in the courtyard?'

Anna frowned. 'Of course he knows. They asked him about it.'

Brianna nodded, then tilted her head to one side. 'Did he happen to say why Vera was at the garage on Thursday?'

'Vera? Here on Thursday? That's the day Shari was murdered.' Brianna nodded.

'Vera was *here*?'

'Mm-hm. It was the strangest thing. I was crossing the floor toward my truck and I saw her. I recognized her immediately. I've met her a number of times at Family Day.'

'What was she doing?'

'She was heading for the break room stairs. She didn't see me. There was no one else around. She looked to each side in this sneaky way before she went through the door.'

'And?'

'And I waited a little bit.'

'For what?'

'For her to come back down.'

'And did she?'

'No, that's the strange thing. I waited a good ten minutes, figuring she'd gone to the ladies' room. When she didn't come back down, I got curious and went upstairs. And guess what?'

Anna shook her head to signify she didn't know.

'She wasn't there.'

'What do you mean, she wasn't there?'

Brianna threw out her hands. 'Gone. Not up there. Not in the break room, not in the bathroom...I even checked the locker room and the showers.'

Anna laughed. 'She must have come back down and you missed her.'

'No,' Brianna insisted, 'that's just it. I never took my eyes off that door. You see, I was curious about what she was doing there. I had never seen her at the garage before.'

Anna gave Brianna a shrewd look. 'You had a good idea why she was here, though, didn't you?'

'Sure. I'm not stupid, Anna. I had a pretty good idea what was going on between Gerry and Shari.'

Anna said nothing. Then, 'So why did you think Vera was here?'

Brianna gave a small shrug. 'To have it out with Shari—that seemed the likeliest reason. Why else would she have come? And why else would she have been sneaking around like that? Because she didn't want Gerry to know she was here. Or maybe some other reason...'

'Like?'

'Like she was waiting to murder her.'

'What! Oh, for Pete's sake.'

'Why not? Anna, *somebody* did it. It could have been Vera as much as anyone. Why else would she have hidden up there? Because I know that's what she did. Maybe in a closet—I should have checked—maybe in one of the bathroom stalls; if you stand on the toilet, no one will see your feet.

'She was waiting for the right moment. You know how it is here in the garage. Sometimes I walk through the building and there's not a soul in sight. She creeps downstairs...makes sure no one's around...sees Shari go out to the courtyard...follows her...and—' Brianna put her hands around an imaginary neck and pretended to squeeze.

'OK, OK, I get it.'

'Ask Gerry,' Brianna said easily.

'Ask Gerry what?'

'Ask him what Vera was doing here. If she wasn't here for some sneaky reason, he'll know she was here, right? And he'll be able to tell you why.' Brianna checked her watch. 'I'd better get goin'.' And she hurried off.

She was right. Anna went directly to Gerry's office

and knocked on the door. When he called, 'Come in,' she pushed it open.

'Gerry,' she said without preamble, 'why was Vera here on Thursday?'

He looked at her sharply and she could practically see the wheels of his brain turning. But his face had already told her what she needed to know: he hadn't known.

He gave her a relaxed smile. 'She came into the city with me, wanted to do some shopping. She met some friends for lunch, shopped some more, then came by for me at the end of the day and we went back home together.' He watched her, his expression saying, 'Is she buying it?'

He didn't have to know she didn't really buy it. 'I'm jealous,' she said with a smile. 'I haven't been shopping in ages, let alone done a lunch with the ladies. I hope she found some nice bargains.'

'On Fifth Avenue? I don't think so. But that's OK. She doesn't shop there very often. Most of the time she's at Loehmann's and the Burlington Coat Factory.'

She laughed, closing the door. As soon as it clicked shut, her smile was gone. How well did she really know Gerry? Not well enough, she realized, to know he wouldn't lie. Well enough, she wondered, to know he couldn't commit murder? She wasn't sure.

Perhaps Gerry *had* confessed to Vera, and Vera took it on herself to eliminate the problem—Shari. Or perhaps together they had planned for Vera to come to the garage. Perhaps that look on his face had been because he knew perfectly well that Vera had come to the garage, but wondered how Anna knew...

Purposefully she marched back to her office, closed the door, flipped open her address book, and found Gerry's home number. Vera answered on the third ring.

'Anna, this is a nice surprise.'

Anna had met Vera several times, both at the garage's Christmas parties and at the annual summer Sanitation Department Family Day picnic.

'How are you, Vera?'

'I'm fine,' Vera replied, already sounding puzzled. 'Is everything all right, Anna?'

'Yes, everything's fine, Gerry's fine. But I need to speak with you about something. Is there any way we can meet?'

'Anna, darling,' Vera said with a laugh, 'I'm out on Long Island. Can't we talk on the phone?'

'I…don't think this is something to discuss over the phone.'

There was a moment's silence. 'All right. I have a sitter in the mornings.' Vera and Gerry had two small children, a boy and a girl. 'I could come in on Monday if that works for you.'

'Yes, that works. You take the train into Penn Station, right?' Anna asked. 'Let's meet there. Say, ten o'clock?'

'Yes, that would be fine.'

'Good, I'll meet your train.'

'All right.' Vera sounded uneasy. 'Monday, then.'

'Oh, and Vera—'

'Yes?'

'I think it would be best if you didn't mention to Gerry that you're meeting me. At least not yet.'

'All right,' Vera said, sounding as if she already knew why.

NINE

ANNA HADN'T TOLD Gloria where she was going today. She slipped out of the apartment and down the stairs to the street.

George was waiting at the curb in a beat-up old Corolla. 'Not very glamorous,' he said as she got in. 'Then again, where we're going isn't glamorous, either.'

It was a gray day, a light drizzle falling. George, who apparently disliked windshield wipers, flipped them on occasionally to clear the glass. Not knowing when he would do it added to Anna's nervousness.

He crossed town and took the Triboro Bridge to Queens. For ten minutes they rode in silence, George consulting a sheet of scrawled directions on the seat beside him. Finally he pulled into the Rikers Island parking lot.

'Now we have to take the shuttle,' he said, and they walked to the stop, where a large number of people, mostly young women, waited with grim expressions. Finally the bus appeared, squealing to a stop in front of the group, who had formed a line.

When everyone was aboard, the driver, a bone-thin woman who looked as if she had driven this route a million times, steered the bus on to the long two-lane bridge that connected Rikers Island and Queens. Through the mist, Anna saw a sewage treatment plant on the left; from the right came the roar of a jet from nearby LaGuardia Airport as it climbed toward the leaden sky. Soon the island that housed the massive prison complex came into view, encircled by barbed wire and high chain-link fences. Beside her, Anna felt George shift uncomfortably.

Leaving the shuttle, they were met by a tall male corrections officer. After leading them into the Control Building, he turned and said: 'Ladies and gentlemen, listen closely, please, and this process will go smoothly—something I'm sure you all want. Now, inmates are allowed three one-hour visits a week. That means if you have already been here three times this week, get right back on that bus. Ditto if you're not a relative of the inmate you've come to see.'

Anna looked at George, who shook his head to say not to worry. 'Tommy put you on his list,' he whispered. 'You're his Aunt Anna.'

'There are to be no more than three visitors per visit,' the officer continued. 'Now, if you'll follow me, please…'

Divided into two lines, the visitors marched stoically into the visitors center. There they presented ID, were frisked by a group of male and female guards, and were then met by an overweight female corrections officer who had brought in a yellow Labrador retriever that began zealously sniffing handbags, legs, and shoes. Satisfied that none of the visitors carried any contraband, the female officer led the group to a locker room and instructed them to leave all belongings behind in coin lockers that lined the walls, including the contents of pockets and even belts and jewelry, 'except for wedding and engagement rings,' she informed them, 'and necklaces with *small* crosses.'

Finally, after passing through X-ray scanners and metal detectors and getting wanded down, Anna and George boarded a bus to the George Motchan Detention Center, where Tommy was being held.

Waiting for him in the visitors' room, Anna scanned the cheap artwork on the walls; it only served to exacerbate the atmosphere of misery. At a table directly behind her and George, a young woman whom Anna remembered from the shuttle sat weeping into her hands. Looking up as a young man approached her table, she forced a smile and quickly wiped her eyes.

When Tommy entered the room a moment after the young man, George let out a soft involuntary groan. In his gray prison suit bearing the letters DOC, Tommy walked slowly over, his shoulders hunched. His face was nearly as gray as the suit, and a thick black stubble covered his face. He embraced his father.

'Thanks for coming, Anna,' he said, sitting opposite them.

George covered his son's hand with his own. 'How are you holding up?'

Tommy merely shrugged. 'We don't have a lot of time,' he said, shooting a look at a nearby guard. 'There are some things I want to tell you. Maybe knowing these things will help you figure out what really happened on Thursday.'

'Tommy,' Anna interrupted him, 'I think I've got a good idea of at least some of it.' And she quickly ran down the scam Shari and Dennis had pulled on Gerry—though without mentioning Gerry's name. 'And they threatened to show the photos to your fiancée unless you paid up, am I right?' she finished.

Tommy nodded. 'Partly. But there was something else she wanted.'

Anna's brows rose. Tommy leaned forward, lowering his voice even further.

'The whole reason Shari wanted to be a sanitation worker was so she could find buildings along her route to burglarize.'

'What?' George said, a little too loudly, and the guard gave him a warning look.

Tommy nodded. 'It's true. She said, "You're going to

give me the money, and you're also going to help me break into some of these places we're servicing." When I asked her how I was supposed to do that, she said I had been working my route long enough to know where she could break in without being seen—alley doors, cellar doors, fire escapes…'

'What did you do?' Anna asked.

Tommy lowered his head in shame. 'I showed her one place on West Forty-Ninth Street—an alley with a Dumpster at the front of it; you can't see behind it. She never used it, thankfully. I guess she would have if she hadn't been killed. Anyway, as soon as I had told her about the break-in place, I regretted it, I felt terrible. Hurting me was one thing. I couldn't help her hurt other people.

'She was expecting me to tell her about other break-in spots. She came up to me in the break room one day and said she wanted the information. I told her I wasn't going to do it, that she could show the photos to Colleen if she wanted to, but I wasn't going to help her.'

'What did she say?' George asked.

'She was furious.' Tommy shook his head, remembering. 'Man, it was scary. Bill and Fred came into the room at that moment, so Shari and I stepped out into the hall, and all of a sudden Shari pulled me into the supply closet. She slapped me and said I *would* cooperate or Colleen wouldn't just see the photos; Dennis would hurt her.

'I slapped her back. I've never hated anyone as much as I hated her at that moment. And I was afraid for Colleen. I mean, these people were ruthless. I believed they would do what Shari had threatened. I told her I would kill her if anything happened to Colleen. When I said that, Shari suddenly looked at me in a new way, almost…*admiringly*. But then she laughed and tried to kiss me. I was disgusted.

I broke away from her and left the closet. That's when you walked by, Anna.'

She nodded, remembering. 'Did she leave you alone after that?'

He gave a mirthless laugh. 'Of course not. The next day, right on the garage floor, she came up to me in my truck—Pierre and I were about to head out—and said she needed to talk to me. I got furious. I jumped out of the truck and screamed at her, told her it was enough. She said she would decide when it was enough. I was so angry that I said again that I could kill her.

'You came over and broke us up, Anna, but once you were gone she came up to me again. She was like an evil tar baby you couldn't shake off. She insisted on speaking with me. I was afraid she would make another scene, so just to shut her up I said I had to go out on my route but that I would meet her later. She said, "When? Where?" I told her to meet me in the courtyard at eleven-thirty. That way I figured it wouldn't look suspicious; people go out there all the time to smoke.

'Pierre and I finished our route and came back to the garage. At eleven thirty I went out to the courtyard and found Shari on the ground. I knew immediately that she was dead. I went up to her. There were dark bruises on her neck. Then I saw that her shirt was ripped open and there was blood on it. I pulled the shirt a little to the side to see more, and that's when I saw the symbol carved into her chest.

'That's when I panicked. You had seen me in the closet with her, Anna. People had heard us fighting, heard me say I could kill her. And I don't know if you know this, but Shari told Rob that she and I were an item but that she was afraid of me sometimes because I could get violent.'

As Shari had told Anna. She lowered her head in disbelief.

'I knew I would be blamed for killing her. I knew no one would believe me. So I ran. Brianna saw me. I ran upstairs, changed into my street clothes, and got on the next subway uptown.'

'Where were you going?' George asked.

Tommy shook his head. 'I don't know. I told you, I panicked. I had to get away before...' He indicated his gray prison jumpsuit. Tears came into his eyes. 'What am I going to do?'

'You're going to keep telling the truth,' George said. 'Worst-case scenario, there will be a trial and the jury will see that there's no real evidence against you. But that's the worst case. Anna and I are going to do what we can to clear you, Tommy. You do realize Colleen's going to have to find out about you and Shari?'

'Yes. Please tell her I love her and that I'm so very, very sorry.'

As if on cue, the guard announced that the hour was up. Anna and George watched Tommy as he left the room. Then, wordlessly, they filed out of the visitors room and got in line for the bus.

ON ARRIVING HOME, Anna opened her apartment door and was greeted by one of the largest flower arrangements she had ever seen, an other-worldly assortment of pink, blue, and white blossoms and curling white branches, all in a heavy blue-and-white Chinese-style porcelain pot.

'Beautiful, isn't it?' Gloria stood a few feet away, taking it in.

'Do you think my table can support the weight?'

Gloria made a face. 'Oh, Anna.' Her expression softened. 'Guess who they're from.'

'Hmm...' Anna put thumb and forefinger to her chin

as if concentrating. 'Who could it be? I'm surprised you accepted them.'

'They're so beautiful. How could I not?'

'What did the card say?'

Gloria had it in the pocket of her jeans. Shyly she brought it out and read: 'You bring beauty to my life. I love you, Gloria. Please come home.' Her voice cracked on the last word. 'Isn't that sweet?'

There was no way Anna would say otherwise. 'Very sweet. Have you thanked him?'

'Not yet. They only arrived half an hour ago. I'll go in the bedroom and call him. Oh—' she said, turning around, 'Mom called. She told me you refuse to listen to reason and come home until this Ankh Killer is captured.'

'That's right. How come she's not bugging you and Beth?'

'She is! We refused, too.' Gloria continued into Anna's bedroom. Looking at the flowers, Anna decided this was extremely encouraging.

She had little appetite. She made some tea for her and Gloria and took her cup out to the living room, switching on the TV. She groaned. On the screen were photos of Lauri Shepard, Carmela Santiago, Crista Sherrod, Paulette Edwards, Shari Baird, and Ruth Wolf.

The photographs faded. A newscaster was interviewing a white-haired man with silver-rimmed glasses who, according to the caption at the bottom of the screen, was Dr Alexander Tobias, a forensic psychologist.

'Dr Tobias,' said the host, 'can you give us some insight into this person? Can we tell anything about him from his crimes?'

'Yes, I think we can tell a lot about him,' Dr Tobias replied. 'First, I think it's safe to say this is a man who hates women. Most likely he was abused by a woman or women as a child; or perhaps a woman—most probably his mother—abandoned him.'

'That's very interesting,' the host said, nodding intently.

'I think it's also safe to say that this man is quite ordinary,' Dr Tobias said.

'Really?' the host asked, looking surprised. 'What do you mean by that?'

'These murders do not only help this man express his hatred for women; they also help him elevate himself to the position of—well, a god. A god can give life and take it away. For this man the taking of life is the ultimate high, because it makes him feel like somebody important.'

'Anything else?'

Dr Tobias thought for a moment. 'Strangulation as the murder method backs up what I was just saying. Strangling these women allows the killer to watch the life seep out of them, so to speak. He can *control* their deaths. As I said, he becomes a god with power over life.'

The host nodded thoughtfully. 'One last thing, Dr Tobias. What do you make of the mark he carves into his victims? This ankh symbol?'

Dr Tobias nodded. 'That…is a message.'

'A message?'

'Yes, a secret one. Because of something in his past, this symbol is meaningful to him. It does, after all, represent life, immortality. This symbol is also meaningful to someone else—someone who may not even be alive any longer. What this man is doing is branding his killings with this secret message. We won't know its full meaning until he's caught.'

'And let's hope that's soon,' the host said solemnly, and the photographs of the six women reappeared on the screen. 'This has been extremely enlightening. Thank you, Doctor.'

With a shudder, Anna clicked the remote; the TV went dark.

From the bedroom came the sound of Gloria talking on the telephone. Smiling, Anna gazed out her window into the deepening darkness of Forty-Third Street and sipped her tea.

FAR ACROSS TOWN, in a rented room in the basement of a crumbling building on West Thirty-Seventh Street, the Ankh Killer watched the TV. He didn't care what that idiot doctor said about him—that he was abused, ordinary... whatever. Now the six women's photographs were on the screen again...

Suddenly with a roar of rage he hurled his beer bottle across the room. It missed the TV screen, instead hitting the plank-and-cinder-block bookcase behind it and shattering, beer and shards of brown glass flying everywhere.

'It's only *four*!' he cried. *'Four!'* His eyes narrowed to slits as he leaned forward to study the women's faces, but they faded away, replaced by an antacid commercial.

'Who is doing this?' he muttered to the well-fed black cat that had just padded into the room. He stroked its sleek fur and it began to purr softly. 'Who is doing this to us, Bastet?' In his lap was a pad of yellow lined paper. His right hand rested on the pad and in it he held his cell phone, which displayed the photograph he had taken of Ruth Wolf just after strangling her and carving the ankh into her chest. Looking at the picture, he moaned.

In his left hand he held a pen. On the pad, his hand jerking violently, he drew an ankh; then, faster, another; and another; and another...

TEN

ANNA WAITED ON a bench in the Long Island Railroad waiting area on Penn Station's middle level. Presently Vera Licari appeared, walking purposefully toward her. Anna had forgotten how very attractive she was—a shapely brunette with pale, soft features and long, slim legs. As she approached, Anna rose to greet her.

'Oh, Anna, I didn't see you!' Vera said breathlessly, and the two women embraced briefly. 'It's good to see you...' She looked at Anna warily. 'I think.'

'There's a little café just over there,' Anna said, and led the way. They took a table at the back and ordered coffee.

'So what did you want to talk to me about?' Vera asked. 'The suspense is killing me.'

'All right, Vera, I'll get right to it. What were you doing at the garage on Thursday morning?'

There was an infinitesimal pause. 'Oh,' she said airily, 'I came in with Gerry. I went shopping, met a few friends for lunch, that sort of thing.'

'Why did you go upstairs?'

Vera gave her head a confused little shake. 'What do you mean?'

'When you were at the garage,' Anna said patiently, 'you went upstairs. Why?'

'Why do you think? I had to use the bathroom.'

'But you never came back down.'

Vera had raised her coffee cup almost to her lips. She set it down. 'I beg your pardon?'

'You went up—someone saw you—but you didn't come down, at least not for a long time. And when the person who saw you go upstairs went up to look for you, you were gone.'

'That's ridiculous! Of course I came back down. Whoever was spying on me must have looked away, because I went to the bathroom, came right back down, and left. I couldn't have been up there for more than five minutes. Anna, what is this about? I demand to know.'

This was delicate. 'Vera, has Gerry told you...?'

'About Shari?' Vera said, her eyes suddenly cold.

Anna waited.

'No, he didn't actually tell me,' Vera said, 'but I know about her.'

'How do you know?'

Vera rolled her eyes and laughed. 'Anna, once you're married you'll find out how dumb men are—or maybe you already know. Gerry was getting calls at home on his cell phone—a lot of them. And every time he got one, he left the room.'

'So you overheard?'

'No, I wouldn't eavesdrop on Gerry!' Vera said, affronted. 'I waited until he was asleep and called the number on his phone.'

'And you got Shari?'

'It took me a while to establish that. The first time I called, she obviously thought it was Gerry calling, because she said, "Gerry, what is it?" When I asked who she was, she hung up. So I copied down the number and called on my regular phone, dialing *67 first so that she wouldn't know who was calling, of course.

'This time when she answered, I changed my voice a little and made believe I was Macy's calling with a delivery for her—a chair she'd ordered. When she said she hadn't ordered a chair, I said the store must have mixed up her records with someone else's. I asked for her address so that I could clear it all up...and she gave it to me.'

'But you still didn't know why she had been calling Gerry.'

'I had a pretty good idea, though I hated to believe it. You see, a short time after we were married, Gerry had an affair with a woman at the company he worked for at the time. It almost broke up our marriage. I prayed it would never happen again. He promised me it wouldn't. But when he started getting these mysterious calls, I decided to prepare myself for the worst.'

'Did you go and see her?'

'Late one afternoon I went to the address she had given me. I thought that if she worked, I would have the best chance of finding her later in the day. It was an apartment building. When I buzzed her apartment, there was no answer. I couldn't very well wait in the hall outside her door, so I sat down on the building's front steps. Every time a young woman came up the stairs, I looked up and said, "Shari?" Finally I hit the jackpot. A very attractive young woman ran up the steps, and when I said, "Shari?" she stopped. She pretended that wasn't her name, that she'd just stopped because she'd heard me say something, but I knew she was the one. I told her I knew. Then I told her that if she didn't speak with me, I would wait on those front stairs until she did. Finally she agreed and we went up to her apartment.

'It was an awful, filthy dump, dust and dirt all over the floor, barely any furniture. But I wasn't there to clean the place. As I said, I was assuming the worst about this woman, so I said, "I want you to stop seeing Gerry."

'When she realized who I was, she started laughing.

She laughed so hard she couldn't stop. I asked her what was so funny—did she think it was amusing to break up someone's family? Then her face got very serious and she said now that I knew about her and Gerry, she had no further interest in him.'

Anna watched Vera closely. 'Did you know what she meant by that?'

'Of course. That now that I had found out about their affair—caught them—Shari would end it. Why are you looking at me that way?'

'Vera, I'm going to tell you the truth. Gerry won't like it, but we women have to stick together. Shari was blackmailing Gerry.'

'She was *what*?'

Anna nodded. 'Their "affair" actually consisted of one afternoon when Shari got Gerry up to that apartment on a pretext—to fix something or other—and seduced him. While they were in flagrante delicto, Shari's accomplice burst in and took pictures. Shari then told Gerry she would show you these pictures if he didn't pay her—a lot.'

Vera was looking at her, stunned. 'And did he pay?'

'Yes. But she wanted more. They fought about it at the garage.'

Vera's pretty face softened. 'And all because Gerry didn't want me to know.'

Anna blinked. 'That's a good thing?'

'Well, of course. He wouldn't have cared so much about my seeing the photos unless he valued me and our marriage.'

'I suppose that's one way to look at it.'

'Anna, how do you know all this?'

'Gerry told me.'

'Why?'

'Because someone had overheard him fighting with Shari. He knew the police would think he had a good motive to kill her. He wanted to get it all out in the open, tell me the truth.'

'Good. So now you know everything,' Vera said briskly, gathering herself together, 'I should start getting back.'

But Anna hadn't moved.

'What is it?' Vera asked.

'You still haven't explained why you went upstairs and never came down.'

Vera's eyes bulged. 'I've already *told* you, I *did* come down.' She laughed. 'What do you think I did, go upstairs pretending to go to the bathroom, hide in a closet or something, and then sneak out at the right time and kill her?'

'It's not out of the realm of possibility.'

'Yes, it is, because it's absolutely ridiculous. I don't know what kinds of silly murder mysteries you've been reading, Anna, but things like that don't happen in real life. Besides, even assuming I had done that, how could I have gotten from upstairs to the courtyard without being seen?'

'That's not difficult. There are many times during the day when the garage is quiet. It wouldn't even have taken a minute to get out there.'

'Oh, for pity's sake,' Vera said, disgusted, and rose. 'Think what you like, Anna. There's just one problem, a rather large one. The police have caught the person who killed Shari. It's that boy, Tommy Mulligan. Gerry told me and it's been in all the papers. So why are you doing this?'

'Because I know Tommy didn't do it, and the only way I can help clear him is to figure out who did.'

'Well, Miss Marple, I hope you have a wonderful time. Just don't bother me again.'

She walked away briskly on her high heels, her trousers stretching attractively across her shapely rear end.

BACK AT THE GARAGE, Anna had no sooner sat down at her desk than Gerry walked in without knocking.

'How dare you speak to my wife?'

She gazed up at him impassively.

'Answer me!'

'I have every right to speak to whomever I want, Gerry. You don't own your wife, and you don't own me.'

His expression of anger was replaced by one of hurt. 'Anna, I confided in you. I *trusted* you.'

'Gerry, she already knew.'

'Knew what?'

'About Shari. Except that she thought the two of you were just having an affair. Vera told you I had spoken to her?'

He nodded. 'Of course; how else would I know. Why did you do it?'

'I wanted to know why she went upstairs Thursday morning and never came down.'

'What! Of course she came down.'

'That's what she said.'

'And you don't believe her?'

'I don't know what to believe. The point is that she could very well have killed Shari.'

'A lot of people could very well have done a lot of things, Anna. That doesn't mean they did them.'

He threw up his hands in exasperation and stormed out.

LATE THE FOLLOWING afternoon, Anna emerged from the subway on to Canal Street. She made her way along the teeming sidewalk until she reached an abandoned storefront. Its door and plate-glass windows had been opaqued with swirls of soap. Above the window, the ghosts of removed letters spelled KATZ'S MEAT MARKET.

Referring again to the scrap of paper in her hand, she went to the door and knocked. When there was no answer she knocked again. After a few moments the door opened a crack and a woman peered out from behind strong eyeglasses. 'The store is closed.'

'I know that,' Anna said, stopping the door from closing by wedging her foot between it and the frame. 'I'm looking for Urban Access.'

The woman stared at her. 'Who are you?'

'My name is Anna Winthrop. I'm here about one of your members.'

'Who?'

Anna sighed. 'I'd like to come in, please.'

The woman spoke to someone behind her; then the door slowly opened. The woman with the bug eyes was petite, unusually thin, with black hair cut in a severe old-fashioned pageboy. Anna judged her to be in her mid-twenties. There were other people standing farther away in the shadows, but Anna's eyes hadn't yet grown accustomed to the darkness and she couldn't make them out.

One of these shadow people stepped forward, an attractive woman with creamy-white features, gray eyes, and a healthy mane of red hair. 'What do you want?'

'My name is Anna Winthrop—'

'I heard that already. What do you want?'

'I'm looking for an old friend of mine and thought you might be able to help me. What is your name, by the way?'

The woman eyed her suspiciously. At last she said, 'Jocelyn Paar.'

'I take it you're the group's leader?'

Jocelyn shrugged, not wanting to answer.

'At any rate,' Anna said, 'my friend's name is Dennis Ostrow. I understand he belongs to your group.'

'You say he's a friend of yours?' Jocelyn said. 'From where?'

Anna had come prepared. 'Actually, I met him through someone else I believe was also one of your members—Shari Baird. You've probably heard about her.'

'Yes.'

'Well, Shari and I worked together on a few temp assignments'—Anna had learned from Shari's file that she had done temp work before coming to the Sanitation Department—'and she and Dennis and I got to be friends. I called the number I had for Dennis but it's been disconnected, and he's not at his address anymore either.'

Jocelyn seemed to consider all of this. Finally she snapped at the bug-eyed woman, 'Patsy, give her Dennis's number.'

Patsy retreated to the back of the store, which Anna now saw was empty except for the people in it. She also realized it was very dirty. She felt grit under her shoes and saw trash—remnants of the meat market—strewn across the floor.

'Here.' Patsy had reappeared, holding out a slip of paper.

'Thanks,' Anna said, smiling. 'I really want to see Dennis. I'm sure he's devastated about poor Shari.'

Jocelyn and Patsy just stared at her. She said goodbye and slipped out through the soaped-up door.

WHEN THE PERSON Anna presumed was Dennis Ostrow answered his phone, he did not say hello. He said nothing. Anna could hear faint breathing and street noises in the background.

'Hello? Is someone there?'

More breathing and street noise; then, 'Who is this?'

'Dennis, this is Anna Winthrop. I was Shari's supervisor at Manhattan Thirteen.'

'What do you want?'

'I want to talk to you.'

'So talk.'

'In person.'

'Why?'

Anna hesitated. 'It's about Gerry Licari and Tommy Mulligan.'

A long silence. 'What about them?'

'Look,' she said, patience gone, 'either you see me or you see the cops. Take your pick.'

'Union Square Park, north-east corner, in an hour.' The phone went dead.

IT WAS PAST nine o'clock and completely dark when Anna emerged from the subway station at Fourteenth Street and walked to the north-east corner of Union Square Park. Across Seventeenth Street, the Barnes & Noble bookstore glowed cheerily. Light poured from the windows of the fourth floor; Anna imagined an author reading was taking place, and for a moment she wished she were there instead of here.

She heard a scraping sound and spun around. Dennis stood only a few feet away. He was on crutches, his left foot in a cast.

'Motorcycle accident?' she said.

'So talk.'

'Wouldn't you like to sit?' she said, pointing to a bench.

He gave a little shrug, hobbled over, and sat down. She sat as far from him as she could. He was good-looking in a shabby sort of way, with that mass of dirty-blond hair, long-lashed eyes, even features, and a becoming five o'clock shadow. He was waiting.

She jumped right in. 'I know what you and Shari did to Gerry Licari and Tommy Mulligan. But that's not why I wanted to talk to you. I'm trying to find out what really happened to Shari, and I think you might be able to help.'

He laughed. '"What happened to Shari?" Don't you know? Seems to me it happened right in your garage.'

'Don't be a wise guy. It did happen in my garage, but it didn't go down the way the police think. In other words, Tommy didn't kill her.'

''Course he did. Shari told me how mad he was, that he even said he would kill her.'

'*If* you and she hurt his fiancée.'

'He killed her anyway. He strangled her and carved that unk into her chest to make it look like that lunatic did it.'

'Ankh.'

'What?'

'It's an ankh, not an unk.'

'Are you saying I'm stupid?'

'There are a lot of things I'm not saying you are. The fact is, I don't care. I just want you to tell me what you can about Shari.'

'What about her?'

'Did she have any family?'

'Nope. She had my number in her pocket and the cops called me to identify the body. I was the one who gave them her picture.'

Anna remembered Shari's smiling photo on the TV news. 'Where was she from?'

He shrugged.

'Where did she live?'

'Upper West Side.'

'Alone?'

'With another chick.'

'Ah. Who?'

'A girl named Taffy. If I give you her number, will you get out of my face?'

Nodding, she brought out paper and pen. He wrote down the number.

'You'll forgive me if I don't stick around,' she said, pocketing the paper and pen. 'There seems to be a bad smell around here.'

She walked away without looking back.

SHE TRIED TAFFY'S NUMBER as soon as she arrived home, but there was no answer, no recording. She tried it again before leaving for work the next morning. This time a woman with a high, squeaky voice answered.

'Taffy?' Anna said.

'Yeah?'

'My name is Anna Winthrop. I was Shari's supervisor at Manhattan Central Thirteen.'

'Yeah?' Taffy sounded puzzled.

'I'd like to speak to you about her.'

'Speak to me? Why?'

'I'll explain when I see you. Please.'

'Well,' Taffy said, sounding uncomfortable. 'When did you have in mind?'

'How about tomorrow? I finish work at two.'

'I start work at four. Come see me there. Marconi Pasta Company, on Eighth Avenue between Thirty-Second and Thirty-Third.'

That wasn't far from the garage. 'You start at four?'

'Uh-huh,' Taffy squeaked. 'What did you say your name was again?'

'Winthrop. Anna Winthrop.'

THE NEXT DAY she stayed late at the garage, catching up on some paperwork, and left a little before four, walking the ten blocks down Eighth Avenue.

The Marconi Pasta Company was on the west side of the street, between a dry cleaner and mobile phone store. Approaching the storefront, Anna saw that it wasn't only a store but also a restaurant, with a menu in the window beside the door and tables inside covered with red-and-white checkered tablecloths. The uneven wooden floor creaked under her feet as she entered. On the walls hung antique posters advertising the restaurant: 'Dine in Old World Charm, at the Marconi Pasta Company.'

The place was indeed charming, and Anna made a mental note to return with Santos.

'Can I help you?'

She turned. An elderly man behind a counter displaying various Italian salads was wiping his hands on his apron. He frowned, taking in Anna's Sanitation uniform.

'I'm looking for Taffy Grant.'

His eyes grew wide. He turned to a young woman a few feet away, who also stared at Anna in surprise.

'Is something wrong?' Anna asked.

'No...uh, no,' the man said. 'Does Taffy know you're coming?'

Anna nodded.

'Have you been here before?' the young woman asked.

How strange, Anna thought. 'No.'

The man cocked his head toward the back. 'Through there, second door on the left, up the stairs.'

Anna frowned. 'To see Taffy,' she confirmed. 'She works here.'

They both nodded.

With an inward shrug, Anna followed their directions, passing through a curtained doorway and part of the kitchen—where a man chopping onions looked up, gave her a funny look—before opening the second door on the left and starting up a steep, narrow staircase that smelled strongly of cigarettes. Nearing the top, she heard a popular disco tune from the seventies.

Stepping on to the upper landing, she began to understand. It was dark up here, even darker than Urban Access's headquarters, the small red lights spaced along the walls providing little illumination. She was standing in a short corridor with a door on each side and one directly in front of her. None of these doors was marked. With a shrug she opened the one on the right and passed through.

The music was louder here—Donna Summer squealing that she felt love…felt love. The air was warm and still, scented with a combination of sweat, cheap perfume, and the cigarette smoke she had smelled on the stairs. It was even darker here. As Anna's eyes adjusted, she realized she was in another corridor, this one longer and with many doors. In front of each door stood a young woman. The one nearest Anna was a stunningly beautiful Asian girl who couldn't have been more than eighteen. She wore the stringiest of bikinis, impossibly high stilettos, and a scarlet ribbon around her long, graceful neck. She sidled up to Anna. 'You here for some fun?'

'Uh…no. I'm looking for Taffy Grant.'

The woman had completely lost interest and was already walking away. 'You a cop?'

'No.'

'Go back out that door and through the middle one.'

She did. This time she found herself looking at a large circular structure with doors all around. She had a pretty good idea what this was. She chose a door at random and went through.

She was in a tiny booth with solid side walls and a darkened Plexiglas wall straight ahead. Next to the Plexiglas wall was a slot for bills. Anna fished a dollar from her purse and fed it in. The dark screen on the other side of the glass slowly rose.

Now she was looking in on a small circular space on to which a number of other booths around the circle had a view. There were men in some of the booths. Inside the circle, a tall woman with curly dark hair gyrated sluggishly. She was completely naked except for a pair of stilettos much like those worn by the young Asian woman. On the floor was a selection of vegetables—a banana, a cucumber, a zucchini. A kinky salad.

Suddenly the gyrating woman noticed Anna. Abruptly she stopped her bumping and grinding, gestured toward the outside, and went through a door. Men's cries of protest came from the other booths.

Outside, the woman approached Anna. Somewhere between her little stage and here she'd donned a wispy pink chiffon blouse that hung to her mid-thighs. 'Are you Anna?' It was the same squeaky voice.

Anna nodded. 'I thought you said you worked for the Marconi Pasta Company.'

'I do.'

At that moment the door to the corridor opened and a man in his late thirties hurried over to Taffy. 'Babe, you'd better get back in there or I'm dockin' you three hours.'

'I'm on break, Dante,' Taffy said, irritated.

Anna looked up sharply, remembering the love note in Shari's locker from someone named Dante.

'Your break doesn't start for another twenty minutes,' Dante said. 'What'll it be, babe?'

All business, Taffy turned to Anna. 'How much can

you give me for one hour? That's long enough for us to talk, isn't it?'

'Uh…I think so,' Anna said, caught off guard. 'A hundred?'

'Done. Gimme a sec.' Ignoring Dante, who shrugged in disgust and went back through the door to the stairs, Taffy disappeared somewhere in back and returned a moment later in jeans, a T-shirt, and sneakers.

'Won't you get fired?' Anna asked her.

'Nah. You think it's so easy to find talent? Besides, another girl can fill in.' As she spoke, the corridor door opened again and the pretty Asian girl entered, walked to the circular structure, and went through a door toward the back. 'See? Come on, we can get some coffee.'

ELEVEN

THEY WENT TO a Dunkin' Donuts across the street and sat at a table by the window. In normal daylight Anna could see that Taffy was quite beautiful, with flawless skin and exotically slanted, almond-shaped eyes. 'I guess you're wondering what a nice girl like me is doing in a place like that?' she said with a squeaky little laugh, and sipped her coffee.

'We all have to make a living.'

'So true,' Taffy said, growing serious. 'It's actually a very nice living. I make a lot more dancing at Marconi's than I made as a secretary at Prudential Insurance.'

Anna remembered the corridor with a girl at each door. 'Is there, uh, room for growth?'

'Oh, sure. Dante has offered me a promotion, but I don't know if I want to do that kind of work.'

That was as far as Anna wanted to take that particular subject.

'What do *you* do?' Taffy asked.

'I'm a garage supervisor for the Sanitation Department.'

'Oh, yeah, you said you were Shari's boss.'

'That's right.'

'It's horrible what happened to her,' Taffy said, and examined a chipped nail. 'At least the cops got the creep who did it. *And* he's the Ankh Killer.'

Anna shook her head.

'No?'

'Neither is true. He didn't kill her, and he's not the Ankh Killer.'

'What do you mean? He threatened to kill Shari. She told me so.'

'He was just angry. He couldn't kill anyone. I know him.'

'Then why did he try to run away?'

'He was scared. He knew he would be blamed.' Anna shook her head impatiently, looked at her watch. 'But I don't want to talk about that. I want you to tell me about Shari.'

'What do you wanna know? She and I shared an apartment, that's all. We weren't, like, close friends or anything.'

'Did you know she was a blackmailer?'

'Oh sure.' Anna looked at her in surprise. 'She and Dennis always had some kind of scam going,' Taffy went on with a laugh. 'I had to hand it to them, they were always trying something!'

'You know they worked together, then? That Shari would get these guys up to the apartment, seduce them, and then Dennis would burst in taking pictures?'

'Mm-hm.'

'None of that bothered you? That they were committing a crime—blackmail is a crime, you know—and using your apartment to do it?'

'*Our* apartment. Listen, my dad always said, "Judge not, or you'll be judged", or something like that, and that's how I live my life. You do your thing; I do mine. We all gotta make a living. It's not like I'm some kind of angel. Besides, all the guys Shari and Dennis blackmailed—when they slept with Shari, they were cheating on their wives, their girlfriends, their fiancées… If they didn't want to get in trouble, they shouldn't have come up to the apartment with Shari.'

Anna considered this convoluted logic, then decided to move on. 'Did Shari and Dennis get along? Did they ever fight?'

'Oh, all the time,' Taffy said easily. 'But if you're saying Dennis might have killed her, forget it. He would have no reason to. In fact, it was the opposite. He needed her for the scam. When he found out about Shari getting murdered, he asked me if I wanted to take her place, but I told him no; I have my job at Marconi's.'

'Who else was Shari close to?'

Taffy thought about that. 'No one, really—at least, that I know of. She wasn't even that close to Dennis. She told me she didn't care one way or the other about him.'

'Really? I thought he was her boyfriend.'

'Hon',' Taffy said, leaning toward her, 'you gotta understand what Shari was like. Shari was out for Shari and only Shari. When all was said and done, she didn't care about anybody else. If you could do something for her, she would be as sweet as pie. If you couldn't, she could be colder than ice.'

Or stone, Anna thought, remembering Shari standing in the shadow of the tires, watching Gerry.

'What about the urban exploration?'

'The what?'

'That group she belonged to, Urban Access.'

'Oh! Yeah, I tried that a few times with her and Dennis. I didn't like it at all.'

'Why did they do it, do you think?'

Taffy pulled down the corners of her pretty mouth, as if she'd never thought about that. 'Good question. Dennis did it first; then Shari started going on missions with him. She told me it was fun, but now that I think about it, Shari would never do something just because it was fun. She needed Dennis for the scams. Maybe she did it to please him, to hold on to him.'

For some reason Anna doubted it, but didn't voice this thought. 'So bottom line, you can't think of anyone in Shari's life who might have wanted to hurt her? Who was angry at her about something? Wanted revenge?'

'Sure, I can think of lots of people!' Taffy said, to Anna's surprise. 'Every poor fool she and Dennis shook down. But I don't know who they are. Shari didn't exactly give me a list. Or it could have been somebody in your garage. For instance, Shari told me this guy you partnered her with—Rob, I think she said his name was—was a real piece of work, all uptight, didn't like her at all.'

'What about your boss, Dante?'

Taffy wrinkled her nose, confused. 'What about him?'

'Was Shari having an affair with him?'

Taffy's eyes grew huge and she let out a loud whoop of laughter. '*Dante?* I don't think so.'

'Why not?'

'Several reasons,' Taffy said. 'First of all, he's married to the most beautiful girl I've ever seen. What would he need Shari for? Second, he would never date one of his girls. He says mixing business with pleasure is always a bad idea. Shari did work at Marconi's for a while, but she didn't like it and left. There was never anything between her and Dante.'

'I see. What about Shari's past? Do you think anyone from her past life might have wanted to hurt her?'

'Sure, in her old line of work there probably would have been people who wanted to hurt her.'

Anna frowned. 'What line of work?'

Taffy laughed. 'Oh, right, I guess you wouldn't know

about that. I can tell you; she's dead, right? Shari used to be a hooker.'

Anna stared at her.

Taffy nodded. 'So there could have been any number of guys who might have been mad at her about something... not to mention her pimp.'

'When did she do this?'

'Right when she got to New York, I think.'

'But she told me she took small jobs to make ends meet. Cashier, waitress, that kind of thing.'

Taffy threw back her head and squealed with laughter. 'And you believed her? I can just see it—Shari taking my breakfast order, or Shari bagging my groceries at the supermarket.' She looked at Anna pityingly. 'Shari was a liar—you gotta remember that. She would tell you what she thought you needed to hear so she could get what she wanted. That was Shari in a nutshell—all about getting what she wanted.'

'And what was that?'

'Money. A glamorous life. Respect. You gotta keep in mind where she came from—a trailer park in Kentucky.'

'Ah, then that part was true.'

Taffy nodded. 'That was the thing with Shari. You never knew what was true because she mixed her lies with bits of the truth. She once told me that was the best way to lie—keep your lies as close to the truth as possible.'

'Taffy, I'd like to see Shari's room at your apartment, if you wouldn't mind. She did have her own room?'

'Yeah, of course. Why do you want to see it?'

'Maybe I'll find something that points to who might have killed her.'

Taffy gulped down the last of her coffee. 'What time you got?'

'Five fifteen.'

'If I take you up to the apartment you're definitely going to need another hour of my time. You up for that?'

'Sure.'

'OK, let's go,' Taffy said, and led the way out to the street. 'It's just around the corner. Convenient for my work.'

The apartment was on Thirtieth Street between Seventh and Eighth avenues, in a nondescript four-story apartment building. Climbing the front steps, Anna remembered what Vera had told her about waiting for Shari to come home. The building's small lobby smelled like cat urine. The two women took a dilapidated elevator to the third floor, where Taffy led the way down a narrow, stuffy corridor and opened a door on the right.

'Home sweet home,' she said, switching on the light.

They were in the living room, which had been furnished with two cheap orange beanbag chairs and a large flat-screen TV propped up on two plastic milk crates. There was no clutter but the floor was filthy, a mass of crumbs and food smears. Anna wondered when the apartment had last been cleaned, if ever. To the left was a tiny kitchen, the sink piled high with dirty dishes on which she spotted several large cockroaches.

'Her room's through here,' Taffy said, leading Anna across the living room and past a bathroom on the right. There were two bedrooms. Taffy leaned into the one on the left, flipped on the light switch, and returned to the living room. Anna turned and saw her pick up a *People* magazine from the floor and drop on to one of the beanbag chairs.

Shari's bedroom was tiny, like many bedrooms in New York City. In one corner of the narrow space stood a twin bed, messy and unmade, the sheets a grimy gray. The room was so small that there wasn't even room for a night table beside the bed.

Not far from the bed was a closet without a door. On the rod hung about half a dozen cheap-looking cocktail dresses, a long wool winter dress coat, and two inexpensive blazers. On the floor of the closet was a jumble of shoes, most of them dress shoes with high heels.

At the end of the room opposite the bed sat a dresser of wood that had been left unfinished. Each of its three drawers stuck out; from the middle one hung a pink sweater, half in, half out.

Clutter covered the top of the dresser. Anna stepped over to have a look. Most of it was cheap make-up. On a small clear-plastic stand hung a few cheap pieces of jewelry—a blue plastic bracelet, some earrings. A can of deodorant lay on its side.

She opened the top drawer and found a tangled mass of underwear. The middle drawer was crammed with jeans, T-shirts, Sanitation uniforms.

The bottom drawer revealed heavier sweaters and sweatshirts. Anna gave a few of them a cursory lift and something gold caught her eye. She lifted a hooded sweatshirt and found a slip of paper. Taking it out, she realized it was a candy wrapper—from a Butterfinger candy bar, specifically—shiny gold on one side, white on the other. On the white side someone had written a sequence of numbers—a telephone number, it looked like—and next to it was a crude drawing of a bell.

Anna frowned. Whatever the number and bell on the wrapper meant, Shari hadn't wanted anyone to find it. With a furtive glance toward the doorway, Anna slipped the wrapper into her purse. Encouraged, she returned to the top drawer and searched it, found nothing, and tried the middle drawer again. Nothing. She moved on to the bottom drawer, carefully lifting each garment. At the back of the drawer lay something about the size of a ballpoint pen, wrapped snugly in tissue and held closed by a piece of cellophane tape. Anna carefully unwrapped it.

At first she couldn't identify the object in the palm of her hand. It was a golden brown color, about four inches long, hard and cylindrical, though irregular in shape, thicker in the center. Frowning, she gave it a poke, rolled it over…and saw the fingernail.

With a gasp she dropped it. It made a sharp sound as it hit the floor.

A finger. A mummified finger. What kind of a monster…?

Instinctively she opened her mouth to call to Taffy, then stopped herself. Chances were excellent Taffy knew nothing about this. Fighting back her squeamishness, Anna picked up the finger, rewrapped it in the tissues, and slipped it into her purse alongside the candy wrapper. Then she put a smile on her face and returned to the living room.

Taffy looked up from her magazine. 'Find any good clues?' she asked in a slightly mocking tone.

'No,' Anna said easily. 'But thanks for the look.'

Taffy rose. 'Not a problem. It's your money. Speaking of which…'

'Oh, right.' Suddenly Anna realized she didn't have two hundred dollars in her purse. 'Is there an ATM near here?'

Taffy looked at her suspiciously. 'You don't have it?'

'Not on me, no.'

'There's one on the way back to Marconi's. I'll show you.'

Anna followed her to the door. Passing the beanbag chair in which Taffy had been sitting, she caught a glimpse of the mailing label on the *People* magazine. It was addressed to a Myra Klotz at this address.

Anna suppressed a laugh. 'So Taffy Grant isn't your real name.'

Taffy squeaked out a laugh. 'No way! How far do you think I'd get in my career with a name like Myra Klotz?'

Her career. They went out to the corridor and Taffy locked the door.

'How did you come up with Taffy Grant?' Anna asked.

'It's my porn name.'

Anna stopped. 'Your what?'

'Haven't you ever heard of it?' Taffy said, summoning the elevator. 'Here's what you do. First you take the name of your first pet that was the same sex as you are. Then you take the street you grew up on. So for me, my first girl pet was our dog, Taffy. And the street I grew up on was Grant Avenue. So...Taffy Grant!'

'Interesting,' Anna said, and as they walked to the ATM she figured out her own porn name. 'My first female pet was my pony, Silky. My parents' house—the house I grew up in—is on Fox Run Lane.'

'Perfect!' Taffy squeaked. 'Silky Fox! You know,' she said, looking Anna up and down, 'you could make a lot of money up there'—she jerked her head in the direction of Marconi's across the street. 'With a body and face like that.'

'Oh, yeah,' Anna said with a laugh. 'Gloria would love that!'

'Huh?'

'Never mind.'

TWELVE

AFTER PAYING TAFFY and saying goodbye, Anna walked back to her apartment by way of Ninth Avenue, stopping at Mr Carlucci's produce stand at the corner of Forty-Third Street to pick up something for dinner. Gloria was still dieting, insisting she was too fat to start dating. Anna decided to pick up some fresh vegetables for a salad.

As she perused the Bibb lettuce, stocky little Mrs Carlucci who never smiled bustled by. 'Good evening, Anna.'

'How are you, Mrs Carlucci?'

With her hand the older woman made a gesture that said, 'So-so.'

Anna nodded. From behind the counter Mr Carlucci smiled and called hello. When he had finished ringing up an order, he hurried over.

'Anna, I've been waiting to speak to you. How are you holding up?'

She gave him a puzzled look. 'You mean with Gloria?'

Now he looked puzzled. 'No, the murder at your garage.'

She couldn't help laughing. Which was worse, Gloria or a murder? She wasn't sure. 'I'm OK,' she said. 'It's very upsetting for everyone, bad for morale.'

He made a tsking noise and shook his head. 'To think that one sanitation worker would kill another...'

'Oh, no,' she hastened to tell him, 'that's not true. Tommy Mulligan didn't kill Shari.'

Mrs Carlucci, busy at the eggplants, turned around. 'Of

course he did,' she said in a tone that said Anna was stupid. 'The police arrested him. Charged him. He's at Rikers.'

'I know that,' Anna said patiently. 'But just because the police charge someone with a crime doesn't mean he's actually guilty. That's why we have trials and juries, right?'

'Wrong. That boy ran away. He's guilty.'

'Ah!' Mr Carlucci waved a hand in her direction. 'Don't listen to her. The fact is, Anna, my wife has been terrified about this Ankh Killer. Now that this Mulligan boy's been arrested, she wants to believe the madman is off the streets.'

'Well, I hate to spoil your sense of security, Mrs Carlucci,' Anna said, 'but the madman is not off the streets, because he didn't kill Shari, either. No way did we have the Ankh Killer working in Manhattan Central Thirteen.'

'Why not?' Mrs Carlucci asked.

'Because—' Anna didn't know what to say. She just knew. Wordlessly she grabbed a package of fresh mushrooms and added it to her basket. When she turned around, Mr and Mrs Carlucci were both looking at her.

'Because what?' Mrs Carlucci said.

Anna took a deep breath. 'Mrs Carlucci, you've had several people working here for years, am I correct? Rosa who rings up my order sometimes, and Pete who moves the produce around?'

'Yeah, so?'

'So what would you say if I told you one of them was the Ankh Killer?'

'I'd say you were nuts.'

'Exactly! Because you know these people. Well, I know the people I work with at the garage, and none of them is the Ankh Killer.'

Mrs Carlucci shook her head and walked away.

Mr Carlucci smiled apologetically. 'I believe you,' he whispered. 'I'll pray for that boy they've arrested.'

'Thank you,' Anna said, and realized tears had sprung to her eyes. Wiping at them, she moved toward the arugula.

SLICING CUCUMBERS, Anna suddenly remembered the candy wrapper she had put in her purse...which reminded her of the mummified finger.

'What is it?' asked Gloria, who sat at the tiny kitchen table. 'You made a face like you'd just seen something horrible.'

'Nothing, nothing.'

Gloria regarded her suspiciously, then gave a little shrug. 'I spoke to Donald today.' Her tone was nonchalant.

Anna spun around, knife in hand. 'You did? I thought you were never going to speak to him again as long as you lived?' As soon as she had said this she regretted it. Better not to remind Gloria about that.

'He called and your machine picked up. It was just before you got home. He sounded so sad, so...forlorn. Before I knew what I was doing, I picked up the phone.'

'What did he say?'

'That he's sorry, that he doesn't know what came over him, that it will never happen again...that he loves me.'

'Well, hey,' Anna said, turning back to her slicing, 'he seems to have said all the right things.'

'Mm,' Gloria said thoughtfully.

'So how did you leave it?'

'I agreed to see him. We're having lunch tomorrow. I figure he deserves at least that.'

Amen, Anna said silently, thrilled at the prospect of having her apartment to herself again.

LATER THAT NIGHT, George Mulligan called. 'I was just wondering if you'd made any progress, Anna, found out anything that might help Tommy.'

'I spoke with Shari's boyfriend, a guy named Dennis Ostrow. He's the one who helped Shari with her blackmail schemes.'

'Yes, I know. Did he admit that?'

'No, of course not. He didn't say anything useful, actually, though he did give me the number of Shari's apartment mate, a—dancer named Taffy Grant.'

He laughed. 'Sounds like a stripper.'

'She let me look around Shari's bedroom.'

'Anything useful?'

'No,' she lied. She hadn't yet called the number on the candy wrapper, she didn't know what the picture of the bell meant, and she wasn't going to tell him about the finger—not yet, at least. Nor had she followed up on the Dante lead. 'I'll keep thinking, George.'

'All right.' He sounded totally dejected. 'Thanks, Anna.'

The image of poor George Mulligan alone in his apartment stayed with Anna as she changed into black jeans, a skimpy red halter top, and a jacket of thin black leather. Twenty minutes later she entered the Marconi Pasta Company. This time she didn't bother speaking to anyone behind the counter, instead making straight for the door at the back and heading up the stairs.

The place was jumping tonight. As Anna climbed the stairs, three men passed her on their way down. Another man behind her was in such a hurry that he said 'Excuse me' and pushed her aside as he ran past her up the stairs.

At the top of the stairs she went through the door on the right, where the girls stood at their respective doors. Once again one of the girls approached her. This one was tall, with golden skin—most of it showing—and high platinum-blonde hair. 'Hey,' she said seductively.

'Hey.'

'You lookin' for some fun? You're cute.'

'Actually, I'm looking for Dante.'

The woman looked at her in surprise. 'You lookin' for a job?'

'No,' Anna said with a laugh, 'I just want to talk to him.'

'And who shall I say is calling?' the woman asked.

'Tell him I'm a friend of Shari's.'

'Who's Shari?'

'Just tell him,' Anna said in the tone she used at the garage when trying to sound stern. With a shrug, the woman turned and walked to the opposite end of the hall, where she went through a door. After a few minutes it opened again and Dante emerged, followed by the golden girl.

'You wanted to see me?' he asked, clearly irritated. He narrowed his eyes. 'Do I know you?'

'I was here to see Taffy earlier today.'

'Yeah, right. What can I do for you? Fifi says you're not lookin' for work.' He looked her up and down appraisingly. 'That's a shame.'

'I've got a job, thanks. Have you got someplace we can talk privately?'

'Sweetie, I'm real busy. State your business and let's get on with it, OK?'

'Suit yourself,' she said easily. 'I want to talk to you about your affair with Shari.'

He jumped and actually raised his hand as if to clamp it over her mouth. 'Follow me,' he said through clenched teeth, and led her down the hall and back through the door at the end.

He showed her into a cramped, windowless office. 'Sit,'

he said, indicating a metal chair with a torn black vinyl seat. He sat behind a small desk. 'Now who are you and what are you talking about?'

'My name is Anna Winthrop. I was Shari's supervisor at the Sanitation garage where she worked. When we opened her locker, we found a love note you had written to her.'

'Oh yeah?' he said, his voice cavalier, his face worried.

'Yeah. You begged her to come back, said you loved her.'

'And what's that got to do with you? What are you, the morals police?'

She shook her head. 'I couldn't care less about your affairs. I'm trying to find out who killed Shari.'

'Who killed Shari! What are you talking about? It's all over the papers. That kid killed her. Mulligan, his name is. He works for you.'

'Yes, he works for me, but he didn't do it.'

'How do you know?'

'I just know.'

'You think you know more than the cops?'

'In this case, yes. I want to clear Tommy, and the only way I can do that is to find out who did kill Shari.'

'Ah!' he said, sitting back in his chair. 'And you think *I* killed her?'

'I didn't say that. I want to know about your relationship. That way I can rule you out.'

'If I tell you, how do I know it won't go any farther?'

'As I just said, I'm not interested in your affairs. I don't even know you.'

'All right, sure, I'll tell you. Shari worked here for a short time; did Taffy tell you that?'

'Yes. She said Shari didn't like the work.'

He moved his head slightly from side to side. 'Well… not exactly. That's what I told Taffy and the other girls.'

He leaned back, crossed his legs. 'It was Taffy who brought Shari up here for the first time. They shared an apartment. Shari was out of work and Taffy suggested that she try to get a job here. Well, I took one look at Shari and knew I wanted her working for me. That girl was gorgeous. I asked her if she was interested, and she said she wouldn't have come up if she wasn't. That's how she talked; she had a smart mouth. It was sexy as anything.

'We always start the girls out with the easier stuff, like workin' the peep show or dancin' in the lounge.'

'Lounge?'

'Yeah, didn't you see that? It's real nice. I'll show you on your way out.'

'No, that's OK. Go on.'

He shrugged. 'Suit yourself. Anyway, I had Shari work the peep show for a while, to see how she did with that. Well, she did real well, lemme tell ya.'

'What do you mean?'

'The guys were comin' out in a daze—you know, shakin' their heads like they couldn't believe it. And they kept comin' back. So I decided to have a look myself. Shari was wild.'

'In what way? Her dancing?'

He looked at her as if she had just arrived from another planet. 'Her dancing? That's cute. No, it was what she did in there.'

Anna remembered the fruits and vegetables. 'You mean the banana…'

'Yeah, and the cucumber, and the celery, and the carrots—I mean, this chick was game for anything. I had never seen anything like it. I told her so one day. That was my first mistake.'

'Why?'

'Because she demanded a raise. I gave it to her—how could I not? She was bringing in a lot of business. You know, guys talk to other guys…So she worked the peep show for a while, but then she got restless.' When Anna lowered her brows, he explained, 'She wanted to move up, she said. She wanted to do whatever made the most money. I told her that wasn't how it worked here, that you had to work your way up the ladder.'

'And how did she react?'

Dante flushed a deep red. 'She…um…grabbed me in a private place and said maybe we could discuss a short cut.'

'I see,' Anna said, uncomfortable. 'And did you… discuss a short cut, I mean?'

'Oh, yeah. I broke my rule of never mixing business with pleasure.'

'Not to mention the fact that you're married.'

'Who told you that?' When she didn't answer, he said, 'My wife and I…we have an understanding. That's not an issue.'

She shrugged. 'OK. So you started an affair with Shari. How did it go from that to "Don't do this to me", "I love you", "Please come back"?'

'Oh, that's easy. Another guy came along.' His face had grown red again.

'You were upset.'

'Upset! Yeah, you could say that.' He leaned forward against his desk. 'Anna, I *loved* Shari. She was the most exciting woman I had ever met. She told me she loved me, too.'

'Who was the other man?'

'Some customer. By this time I had her working the corridor—that's what we call—'

She raised a hand. 'I knew what you meant.'

'This guy kept comin' to see her. Which happens, believe me. But I had no idea they were gettin' so serious. But she fell for this guy big-time. He was a biker type.'

'Was his name Dennis?'

'Yeah, how'd you know?'

'I met him at the garage.'

'So they were still together right up to when she was killed,' he said, nodding sadly. 'Not long after she met this guy, she left her job here. I guess that was when she went to work for you at the Sanitation Department. I gotta tell ya, that really threw me. A knockout like that and she wants to haul garbage? Then again,' he said with a sly smile, 'you're a knockout yourself and I guess that's what you do.'

'Did. I'm a supervisor now.'

'I don't get it. Maybe you can explain it. Why would anybody want to do that?'

'It happens to be extremely interesting work. Did you know that every week, New Yorkers throw away 64,000 tons of garbage? That's not even including the stuff that gets thrown away in offices, in factories, on construction sites... It's my job to help make that garbage go away.'

'It boggles the mind,' he said, looking sorry he'd asked. 'Well, like I told ya, I was blown away when I found out what her new job was. There was plenty of room for advancement here.'

'Especially if she took some of those short cuts,' Anna said.

'Hey, I won't deny it. I was ready to do some special things for her—maybe give her her own show in the lounge, that kind of thing. But believe me, she would have deserved every bit of it. She was unbelievable. I begged her to come back, as you know.'

'But she refused, obviously.'

'She said there were more opportunities at the Sanitation Department than I thought. Plus she was with this Dennis guy now.' His shoulders rose and fell. 'And that was that.'

'When did you send her that note?'

'Oh, early on. Right after she left. I sent it home with Taffy.'

'Did she respond?'

'No. Then I called her. I asked her to meet with me, but she said no and told me to stop calling.' He lowered his gaze. 'I told her I loved her, more than I'd ever loved anybody, but she said she didn't love me. She said she never had. Shari could hurt you that way. I told her she was lying, that she was just saying that because she wanted me to leave her alone.'

'What did she say to that?'

'Nothing. She hung up.' He leaned toward her. 'I'm telling you, there was no way I could have hurt Shari. I would have done anything to have her back.' He rose. 'You got any more questions?'

'No. Thanks for your time.'

'Not a problem. And listen, if you change your mind about a job here, you call me, you hear? I think you could really go places.'

THE NEXT DAY—Thursday, which Anna had off—she called the number—which she wasn't even sure *was* a phone number—scrawled on the candy wrapper she had found in Shari's dresser.

'Arabella Farnham's office.'

Anna frowned. Arabella Farnham was a superstar TV personality who had just gotten her own show, a much-talked-about combination talk show and reality show. It couldn't be the same person...

'Hello?' said the person on the line.

'Uh, yes, sorry. Is it *the* Arabella Farnham, with the TV show?'

'Yes, that's right. Who is this, please?'

'My name is Anna Winthrop. Can you tell me if the name Shari Baird means anything to you?'

There was a moment's silence. 'I think you'd better speak to Arabella. Please hold.'

Before Anna knew what was happening, Arabella Farnham herself came on the line and said hello in her famous husky tones. 'Did you tell my secretary that you're calling about Shari Baird?'

'Yes, Ms Farnham. I take it you knew her?'

'Yes, I knew her.' She didn't sound very happy about it. 'And who are you?'

'Anna Winthrop. I'm a garage supervisor for the Sanitation Department.'

'The Sanitation Department…Didn't Shari—?'

'Yes, she worked for me. You know what happened to her, of course.'

'Of course. Why are you calling?'

'Do you mind if I ask what your connection to Shari was?'

'Um…Anna, why don't you come and see me? I can explain it better in person.'

'All right. When?'

'How about now? We don't start today's taping until late this afternoon.'

Anna agreed and took down the address of Arabella's office at CBS headquarters on West Fifty-Second Street. Twenty minutes later she was entering the star's reception room, on whose wall was displayed the star's well-known logo: *ArabellA!* She was ushered immediately into Arabella Farnham's office.

Arabella Farnham did not look like a star, with her

famous mop of curly black hair and thick eyebrows. But she was beloved by millions, who perhaps saw her as one of their own and not the superstar she really was.

'Thanks for seeing me,' Anna said, shaking Arabella's hand. The two women sat in a little conference area to one side of the huge office.

'Now,' Arabella said, smiling her famous warm smile, 'you knew Shari. Worked with her, you said.'

Anna nodded. 'I was her supervisor.'

'I see. Before I explain my connection to her, would you mind telling me how you came to call me?'

Anna explained finding Arabella's number among Shari's belongings.

'Yes, that makes sense,' Arabella said. 'That was the trouble—she wouldn't stop calling.'

Anna frowned, not understanding.

'Let me back up. About a year ago, we were putting together a show about young women who come to New York from other parts of the country—which ones succeed, which ones don't…you get the picture.

'My producers interviewed a lot of women, easily a hundred. Shari got on the list because she was doing temp work here at CBS. She seemed like a bright, personable young woman. Ambitious…'

That's for sure, Anna thought.

'…well spoken. We interviewed her twice, actually, and she almost made the cut.'

'Almost?'

Arabella nodded. 'We needed only eight women in all, and in the end Shari wasn't chosen.'

'Let me guess,' Anna said. 'She wasn't happy about that.'

'That's putting it mildly. When Ellie, one of my producers, called Shari to let her know she hadn't been chosen, she flew into a rage. She said we had misled her, that we had promised to have her on the show, that she had told everyone she knew she was going to be on, that she was counting on this helping her career, whatever that was.

'Which was insane, of course. At no point had we told her she would be chosen. At any rate, Ellie said she was sorry it hadn't worked out and that was that—we thought. Fortunately, Shari's temp job here had ended. We thought we had seen the last of her.

'That's when the craziness really started. At first Shari just kept calling, at least once a day. She would demand to speak to me, say I was a liar. We warned her that if she didn't stop, we would call the police.'

'And did she stop?'

'Yes, she stopped. That's when the letters started to arrive.'

'Letters?'

'Mm. Not that she signed them, of course, but we knew they were from her. They were full of the same crazy accusations as her phone calls, except now there were threats. She knew where I lived—which I don't think she really did—she was watching me…I wasn't safe, that kind of thing. We got at least one of these letters a day.'

'What did you do?'

'We called the police. We had her address, you see, from when she applied to be on the show. The police went to see her, told her that if she didn't stop they would charge her with harassment.'

'Did she stop?'

'Oh, she stopped. And started up the calls again, except now she was careful to call from pay phones—I didn't even know there *were* any of those in New York anymore—and she kept the calls very short. She would say things like, "Liars die, you know", or "People who make promises they don't keep had better be careful crossing the street." Crazy stuff. Of course, it was my poor assistant Roberta outside at the desk who had to field all of these calls.

'We called the police again. This time when they went to see her she had moved, and no one knew where.'

'So she just kept calling?'

'That's right. In fact,' Arabella said, thinking for a moment, 'the last call came the morning of the day she was murdered. So you'll forgive me if I say that although I wouldn't wish what happened to her on anyone, I'm not sorry she's gone.'

'I guess I don't blame you,' Anna said, as Roberta from the front desk poked her head in.

'Bell, I've got Ralph on the line...'

Bell...

'I think we're done here,' Arabella said, and gave Anna her famous smile as they shook hands. 'Thanks for coming up.'

'Uh, one more thing, if you don't mind. Did Shari call you Bell?'

'Yes, that's right.'

'Wasn't that rather...familiar? I mean, for your assistant to call you by your nickname is one thing, but a temp?'

Arabella laughed. 'That's just how things are here. We're all friends!'

THIRTEEN

THE FOLLOWING MORNING, Anna sat down opposite Taffy Grant in the Dunkin' Donuts across from the Marconi Pasta Company, Anna having opted not to meet the younger woman at work this time. 'I've told you everything I know,' Taffy squeaked.

'Maybe not,' Anna said. When Taffy looked confused, Anna said, 'I want to talk about Dante...What is his last name, by the way? I never found out.'

'What do you think? Marconi.'

'Ah, yes, a family business.'

'What do you want to know?'

'About Dante and Shari.'

Taffy's eyes floated heavenward. 'There's nothing to tell. They weren't having an affair, I told you that.'

'Actually, they were.'

'Huh?'

'Dante admitted it—but I'd appreciate it if you'd keep to yourself that you know that. Apparently, Shari left Dante for Dennis.'

'So that's it, then! Nothing more to know.'

Anna shook her head. 'I think there is. There was something not quite right about what Dante was telling me. Something...seemed to be missing.'

Taffy considered this. 'Well, if anybody is going to know anything, it would be Lola.'

'Who's Lola?'

'Dante's secretary.'

'He's got a secretary?'

'Sure. Marconi's is a business, just like any other.'

'Not quite.'

'Well, she is his secretary, and she knows everything about him. You should talk to her.'

'How can I reach her?'

'You can come upstairs with me now if you like. I can take you to her.'

'Thanks, but I'd rather not go up there again.'

'It's all pretty shocking to someone like you, huh?'

'It's not that. I don't think Dante would appreciate seeing me there again.'

'Gotcha. I have her number in my purse—I'm always calling her about problems with my paychecks.' Taffy rummaged around in her overstuffed bag and finally pulled out a crumpled dry-cleaning ticket. 'Here you go,' she said, flipping it over, and read a phone number from the back. Anna jotted it down.

'OK, then,' Taffy said, rising, 'good luck.'

But Anna remained in her chair.

'Are you staying?' Taffy asked.

'Yes. I need you to help me with one more thing.'

Taffy blew out a sigh of exasperation. 'Honey, I gotta earn a living, you know? I've told you everything I know.'

'I'm sure you have,' Anna said. 'But there are some people who I think can tell me more, and I want you to help me get to them.'

Looking puzzled, Taffy fell back into her seat. 'Who?'

'Urban Access.'

'What could *they* tell you?'

'I don't know. Maybe nothing. But Shari and Dennis

have both been involved with this group. Dennis won't tell me anything, so I'll ask the others.'

'So ask them,' Taffy said simply. 'You said you already went there. That's how you got Dennis's number, isn't it?'

'You don't understand,' Anna said. 'I want to *join* Urban Access.'

'*Join?* Why?'

'I have to get them to trust me before they'll tell me anything useful about Shari. And they won't trust me unless someone they know vouches for me. Dennis isn't about to do it…which is why I'm asking you.'

'Me?'

'They know you. You said you had gone on some explorations with the group. They know you were Shari's apartment mate. If you say I'm OK, maybe they'll let me in.'

Taffy's gaze wandered as she took all of this in. Then she looked at Anna. 'All right. How much?'

'Two hundred dollars,' Anna said.

'Five hundred.'

'Three hundred.'

'Four hundred.'

'Deal,' Anna said. 'Let's take another walk to the ATM.'

IT WAS NEARLY DARK when Anna and Taffy came up the stairs from the subway and made their way along Canal Street to the store-front headquarters of Urban Access. This time Anna let Taffy knock on the door, and this time Patsy, the bug-eyed woman with the black pageboy who guarded the door, actually smiled. 'Hey.'

'Hey, Patsy, how's it goin'?'

Patsy opened the door wider and opened her mouth to reply, then saw Anna and froze. 'What's going on?'

'You've met my friend Anna. She was here looking for Dennis's phone number.'

'I know. So?'

Taffy lowered her voice. 'Can I talk to you a minute? Privately?'

Patsy gave her a wary look but eventually nodded and allowed Taffy in. Anna waited outside for a good ten minutes before the door opened again and Patsy said, 'Come in.'

Inside, beautiful Jocelyn Paar stepped forward with the majesty of a queen, which Anna supposed in a way she was. 'So you're interested in joining us.'

'Absolutely,' Anna said. 'Shari and Dennis told me about what you do and I think it sounds fascin—really cool. By the way, have you seen Dennis lately?'

Jocelyn shook her head. 'He broke his ankle on his bike. It'll be a while before he's ready to go on a mission again.'

Good: There was no danger of Dennis telling the group that Anna wasn't really his friend.

'Here's what we'll do,' Jocelyn said. 'You'll come with us on a mission and see how you like it. If you do, we can talk about your becoming a member.'

'Fair enough,' Anna said. 'When?'

'Tomorrow night. We're doing something in Chinatown. Are you up for that?'

'You bet.'

'Good. You've already met Patsy. Let me introduce you to the others.'

'The others' were the shadow people at the perimeter of the room. Now they stepped forward, a woman and two men.

'This is Lynda,' Jocelyn said, and the woman, an attractive blonde with open Scandinavian features, smiled and shook Anna's hand.

'And this is Marco,' Jocelyn said, and one of the men approached Anna and took her hand.

'Hey, Anna.' He was exceptionally good-looking, with dark, close-cropped hair, sharp features, and eerily light eyes.

By contrast, the other man, Dave, was rather average-looking, with a round face and a soft-looking body. He was bald except for a rim of dark hair. Anna guessed he was the oldest of the group, probably in his thirties. 'Nice to meet you, Anna,' he said.

Jocelyn said to Anna, 'Meet us here tomorrow at nine. Bring a flashlight.'

'OK, then,' Taffy said in her high sing-song voice, and led the way to the soaped-up door. As Anna slipped out, she could feel the group's eyes on her, as if this were the beginning of a test.

'What did you say to Jocelyn?' Anna asked Taffy when they were half a block from the storefront.

Taffy shrugged. 'Just that you were Shari and Dennis's friend and that you're OK, that they can trust you. I'm getting a cab. Listen, Anna, don't take this the wrong way, but don't call me again, OK? There's nothing else I can do for you.'

Surprised into silence, Anna watched Taffy hail a taxi and ride off, her mass of dark curls visible in the rear window.

BEFORE SHE HEADED DOWN into the subway, it occurred to Anna to check her cell phone. Santos had called. She called him back.

'Hey, where you been?' he asked.

'Oh, nowhere in particular. Why?'

'Just asking,' he said. 'Have you eaten yet?'

'No,' she answered truthfully, and they agreed to meet at Sammy's, their favorite coffee shop, in half an hour.

When she arrived at Sammy's Coffee Corner at Forty-Fifth and Tenth, Santos was waiting in a booth reading the *Times*. He rose and kissed her when she reached the table. 'How are things going?' he asked as she sat down. 'Things must be tough at the garage.'

'It's certainly different. No one's saying much to one another, which is good in a way. There haven't been any fights since Shari—since it happened. Then again, most of the fights were *because* of Shari.'

'True. Have you heard anything from George Mulligan about Tommy?'

She had told him about their visit to Rikers. 'George called me but didn't say anything about Tommy. I figure the poor kid is the same as he was when we saw him—utterly miserable.'

Santos shook his head sadly. 'Like I said to you before, Anna, it doesn't look good for him.'

'I wish you would stop saying that,' she said peevishly, just as Sammy approached the table with menus.

'Hey, whoa!' he said, smiling. 'No arguments when you're here. Only peace and love.'

They couldn't help smiling. 'All right, Sammy,' Santos said, 'peace and love.' They ordered sandwiches and coffee, and Sammy went to get the coffee pot.

'Sorry, Anna,' Santos said softly. 'I didn't mean to upset you. I'm just trying to be realistic.'

'I know,' she said, 'but don't, all right? I don't want to hear it. Tommy is innocent and we've got to trust he'll be *proven* innocent, that the truth will come out.'

He nodded but said nothing.

Sammy poured their coffee and a busboy brought water. 'Hey,' Santos said, taking a sip of coffee, 'I did a little research into this group Shari and Dennis were involved in, Urban Access. Like I told you, I haven't had any experience with them, but a friend of my friend Margolin—works out of the Fifth Precinct—has had some run-ins with them, so I went to see him. Interesting what he said.'

'Oh?'

'Yeah. It seems the general assumption among the cops there is that these people are up to no good.'

'What do you mean?'

'Well, the cops have been told third-hand that these people are more interested in burglary than in urban exploring, that the urban exploration part is just a cover. Apparently these people are good at covering their tracks. So until they're actually caught in the act, there isn't anything that can be done.'

'But you just said the police have been told they're into burglary.'

'Being told isn't enough. We're told a lot of things. Like I said, we need to catch them doing it.' He took another sip of coffee. 'It makes sense, though, doesn't it? I mean that these people would be into burglary, because it ties into what Tommy told you about Shari trying to get him to show her places to break into buildings. That's probably why Shari got involved with these people. From what you've told me, she didn't sound like the intellectually curious type.'

'No, not at all,' she agreed. 'Anything else?'

'I did what I could to get the cops in the Fifth to keep a closer eye on the group. They sound like a dangerous bunch of people, don't they?'

'Mm,' Anna said, and took a long drink of water. She was grateful when Santos changed the subject.

'By the way,' he said, 'thanks for talking to Libby.'

'It was my pleasure. How are things going with her and Hector?'

'We're not sure yet. Hector says she hasn't missed any classes since you spoke to her, so that's a step in the right direction. But she still seems...down.'

Anna thought for a moment. 'Do you think she could be depressed?'

'I don't think so—not in the sense that she would need medication, at least. The psychologist at her school didn't think so, and neither did the one Hector took her to see.'

'Down...' Anna said pensively. Then she looked up. 'Santos, do me a favor and ask Hector if Libby has any no-school days coming up.'

'All right. What do you have in mind?'

'How do you think Libby would like to shadow me for a day?'

He drew down the corners of his mouth, considering this idea. 'I don't know...It might be good for her. She could see what it's like in the real world. I'll ask Hector.'

'If he likes the idea, ask him for Libby's cell phone number.' She smiled. 'I know I can reach her that way.'

SANTOS CALLED HER as she turned on to her block. 'Hector says Libby is off from school this Monday. It's a teachers' in-service day.'

'Perfect. Did you ask Hector about my idea?'

'Yes, he thinks it would be great for Libby.'

He gave her Libby's cell phone number. When Anna called it, she got Libby's voice mail: 'Hey. Leave it.'

Anna left a message asking Libby to call her. To Anna's surprise, her phone rang less than five minutes later.

'Hey, Libby, how's it going?' Anna asked.

'All right.' The girl sounded wary. 'You wanted to talk to me?'

'Yes. I had an idea. I understand school is closed on Monday. How would you like to spend the day with me at work?'

'At your…garage?' Libby asked, clearly surprised. 'Why would I want to do that?'

'You asked me what I do here. I thought you might like to see for yourself.'

'I don't know…' Libby said. Anna could tell she wasn't interested but didn't want to be rude.

'Do you know who Caitlin Whitelaw is?' Anna said.

'What? Of course I do. What has she got to do with this?'

'Caitlin is doing her community service with us.'

'That's *your* garage?'

'Mm-hm. You would have a chance to meet her, maybe talk with her.'

'Well, I guess I could do it…' Libby said.

Anna smiled. 'Great. Check with your father to make sure he's all right with it—though I doubt he would object.'

'OK. What time should I be there?'

Anna smiled. 'You're going to have to get up early. I start at six. Caitlin starts at seven, but the media circus doesn't die down until around twenty past. Why don't you come at seven thirty?'

'OK,' Libby said, a note of excitement in her voice. 'I'll be there.'

There was a note on the dining room table.

Anna—
I've gone back to Donald. We're going to give it an-
other try. How can I ever thank you for being you?
Your loving sister,
Gloria

P.S. I was wearing heels and must have been making too much noise because Mrs Dovner banged on her ceiling. Sorry!

The giant flower arrangement was still in the center of the table, vivid and fresh. Anna leaned over to smell a rose, smiled, and went to take a nice long bubble bath.

FOURTEEN

PEDESTRIANS HURRIED past Anna in each direction as she approached the headquarters of Urban Access on Canal Street. Jocelyn and her crew were already there waiting. When Jocelyn saw Anna, she strode toward her, smiling. Behind her were Patsy and, walking together, handsome Marco and beautiful Lynda. They all greeted her with smiles.

'So, are you ready?' Jocelyn asked Anna, who nodded. 'Let's go, then.'

They walked east on Canal Street and turned south on to Mott Street—narrow, busy even at this hour, Chinatown's unofficial Main Street.

Jocelyn, walking beside Anna at the head of the group, said, 'Have you ever heard of the Chinatown Tunnels?'

Vaguely, Anna thought she had, but she shook her head.

'You've heard of the tongs, right? The Chinese secret societies that were always feuding?' Anna nodded as Jocelyn led the way across Bayard Street. 'From the late 1890s to the 1930s, the tong wars were especially bloody. A network of tunnels was created so feuding tong members could move around secretly and also hide. This way,' Jocelyn said, and they turned left on to narrow Pell Street.

When they had walked only a short distance, Jocelyn pointed to a sign on the right that read DOYERS STREET. They turned on to this street and Anna found herself on an even narrower passage, barely wide enough for a car squeezing its way through. After only a few yards, the street took a sharp right-angle turn to the left and disappeared from view. A hectic, colorful patchwork of restaurants, barbershops, and hair salons lined the street.

Marco caught up with them. 'This street was called the Bloody Angle,' he told Anna, 'because the tong wars that took place here were so violent.'

'We're going to the most famous of the tunnels,' Jocelyn said. 'It connected the basement of the Chinese Opera House here with an actor's house on the Bowery—that's the street Doyers runs into. Other tunnels ran off of this one. Half the buildings in this neighborhood have tunnel entrances in their basements.'

Taking in a confusion of signs in Chinese and English—EXCELLENT PORK CHOP HOUSE…NOM WAH TEA PARLOR…VIET NAM RESTAURANT—Anna frowned. 'I don't see an Opera House.'

'It was here,' Dave said, and pointed to a tiny clothing store. Its sign, ornate orange lettering on a yellow background, read 'CC Fashion'.

'But that's not the way into the tunnel,' Jocelyn said. 'It's this way.'

They followed her farther along the street to another ordinary-looking storefront, this one a confusion of red, yellow, and white signs, mostly in Chinese lettering of varying sizes. On closer inspection Anna realized that there were in fact two separate establishments. On the left, above a graffiti-covered red door, a sign read WINNER EMPLOYMENT AGENCY. On the right, a sign above the window announced the BEAUTIFUL & HEALTHY HAIR SALON.

'Over here,' Marco said, standing before the door of the hair salon. When he saw Anna look up and down in puzzlement, he said, 'This isn't the hair salon. That's just one of many stores down here. This is actually the back entrance of the Wing Fat Shopping Arcade. That's what the tunnel is now.'

He led the way in, followed by Lynda, Patsy, and Dave. Anna went next, Jocelyn taking up the rear. Inside, they descended a steep concrete stairway and found themselves looking down a narrow snaking corridor lined with tiny shops: a herbalist, a video store, a language school, a shop offering massage, a travel agent, an adviser on feng shui. It was a miniature underground street, signs in Chinese hanging from the ceiling. Fluorescent fixtures in the ceiling provided harsh, unnaturally bright light. People went in and out of the shops, some heading off down the tunnel in the opposite direction, some coming toward Anna and the group to mount the stairs to Doyers Street.

'I'll bet you didn't know this was here,' Dave said, suddenly at Anna's side.

'No, I sure didn't,' she replied, stepping back. Jocelyn had already started down the tunnel. They all followed.

After Jocelyn had gone about thirty feet, she abruptly stopped. So did the others. They were at a bend in the tunnel where there were no shops except for one that had been boarded up and abandoned. She turned to Marco. 'Ready?' she said quietly.

Looking in each direction to make sure no one was coming, he gave one nod and stepped over to a scratched, gray-painted door on the left that Anna hadn't noticed. On a flimsy-looking hasp hung a large padlock. Jocelyn, Patsy, Lynda, and Dave kept watch while Marco approached the door, removed a large screwdriver he had been concealing in a pocket of his carpenter pants, and inserted it in the padlock. Suddenly he yanked the screwdriver down hard; the lock split open.

'OK, come on,' Jocelyn said, 'hurry up,' and she stood to the side as they all filed quickly through the doorway.

She came in last. Marco pulled the door shut and there was utter darkness.

Now everyone whipped out flashlights and Anna followed suit. The collective beams revealed that this offshoot tunnel was narrower than the main one. There were no shops here, only crude walls of plain concrete.

Silently Jocelyn led the way down the passageway. Anna and the others followed silently. When they had gone about twenty feet, a new tunnel appeared, branching off to the left. Jocelyn said, 'This way,' and they all took the turn. Soon, on the left, doors appeared, some chained, some gated, some padlocked. Anna was aware that Jocelyn had moved to the back of the group to stand beside her, as the others moved quietly forward as if by common agreement. When everyone else was far ahead, Jocelyn said, 'How do you like the Chinatown Tunnels so far?'

'They're extremely interesting,' Anna replied. She wasn't lying. She found these hidden tunnels fascinating and wanted to learn more of their history. 'Where do all these doors lead?'

Jocelyn smiled. 'Into the backs of all the shops you saw in the main tunnel. That's interesting, too, don't you think?'

Anna was aware that the other woman was watching her closely. She nodded.

'Tell me,' Jocelyn said, leaning against the wall, 'Taffy said you and Shari were quite close. Is that true?'

What was the right answer? Anna shrugged noncommittally, gave a half-nod, and hoped her response could be taken either way.

After a long moment Jocelyn said, 'So I guess Shari told you all about our...adventures. The kinds of things we do? The kinds of things she and Dennis did?'

Anna knew the right answer to this one. 'Yeah, sure.'

'You know,' Jocelyn said, reflecting, 'I loved Shari, but things weren't working out with her. She had become too unpredictable, too…volatile. She was a loose cannon. Do you know what I mean?'

Anna nodded.

'With Dennis out of commission because of his broken ankle and Shari dead, I'm looking for people to replace them. Do you think you might be interested in doing…the kinds of things Shari and Dennis did? I'm sure you would find it…interesting.'

How Anna yearned to ask exactly what those things were. But she couldn't, of course. 'Let me think about it,' she said instead, trying to look interested.

Jocelyn nodded thoughtfully—still watching closely—and then gave Anna her beautiful smile. 'Fair enough. You let me know. Now let's join the others. There's something I want to show you.'

They continued along the tunnel and found the rest of the group standing in a cluster about thirty feet ahead. Patsy stood at the left wall, stooping slightly, peering into a hole in the tunnel wall. 'Here, Anna, have a look,' she said, stepping aside.

The hole was about three inches in diameter, drilled into the concrete. Anna took a look.

She found herself gazing into the back of a shop, a brightly lit room with boxes piled against the right wall and an old yellow Formica and chrome dinette table against the left. Around the table were three chairs upholstered in yellow vinyl; in one of the chairs sat an elderly Chinese woman in a black jogging suit, her face shriveled and deeply lined. Her hands moved rhythmically; Anna realized she was crocheting.

Puzzled, she drew back and looked at the others.

'There are lots of holes like this one,' Marco said, and

his finely shaped brows rose slightly. 'We can pretty much see everything these people are doing... What they've got back there... When they're there... When they're not...'

'Like I said...' Jocelyn murmured softly, her eyes fixed on Anna. 'Interesting.'

EMERGING INTO the main tunnel, they turned left rather than going back the way they had come. Eventually more shops appeared, and then there were stairs up and a door to the street.

Outside in the cool night, Anna realized she was in the open spaces of Chatham Square, with its pagoda-style bank, statue of Lin Tse-hsu, and arch 'IN MEMORY OF THE AMERICANS OF CHINESE ANCESTRY WHO LOST THEIR LIVES IN DEFENSE OF FREEDOM AND DEMOCRACY.'

'Anna—'

She turned. Jocelyn stood a little to the side of the tunnel entrance, an Off-Track Betting parlor behind her. 'Get back to me, OK. Let me know if you want to be involved.'

INTERESTING, INDEED, Anna thought on her way to the subway. She saw now that Shari had been all about access— access to places she could burglarize...access to shops off the Wing Fat tunnel...access to the backs of buildings along her collection route...

She started down the steps to the subway.

If Shari had been a burglar, she certainly hadn't kept any of her loot in her apartment. Perhaps she hadn't trusted Taffy. Perhaps she hadn't trusted anyone. Then where *had* she kept her ill-gotten gains?

And where had she gotten that finger?

Anna decided to ask Dennis Ostrow. No time like the present, she thought, and brought out her cell phone.

The first time she dialed his number, her call went

directly to voicemail. The second time, someone answered
and immediately hung up. The third time, Dennis Ostrow
growled, 'What do you want!'

'I want to talk to you.'

'I already talked to you. I'm not talkin' to you anymore.'

'Yes, you are.'

'Oh, yeah? Why?'

She took a chance. 'Because in my purse is a finger.
A mummified finger. You've got a choice: Tell me how
Shari got it…or tell the cops.'

There was a moment's silence. Then, 'Where are you?'

'At Chatham Square. I'm about to get on the subway.'

'Get off at Thirty-Fourth Street. It's near where I live.
I'll meet you on the corner of Thirty-Fourth and Sixth.'

'All right. Oh, and Dennis? If you're not there, I go directly to the police.'

He hung up.

When she reached the designated corner he was already there, sitting on the edge of a stone planter in front
of an office building. His crutches were propped a few feet
away. Without preamble she began digging in her purse.

He put up a hand. 'It's OK, I don't need to see it.'

'Yeah,' she said, 'I figured you'd seen it already.'

He stared at her expressionlessly.

'Well?' she said. 'Me or the cops?'

At last he gave an insolent shrug. 'Sure, I'll tell you.
You can't prove anything, and Shari's dead anyway.'

'The truth.'

He nodded. 'One night about two months ago, Shari
and I were on a mission with the group. There's a tunnel between Chatham Square and Doyers Street in Chinatown. It's kind of an underground mini-mall. There's a
smaller tunnel off of it that goes behind a lot of the shops.
That night we all went into that tunnel. Well, come to find

out, somebody drilled holes in the wall behind the shops. You can look through and see what the people are doing.

'Shari and I were looking through one of the holes into a jewelry store. The others were way up ahead. All of a sudden Shari looked at me and whispered, "I want to go in there." I told her she was crazy, that we couldn't do that, but she wouldn't let go of the idea. Jocelyn and the others were way up ahead. Shari said we would just pop in for a minute and have a look around.'

'A look around,' Anna said.

'I know. It was pretty clear what she was going to do. But...well... We looked through the hole for a while to make sure no one was back there—the room was dark— and when we were sure, I forced open the lock on the back door of the shop and we went in.

'Shari got all excited, shining her flashlight into all the cases, looking at all these diamonds. That's when I thought it was weird.'

'What?'

'That the diamonds were in the cases and not put away in a safe for the night. All of a sudden, Shari picked up a chair and smashed it into one of the cases. It made a terrible crash. Glass flew everywhere. I freaked out. I told her we had to get out of there.

'She told me to shut up and called me a spineless coward. She was like a maniac, scooping up the diamonds and stuffing them into her pockets. She was breathing hard and laughing at the same time. That's when it happened.'

Anna waited, watching him.

'The overhead light suddenly came on and there was this old Chinese guy—the owner—standing there. He had a gun. His hands were shaking badly. I was standing off to the side of the room, but Shari was only a few feet away from him.

'Suddenly she screamed and at the same time she kicked the man hard in the shin. He cried out and dropped the gun. I thought Shari would grab it and use it on him, but she—she jumped on him.'

'Jumped on him?'

'Yeah,' he said, wonder in his voice. 'He was on his back. She sat on top of him, grabbed the chair she'd used to break the jewelry case, and smashed it down on his face. He cried out, blood went everywhere, but he just kept struggling, trying to get her off him. Shari picked up the chair again and this time she kept bringing it down on him, over and over and over again, until I finally had to pull her off him.'

'I see. And that's the first time you reacted.'

He made no response, just looked at her coldly. 'He was dead. I told her we had to leave, I tried to pull her out, but she yanked her arm away. Then she spotted a pair of pliers—the big, sharp kind—on top of a counter. She grabbed them. Next thing I knew, she was sitting on top of this guy again, kind of hunched over. I didn't know what she was doing at first. Then she let out this scream like an animal and stood up. She was holding one of his fingers. She had wiped her face with her hands, so this guy's blood was all over her. Finally she came with me.

'I couldn't let Jocelyn—she's the leader of the group— or any of the others see her like this. So I took my sweat-shirt and wiped the blood off her face; then I dragged her back to the main tunnel and we ran out through the door on Doyers Street.

'No one in the group saw us, but you can bet the mur-der was in the news, and Jocelyn and the others figured it out. It wasn't difficult. Jocelyn said Shari and I couldn't go out with the group for six months. She said Shari was a ticking time bomb, too dangerous, and that after the six months she would decide whether to let Shari go out again. I knew she wouldn't. I think Shari knew it, too.'

He held out his hands. 'And that's the story of the finger. Satisfied?'

'Not quite. Where are the diamonds?'

'How should I know? Shari had them, not me. You can bet she hid them as soon as she got home. And they'll stay hidden now, because only Shari knew where they were. I'm going now,' he said, rising. He grabbed his crutches and began hobbling away.

Anna watched him go. Just as she was about to turn away, a movement to her right caught her eye. A man had stepped from the shadows of the adjacent office building and fallen into step behind Dennis—following him, she was sure of it.

Curious, she followed the man, keeping a safe distance. Dennis started along a quiet block whose shops were dark and shuttered. It was then that the man from the shadows quickened his pace and placed his hand on Dennis's shoulder. Dennis froze. When he turned, he looked surprised and—yes, afraid. Anna watched.

Dennis and the man began to argue; she could hear them even at this distance. At one point Dennis pushed the man hard in the chest. The man pushed back, and Dennis lost his balance and fell, his crutches flying. Indifferent, the man walked away.

Now he was coming back toward Anna. Immediately she turned around, heading in the same direction as he was. Pretending to look in a store window, she let him pass. Then she fell into step behind him.

They walked like this for several blocks, the man walking at a steady pace, his hands shoved into the pockets of his windbreaker. To Anna's right, a woman was dragging her spaniel to the curb; the dog let out a yelp. When Anna looked back, the man was gone.

She quickened her pace, looking right and left, but he seemed to have vanished into thin air. He must have gone into one of the buildings on this block.

A hand thumped down on her shoulder. She gasped and spun around.

It was the man. He was a little taller than she was and thin but stringy and strong-looking, with a leathery brown face deeply pocked with acne scars and a sandy-colored flat-top haircut.

'You lookin' for me?' His voice was low and raspy, ugly-sounding.

'Who are you? Get your hand off me before I scream.'

He laughed. 'Go ahead and scream.'

'What do you want?' she asked.

He laughed again. 'What do *I* want? Lady, you've been trailin' me for blocks. What do *you* want?'

What could she say? 'I was talking with Dennis and then I saw you and him arguing.'

'So?'

She shrugged, shook her head.

He frowned, studying her. 'I don't know what your game is, but your business is with Dennis, not me.' Suddenly his face was inches from hers. 'You try that again and next time you'll be the one who disappears.'

'Hey, lady!' They both turned. It was the woman with the spaniel. 'Is he giving you a hard time?'

He spun around and gave the woman a nasty snarl. She recoiled in shock; so did her dog. 'You mind your business, too!' he snapped, and walked away.

The woman hurried up to Anna. 'Are you OK?'

'I'm fine. Thanks.'

'All right,' the woman said, looking uneasy. 'You have a good night now.'

Anna wished her a good night as well and resumed walking. Anger made blood rush to her face. The man was at least two blocks ahead now. No doubt he thought she would never follow him now.

He was wrong. This time she kept an extra long distance, hugged the shadows of the buildings, never took her gaze from him. He turned; she turned with him. Now he was on a dark, residential block lined with shabby brownstones. Abruptly he stopped and entered one of them.

She moved carefully forward, taking note of the building's address. Then she waited. A few minutes later, a light went on on the third floor and the man passed in front of the window. She drew back out of sight. Then she turned in the other direction and hurried away.

FIFTEEN

SHE WASN'T SURE why she thought this man might lead to something, but she did. The next day, Sunday, she got up early and by seven was back in her surveillance spot, watching the front of his building.

Her patience was rewarded when, at 7:25, he emerged from the front door and hurried down the steps. Then he began walking toward Seventh Avenue.

The previous day, the man had waited until Dennis had reached a quiet block to confront him. Anna now did the opposite, waiting until the man had reached Seventh Avenue, bustling with stores and coffee shops, before hurrying up to him. She didn't plant her hand on his shoulder, worried that he would spin around and sock her. Instead she stepped in front of him, blocking his way.

His eyes bulged in amazement. 'You got a death wish, lady?'

She laughed. 'Tough guy.'

'What is it you want, exactly? Do I know you?'

'No, and you aren't going to. I want some information.'

'What kind of information?'

'Your name, for starters. And your connection to Dennis. If I believe you, I won't scream rape.'

He shrugged easily. 'Willy Sothern.'

'Show me ID.'

Again his eyes grew wide as he withdrew his wallet from his back pocket and flipped it open to reveal his driver's license. He was indeed William Sothern, his address that of the building he had just come from. She nodded and he put the wallet away.

'How do you know Dennis?'

'Easy. We both belong to the same group.'

'What group?'

'You ever heard of urban exploration?'

She nodded.

'That's what the group does. It's called Urban Access. I hadn't seen Dennis in a while, so when I saw him on the street last night, I said hello, asked him how he hurt his ankle.'

'Why were you arguing?'

'Oh, you saw that?'

She waited.

'I heard he had said some bad things about me, and I didn't appreciate it. So I took it up with him. He denied it, but I know he did it.' He gave her a quick smile. 'And that's it. Now I gotta go. You wanna cry rape, you go right ahead.'

Helplessly she watched him disappear down the stairs to the subway. She walked a few blocks in the direction of the garage and then took out her cell phone and dialed Dennis Ostrow.

'I don't believe it,' he said. 'Lady, it's Sunday. I'm trying to sleep here.'

'Then wake up, Sleeping Beauty. I've got more to ask you.'

'When is this going to stop?'

'When I say so. I want to ask you about Willy Sothern.'

'Willy? How do you know Willy?'

'Oh, we're old friends,' she said blithely, then grew serious. 'I saw you arguing with him last night. Tell me what the argument was about.'

'Did Willy tell you?'

She wouldn't answer that. 'What were you arguing about?'

'I don't remember.' There was a long silence on the line.

'I'm waiting.'

'Wait as long as you like. I don't remember.'

He wasn't going to tell her. 'All right,' she said. 'Willy said you had said some bad things about him. Is that true?'

'Yeah, they were bad things. They were also true.'

'What were they?'

'I told Jocelyn he's a hoodlum and that we shouldn't let him stay in UA.'

She let out a laugh. '*He*'s a hoodlum! Has he killed anyone with a chair, cut off any fingers...?'

'Hey, you asked me; I told you.'

And he hung up.

She called him again. 'Hang up on me again and the next voice you hear will be reading you your Miranda rights.'

'What is it you want?' he asked, exasperated.

'I want the truth!' she shouted. Several people passing on the sidewalk turned to look at her. She paid no attention. 'So what'll it be, pal? You tell me.'

'All right, all right. There's a little park a block from where I live. On Thirty-Fourth between Seventh and Eighth. I'll meet you there. Half an hour. I can't move very fast with these crutches.'

'Fine. You'd better be there.'

HE WAS THERE, sitting on a bench near a waterfall, a steaming cup of coffee on the seat beside him. 'You'll forgive me if I didn't get you a cup.'

'Talk.' She sat at the bench's extreme other end.

'Can I ask you a question? Why do you care about all

this? What has it got to do with you? It's clear you didn't like Shari.'

'That's true, I didn't like her at all. I don't like you either, for that matter. But someone I do like—someone I care about—has been charged with Shari's murder. The cops seem to think they've got the whole case wrapped up. So I'm doing what I can to find out who *did* kill Shari and prove this person innocent.'

'Ah, I get it! It's that Mulligan kid. He worked for you.' He looked down his nose in amusement. 'What's the matter, you can't believe someone on your crew would do something like that?'

'No, I can't believe *Tommy* would. So now you know. Talk.'

'What do you want to know?'

'I told you—the truth. Whatever you haven't told me. For instance, what really happened to the diamonds?'

He gazed down into his coffee cup. Finally he shrugged. 'I'll tell you, 'cause like I said, Shari's dead and you can't prove anything. I would deny it all. I took the diamonds.'

'You took them?'

'Sure. Think about it. What Shari did put us both in a lot of danger. She nearly got us caught. I told her those stones were no more than my due. And I took them.'

'How did she react?'

'Like a hellcat, how do you think? She almost scratched my eyes out.'

'And that was that? Why do I think it wasn't?'

He smiled. 'Because you knew Shari, that's why. And you're right. She hired Willy.'

'To do what?'

'The truth? To kill me,' he said simply. When she stared at him, he went on, 'Willy's a part-time hit man. When I said he was a member of Urban Access, I wasn't lying.

That's how Shari and I knew him. Shari promised to pay him if he would kill me; that way she could get her hands on the diamonds. But before Willy could even try, Shari got herself murdered. Now there was no one to pay him.'

'So he gave up on killing you.'

'Not quite,' Dennis said. When Anna frowned, he raised his broken ankle. 'How do you think I got this? Willy found out about the diamonds and now *he* wanted them. One night I was sound asleep and the door of the room I rent burst open. It was Willy. He said that if I didn't give him the diamonds, he would kill me. I told him to take a hike.

'He attacked me, beat the living daylights out of me. We struggled. Somehow we ended up in the hallway. We fell down the stairs. Other people from the building came to see what was going on. Willy wasn't hurt. He got out of there. Me—I had a broken ankle. I had to go to the emergency room.'

'But Willy still wasn't finished with you?' Anna said. It was more a statement than a question.

'You catch on fast. Last night, after I left you, he surprised me on the street, said he was giving me one last chance to give him the stones. If I didn't, he was going to tell the cops I stood by and did nothing while Shari killed the jeweler. *That*'s what we were arguing about.'

'So now what?' Anna asked.

He looked at her. 'What do you mean, "Now what"?'

'What are you going to do? Willy is just going to attack you again.'

He smiled in mild amusement. 'You worried about me?'

'No, just curious.'

His face turned cold. 'He can't kill me if I kill him first.'

A chill went through her. These people were monsters,

each one worse than the last. 'I had a feeling you would say that.'

'Have you got any idea what those stones are worth? I do. I had them appraised. It's a lot, believe me. Well worth killing for.'

'Shari already did.'

He blinked once. 'And now it's my turn.'

She left him then, simply got up and walked away. Let them kill each other off, for all she cared.

AT SEVEN-THIRTY the following morning she went out to the garage entrance in time to see Hector turn on to the block and pull up to the gate. Libby looked apprehensive as she said goodbye to her father and got out.

'Who are all these people?' Libby asked Anna as Hector drove away.

'Reporters.'

'I thought you said they would be gone by now.'

'No, I said the circus would have died down. When Caitlin's limo pulls up they go wild. This is nothing.'

Nodding, Libby followed Anna inside and down the corridor to her office. 'This is me,' she said, and indicated the yellow love seat. 'Relax. Want some coffee?'

'No, thanks.' Libby cast her gaze about the small room.

'I know,' Anna said with a laugh, 'it's not very glamorous.'

'No, I wasn't thinking that,' Libby said. 'I was thinking how cool it is that you've got your own office.'

Anna nodded. 'I'm not here much, of course. A lot of my job involves moving around the garage, not to mention checking on my section from time to time, make sure everything is going well.'

'You walk around the neighborhood doing that?'

'Not usually—I don't have time. I have a Sanitation

vehicle.' Anna rose from her chair and pointed out into the garage. 'If you look over there, that white car with the red and blue stripe is mine.'

'Wow, your own car, too,' Libby said, her eyes wide. She continued to peer out into the garage, her eyes darting right and left.

'You're looking for Caitlin,' Anna said with a laugh. 'Come on, I'll introduce you.'

They found her upstairs, cleaning in the break room. She had her back to them as she mopped a corner of the floor.

'That's her?' Libby whispered, taking in Caitlin's faded jeans and gray T-shirt.

Anna nodded. 'Caitlin,' she said, and the socialite turned, smiling. 'I'd like you to meet a friend of mine, Libby Reyes.'

'Well, hey, Lib,' Caitlin said, and reached forward to take the other young woman's hand. 'Great to meet you. You doin' time here, too?'

Libby frowned, not understanding.

'No,' Anna said, 'she's just visiting for the day.'

'Gotcha,' Caitlin said. 'You don't need to do any of this, then.' She indicated her mop and bucket.

'I—I don't mind,' Libby said, and looked at Anna.

Anna was surprised but recovered quickly. 'Would you like some help, Caitlin?'

'Are you kidding? The only person I've got to talk to is Lorraine, and she and I don't get along very well.'

'Who's Lorraine?' Libby asked.

'Someone else who's working here,' Anna explained. 'Come with me,' she said, and led the way out of the room to the supply closet in the hallway. In it she found another mop and bucket for Libby. 'I'm sure Caitlin will be glad to show you the ropes.'

Libby nodded and returned to the break room.

'OK, then,' Caitlin said, hands on hips. 'You gotta get some soap stuff from that closet you were just in. Pour a glob in the bucket and then fill the bucket with water—there's a sink in the closet; I don't know if you saw it. Then come on back in and we'll have a mopping party!'

Anna stood quietly in the hallway as Libby followed Caitlin's instructions. 'I'll see you later,' she told Libby, who nodded and returned eagerly to the break room.

After a brief silence, Caitlin's voice floated out to the hallway. 'I guess you know why I'm here. The judge said I had to do one hundred hours of community service. The people here are real nice—well, most of them, anyway.'

Anna knew she meant Lorraine.

'So how old are you?' Caitlin asked Libby. 'Eighteen?'

'No,' Libby replied with a little laugh. 'Fifteen.'

'That's cool. Are you in school?'

'Yeah, but we're off today.'

'What are you going to do after you get out—of school, I mean?'

'I don't know...' Libby replied, and then there was the slosh of water hitting the floor. 'Maybe go to art school.'

'Really? Wow, I'd love to do something like that. I never went to college, but my dad says I should. He thinks it would help me with my business—I design clothes and jewelry and stuff. That's a fantastic bracelet, by the way. Where'd you get it...?'

Smiling, Anna returned downstairs.

'AND THAT'S IT,' Anna said, laying her hands on her desk.

Santos was looking at her in angry disbelief. 'I guess you weren't in any hurry to tell me any of this.'

She had picked up the sandwich he had brought her

from the local deli, but now put it back down again. 'What's that supposed to mean?'

'That you should have come to me sooner. We're talking about murder here, Anna, not some sleuthing game.'

'Sleuthing game!' she said, her voice rising. 'Is that what you think I'm doing—playing a game? You people have arrested an innocent young man, tossed him into that god-forsaken place to rot. You've ruined his life.'

'Ah, so it's "you people" now, is it?'

She said nothing.

'Anna,' he said, setting down his own sandwich and leaning forward, 'you don't know that Tommy is innocent, not really. You think he's innocent because you know him, don't think he's capable of murder. But you're not a cop; you haven't seen the things I have. The fact is, anyone's capable of anything if the right emotion meets the right moment.'

'I know that,' she said patiently. 'But you have no more proof that he's guilty than I have that he's innocent. And last time I looked, in this country a person is innocent until *proven* guilty. Remember that?'

'Don't patronize me, Anna. Prove him guilty is exactly what the prosecutor will do at Tommy's trial.'

'But how do you *know* he's guilty? How can you be so sure? You've gone from "It doesn't look good" to "We'll prove him guilty".'

'Because there's no one else it could have been!'

She gaped at him. 'Then you haven't been listening to me. Santos, everyone in this garage hated her! It could have been— No, I'm not going to do that. I'm not going to give you any more suspects; who knows how many more people you would arrest. But I know who they are.'

He shrugged. 'Suit yourself. In the meantime, I've got to do something about what you've just told me. I remember when that Chinese jeweler was murdered. It was in all the papers. His name was Lok Huang.

'We're going to have to keep watching this Urban Access group,' he went on. 'They're definitely bad news. But we *can* pick up this Ostrow character—in spite of the fact that he thinks he can simply deny everything—and charge him as an accessory. By the way,' he said, brows lowered, 'how did you ever get him to tell you all this?'

'Easy. I told him if he didn't I'd go to the cops.'

'Which you've now done.'

She let out a derisive snort. 'You people lie all the time. You're famous for it.'

'Oh, I'm not criticizing you. I'm just surprised. I didn't think you were capable of lying.'

She raised the corners of her mouth in a minuscule smile. 'You haven't known me very long. There are a lot of things I'm capable of. As you just said, all it takes is for the right emotion to meet the right moment.'

His eyes were on her appraisingly as he chewed the remainder of his sandwich.

WHEN SANTOS HAD GONE, Anna found the phone number Taffy had given her for Lola, Dante's secretary at the Marconi Pasta Company. The call was answered on the first ring.

'Marconi. Lola Wentworth speaking.'

Anna wondered fleetingly if this was her porn name. She introduced herself, explaining that she had gotten Lola's number from Taffy.

'Are you looking for a job, Miss Winthrop? Nice name, by the way. Very...New England. We could play up the whole Puritan angle, maybe put you in a bikini and a tricorne hat.' Lola had a low, smooth, sexy voice, like cool liquid chocolate. Anna wondered if she had ever been one of Dante's 'girls'.

'I'm not looking for a job,' Anna replied. 'I'd like to speak with you, if possible.'

'Speak with *me*? About what?'

Anna hesitated for a moment, unsure of the best approach. Finally she said, 'About Shari Baird.'

'Shari? She's dead. She was murdered.'

'I know that. That's what I want to talk to you about.'

'Miss Winthrop, I'm very busy—'

'No, wait, please. Your boss was willing to talk to me. It will all make sense if you'll just give me a few minutes.'

Anna heard her sigh into the telephone. 'All right, but just a few minutes. When do you want to come up?'

'Actually, I—I can't come up.'

'Why not?'

'I'll explain when I see you.'

'Well, where, then?'

'How about the Dunkin' Donuts across the street from your...office? Three o'clock?'

'All right. I'll see you there.'

Anna left her office and went in search of Libby, who—though Anna hadn't planned it this way—had spent the entire day helping Caitlin clean. At two o'clock, as Caitlin prepared to leave, Anna saw the two young women embrace.

'I wish you could come back tomorrow,' Caitlin said. 'Talking to you made the time go twice as fast.'

'I had a great time, too,' Libby said, clearly sad that her day was over.

'Hey,' Caitlin said, 'when I'm done doin' my time here, why don't you and I have lunch?'

'Sure!'

'OK, gimme your cell and I'll call you when I'm sprung.'

Libby gave her the number, Caitlin entering it directly into her own phone.

Caitlin glanced in the direction of the garage entrance. The silver Rolls stood at the curb, her chauffeur waiting at the rear passenger door. 'I'd better get going,' she said, and stopped momentarily, visibly bracing herself, before leaving the building. Then she stepped outside and instantly her trademark brilliant smile appeared as the paparazzi came to life.

'Caitlin! Over here, Caitlin! How was your day today, Caitlin?'

Libby watched, mesmerized, as the Rolls pulled on to the street. Then, turning, she saw Anna and came over.

'It's after two,' Anna said, checking her watch. 'That's it for you, too. I never got to show you what I do.'

'That's OK,' Libby said quickly, and glanced back in the direction of the still-teeming paparazzi. 'It was awesome.'

BACK IN THE Dunkin' Donuts across from the Marconi Pasta Company, Anna watched the door. She was playing a little game, trying to guess which of the numerous young women coming into the shop was the velvet-voiced Lola Wentworth.

'Miss Winthrop?'

Anna spun around. Standing beside her table was a woman who must have weighed at least 350 pounds. Of medium height, she had honey-blonde hair that flipped at her shoulders, and beautiful dark-brown eyes. She wore a loose-fitting navy-blue and white cotton dress.

'Yes,' Anna said, shaking her hand. 'You're Lola.'

'That's me,' Lola said, and began squeezing into the seat opposite Anna. Like all of the seats in the shop, it was attached to the table. Inwardly Anna winced as Lola wedged herself in.

'Coffee?' Anna asked.

'Yes, please. Cream, no sugar.'

When Anna returned with two coffees, Lola smiled up at her. 'You're cute. You sure you don't want a job?'

'Thanks, but I've got one.'

'Oh, yeah? What do you do, pretty girl like you?'

'I'm a section supervisor at a Sanitation garage.'

'Sanitation…Isn't that where Shari went to work?'

'Yes, I was her supervisor.'

'And someone else at your garage killed her—a young guy. He tried to make believe the Ankh Killer did it.'

'Actually, no, he didn't.'

'I beg your pardon?'

'Tommy Mulligan was arrested for Shari's murder, but he didn't do it. I'm trying to clear Tommy by finding out who did.'

Lola's eyes widened in comprehension. 'And you think Dante did it? That's why you wanted to talk to me?'

'I don't think anything. I'm just trying to get all the facts.'

'About *what*?' Lola asked, her patience clearly running out. 'You said you've already spoken with Dante.'

'I want to know about him and Shari.'

Lola looked at her shrewdly. 'So he told you. That's surprising.'

'Why?'

'There's a lot of bad blood there.'

'Oh?'

'Well, yes, with her trying to start her own club and all.'

'Her own club?'

'Oh,' Lola said with a knowing smile, 'so he didn't tell you everything.'

Anna waited.

'Did Dante tell you why Shari left?' Lola asked.

'He said it was because of Dennis Ostrow.'

Lola was shaking her head. 'No… You see, Shari was… ambitious; I guess that's the word. She was always playing the angles. Well, one of our customers was this guy named Petrov. Avel Petrov.' She pressed her nose hard to one side. Lowering her voice, she said, 'Russian mob.'

'How do you know?'

Lola laughed. 'We know, believe me. Everybody knows. Anyhow, this guy starts asking for Shari every time—which happens, of course—but in this case it didn't go down so well with Dante because he could tell things were getting personal between Shari and Petrov, which is against the rules, and besides, Dante already had something of his own going with Shari.'

'Did Dante do anything about it?'

'Sure, he told her to stop seeing him.'

'But how could she stop if Petrov kept asking for her?'

'Easy. You tell everybody that if he comes in, Shari's not there—it's not her shift. That's what Dante told Shari to do, but she refused. She said Petrov was paying her big money in tips, and unless Dante was willing to give it to her instead, she had no intention of stopping.

'Well, it just got worse and worse. Shari and Dante were at each other's throat all the time. One day Dante went into Shari's room—we've got these little rooms, you see—'

'Yes, I know.'

Lola shrugged. 'He went into her room and we all heard shouting and then a lot of banging and bumping. Dante beat her up something awful. She was so mad at him she didn't come to work for three days; besides which, she was all bruised. She had big black-and-blue marks around her neck. She tried cover-up make-up but it wasn't enough. She just had to wait for the marks to fade. Guys—well, most guys—don't want a girl all marked up like that.

'That wasn't the only fight, either. It happened again, and this time Shari left and didn't come back for a week. Then it happened again and Shari left…and never came back.'

'But what about Shari starting her own club?'

'That's why she never came back. She'd gone into business with Petrov. He was going to open a place just like ours. He had already rented the space and was having it renovated. It was going to be really fancy, and much bigger than Marconi's.'

'How did Dante find out about it?'

'Shari called and told him! She was like that—spiteful. She wanted him to know she didn't need him anymore. She wanted to stick it to him that she was going to be competing with him, and with this mob guy, no less.'

'How did Dante react?'

'Unexpectedly,' Lola said, and sipped her coffee. Setting it down, she said, 'I heard him on the phone. This was the first time he had heard from her since she left, of course. I expected him to yell and scream and call her terrible names, but he didn't. Instead he started telling her how much he loved her, begged her to come back to him.'

Anna frowned in puzzlement. 'What do you think of that? Do you think he meant it?'

Lola gazed into the near distance for a moment, chewing her lower lip. 'You know, it's not a black-and-white thing. I do think he loved Shari very much, even while he was so angry at her. So yes, he wanted her back. But he also thought that if she came back, she would give up her plans to build a club with Petrov. So to answer your question, I do think he loved her, at the same time that he was trying to manipulate her. Like I said, not black-and-white.'

'Did she come back?'

'No,' Lola said sadly. 'She was really cruel to Dante. She told him she was with a man who really knew how to—well, you know—and that she would never come back. Then she told Dante he might as well shut his place down, because within a year he would have to close anyway because nobody would come to Marconi's and our skanky girls—that's what she called them—once they had a taste of Paradise.'

'Paradise?'

'That's the name of the new club.'

'Did it ever get off the ground?'

Lola laughed, her ample shoulders shaking. 'Get off the ground! It's a huge success. It's on West Forty-First street; I can't believe you've never seen it. And Shari was right—it's taking a big bite out of our business.'

'So Petrov will have to go on without Shari.'

Lola nodded. 'All he really needed her for was to learn all of Dante's trade secrets. You know, how he did business. Once Petrov had that, Shari was just window dressing.'

'I'm confused,' Anna said. 'You make it sound like she worked at this new club. But not long after leaving Dante, she came to work for the Sanitation Department.'

'She must have been doing both,' Lola said. 'You know, showing up at the club when she wasn't working for you. She didn't do a lot at this new club—mostly greeted customers. A lot of them knew her from Marconi's. She wasn't seeing guys one-on-one anymore; Petrov wouldn't have that. So it was a nice set-up for Shari—a lot of money for not doing much.'

'Yes,' Anna said drily, 'that would appeal to Shari.'

Lola checked her watch. 'I told Dante I was running out to pick up some things at Duane Reade. I'd better be getting back.'

AROUND NOON the following day, Allen Schiff approached Anna in the corridor outside Anna's office. 'Before the princess gets back from lunch, I wanted to give you this list of cleaning jobs I've come up with for her.' He handed her a sheet of paper.

She scanned the list. '"Clean spilled oil near rear garage door"? That's not an easy job.'

He shrugged. 'This is community service, Anna, not a coming-out party.'

'Fair enough. What about Lorraine?'

'What about her?'

'You only said the princess.'

'Well, of course Lorraine, too. In fact, from the looks of her, she shouldn't have a problem with any of these jobs.'

'Why, because she's overweight?'

'Whoa, you're snappy today.'

'I'm not snappy,' she snapped. 'Lorraine may not be rich and beautiful, but she's every bit as important as Caitlin. She's a person just like Caitlin.'

Allen took a step back, keeping away. 'I've got no arguments with that. Uh...thanks.' He walked quickly back to his office and closed the door.

Anna looked again at the work list. Caitlin had been going out for lunch lately, often with her father; but Lorraine never did. She would be in the break room now. Anna made two photocopies of the list, then went up to speak to her.

Lorraine was alone in the bare space, finishing her dessert, a small Dannon yogurt. She smiled as Anna came in.

'How are you, Lorraine?'

'Just fine, Anna. You?'

Anna shrugged. 'I've been better. Listen,' she said, before Lorraine could ask what she meant, 'I've got a list here of some cleaning jobs that need to be done here in the garage. I'm going to give a copy to Caitlin, too.'

Lorraine took the sheet of paper and laid it on the table. Spooning some yogurt into her mouth, she scanned the list and nodded. 'OK, not a problem,' she said, looking up with a smile.

'I'm not sure about number three,' Anna said, referring to the oil clean-up. 'I may have to order a special degreaser for that. The spill is pretty big, and it's old. But give it a try, see what you can do.'

Lorraine threw her trash into the nearby wastebasket. Rising, she folded the list in half. Before she could tuck it into the pocket of her jeans, Anna said, 'Oh, and about the corridor floor. I'm not sure Allen has the right product down for that. What has he got down?'

Lorraine took a deep breath. Slowly she took the list from her pocket, opened it, and gazed down at it, brows lowered. 'I'm not sure…' she said.

Anna frowned, holding out her hand. 'May I?'

'Sure,' Lorraine said, handing her the list.

'Here it is. He wants you to use the powdered detergent. See?' Anna pointed to item number eight.

This time Lorraine didn't look. Lifting her gaze, she said, 'I don't know what he's got down there, Anna. I don't know what he's got down anywhere. The fact is…I don't know how to read.'

Anna's mouth dropped open. She didn't know what to say.

'Don't be embarrassed,' Lorraine said kindly. 'I'm embarrassed enough for both of us.' She shook her head.

'When I was in the first grade, my teacher told my parents I was slow. All the other kids were reading, but when I looked at those letters all I saw was…lines! Everybody hoped I'd start getting the hang of it by the second grade, but…' She shook her head. 'Then my mother died. I was one of seven kids. My dad barely had enough time to hold down his two jobs, let alone teach me how to read. And my teachers…I don't know, they just gave up on me. Schools aren't the way they are now, all this No Child Left Behind stuff. I got left behind big-time. The years passed, I got older, somehow made it through the ninth grade, and gave up, went to work. And those letters were still lines.'

There were tears in Lorraine's pretty brown eyes. Anna's heart went out to her. Before she knew it, she was saying, 'I would be happy to teach you.'

Lorraine's gaze snapped to her in surprise. Then her face softened. 'That's sweet of you, Anna, but I'm sure you've got plenty of things to do besides give me reading lessons.'

'No, really,' Anna said. 'I would love to do it. I've never done it before—I would have to look into the right books and everything—but I would love to try.'

The tears in Lorraine's eyes welled up and ran down her cheeks. 'No one has ever offered to do that before.'

Anna smiled. 'Maybe that's because no one knew.'

'True enough, true enough. All right,' Lorraine said, 'let's give it a try.'

'Fantastic. How about once a week? I could come to your place.'

'No,' Lorraine said, a bit too quickly. 'That won't work. How about the library?'

'I've got a better idea. You come to my place.' Gloria had gone back to Donald; why not?

'All right. When?'

'Let's say every Tuesday night at seven. We could start tonight. Would that work?'

'Beautifully. Thank you.' Then, 'Anna…'

'I know,' Anna said. 'Our secret.'

Lorraine breathed a sigh of relief. 'Right. Our secret.'

SIXTEEN

BUT GLORIA was back. 'Hi,' she said glumly as Anna opened the apartment door.

'What happened?'

'Donald and I had a fight.'

'About what?'

'What do you think?'

'But I thought you'd made up. The flowers...' Anna indicated the arrangement that dwarfed the dining table.

Gloria made a dismissive sound. 'All the flowers in the world mean nothing if you don't really mean you're sorry.'

'He didn't mean he was sorry?'

'I don't think so, no. Not when we got to talking about what he did and he started putting the blame on me.'

'On you! How was it your fault?'

'He said I can be...bossy and closed-minded. Have you ever heard anything so ridiculous?'

Anna wasn't going to touch that one.

'You're not answering.'

'So because he thinks you're bossy and closed-minded, that gives him license to cheat on you?'

'I know!' Gloria said, nodding rapidly. 'Can you believe that? But that's basically what he was saying. That I drove him into Helene's arms.'

'Is that how he put it? You drove him into her arms?' When Gloria nodded, Anna said, 'He's so melodramatic.'

Gloria made no response, walking over to the sofa and sitting down. She took an oversized throw pillow and hugged it to her. Then she started to cry. 'I don't know what I'm going to do, Anna. I thought Donald and I had worked everything out, that we both wanted to start over, but he's not ready to do that, that's pretty clear. He says the problem is *me*.'

'Well...' Anna said, treading carefully, 'couldn't you tell him you'll work on...um...those qualities?'

Gloria looked up at her beseechingly. 'Then you do think I'm bossy and closed-minded.'

'Honey,' Anna said, sitting down next to her and putting her arm around her shoulders, 'you know I love you dearly, but a shrinking violet you ain't. Take, for instance, the way you're always trying to get me to leave the Sanitation Department and pursue a more "appropriate" career.'

'But you should—' Gloria began and stopped herself, her eyes wide. Then, 'It's true, I am those things. But I can change, Anna. I'm no dummy; I can work on it. I can be a better person. I only hope it's not too late.'

'I sincerely doubt it's too late,' Anna said, giving her a squeeze. 'Donald loves you. It's not over. Give him a bit more time and then speak to him again. Tell him you heard what he said and will work on being...more open to other people's points of view.'

'OK,' Gloria said, energized, and jumped up. 'What do you say we go out for big greasy cheeseburgers?'

'I would love to, but I've got to get ready. Someone's coming over.'

Gloria frowned. 'Who? Santos?'

'No, a woman who works at the garage. Lorraine Canady.'

'Why?' Gloria looked baffled.

Anna sighed. 'It's supposed to be a secret, but since you'll be here, you'll find out anyway. I'm going to teach her to read.'

'To read! She can't read?'

'Obviously not, if I'm going to be teaching her.'

'Unbelievable. What are you, Anna, Social Services?'

Anna raised a forefinger. 'Gloria…'

'I know,' Gloria said, chastened. 'Not bossy. Open-minded.' She gave it some thought. 'Actually, it's sweet what you're doing. You've got a good heart, sis. Now, what can I do to help?'

'I'll tidy up, you run the vacuum.'

On the way home from work, Anna had stopped in a bookstore and bought several children's easy-reading books. After moving Donald's gigantic flower arrangement to the kitchen counter, she spread out the books on the dining room table.

Lorraine arrived at seven on the dot. She wore a pretty navy-blue skirt and a light-blue top and had pulled her hair to one side in an attractive style. She shook Gloria's hand with great enthusiasm.

'Let's all have some refreshments before we start,' Anna said, and carried to the living room coffee table a cold pitcher of iced tea with fresh mint that she'd made that morning, along with some butter cookies from the supermarket. Lorraine and Anna sat on the sofa, Gloria in one of the chairs.

'So you work together,' Gloria said, making small talk.

Lorraine nodded politely. 'I've only been working at the garage for two weeks.'

'I see,' Gloria said. 'What did you do before that?'

'Cleaned at other Sanitation garages. Also in the WEP.'

Gloria frowned. 'WEP?'

'Work Experience Program,' Lorraine said.

Gloria shook her head. 'I don't…'

'It's a city program,' Lorraine began. 'It's so welfare recipients can earn their benefits.'

'Oh, I see.' Looking uncomfortable, Gloria sipped her iced tea.

Anna was about to suggest that she and Lorraine start their lesson when Gloria piped up again. 'Are you a widow, Lorraine?'

Lorraine looked at her in puzzled surprise. 'No.'

'Divorced?' Gloria said, undeterred.

'Gloria,' Anna said through gritted teeth, 'I think that's Lorraine's private business.'

'No, it's OK, Anna,' Lorraine said, and met Gloria's gaze. 'If you must know, my Bradley is in prison.'

Gloria's mouth snapped shut; Anna figured Lorraine had known her revelation would have that effect. There was an uneasy silence.

'Well,' Gloria said, rising, 'I should leave you to your lesson. Lorraine, it was a pleasure to meet you.'

'A pleasure to meet you, too,' Lorraine said, her smile forced, and she kept her gaze fixed on Gloria as she left the room.

'I'm sorry,' Anna said immediately. 'My sister can be…'

'Inappropriate?' Lorraine said.

'Yes, I'm afraid so. Shall we start our lesson?'

She found Lorraine bright and quick; the only reason she couldn't read, Anna realized, was that no one had bothered to teach her. The hour passed quickly. By eight o'clock the two women were laughing, the earlier tension gone.

'I've enjoyed this,' Anna said sincerely, closing the book they had been using.

'Me, too, Anna. I can't thank you enough.'

An unfamiliar phone began to ring. Lorraine reached into her purse for her cell phone. 'Excuse me.' She listened for a moment, then said, 'Just pull up in front. I'll be right out.

'It's my son, Jordan,' she explained to Anna. 'He's giving me a ride home. He can't find a parking space.'

'We'd better get down there. Here,' Anna said, handing Lorraine tonight's book, 'why don't you take this home to look at?'

Lorraine thanked her and tucked the small book into her purse.

Downstairs, the same forest-green Ford Explorer in which Lorraine had arrived at the garage on her first day idled at the curb. As soon as the two women started down the building's front stairs, the driver's door opened and a handsome African American man in his mid-twenties got out and came around to the sidewalk. He wore tan slacks and an attractive retro black-and-tan bowling shirt.

'What have you done to your face?' Lorraine asked, pointing to a dark scratch on her son's cheek.

'The cat scratched me,' he replied, opened the back door of the SUV, and indicated a pet carrier on the back seat. Inside was a fluffy white cat.

'Oh, that's right,' Lorraine said, and turned to Anna. 'Jordan has just picked up Wilson from the vet. Wilson always scratches us when we try to put him in the carrier. Anna, I'd like you to meet my son, Jordan.'

'How do you do, Jordan?' Anna said, putting out her hand, but to her surprise Jordan did not take it, simply looking down at it instead.

'Jordan!' Lorraine whispered fiercely under her breath.

Now Jordan took Anna's still outstretched hand, but only for a second and with the weakest of grips.

'We've had a wonderful lesson,' Lorraine told Jordan. She opened her purse and brought out the book for her son to see.

'A Day at the Zoo,' he read, and let out a derisive laugh.

'Gotta start somewhere, right, Anna?' Lorraine said.

'Right,' Anna said.

Jordan stared at her. 'Let's go,' he said to his mother, and ran back around to the driver's side and got in.

'I'm so sorry, Anna,' Lorraine said softly. 'Jordan is very protective of me. He's also a very proud person.'

'Clearly I'm no threat,' Anna said. 'And when you say proud, do you mean he's embarrassed that I'm teaching you to read?'

Lorraine gave a simple nod.

It occurred to Anna to say she was surprised Jordan had never taught his mother to read, but she only smiled. 'I'll see you tomorrow at the garage.'

With a smile and a nod, Lorraine got into the SUV and it zoomed away from the curb. Anna watched until it disappeared on to Tenth Avenue, then turned to go back inside.

Mrs Dovner stood behind the glass of the front door, leaning on her cane, watching.

'Hello, Mrs Dovner,' Anna said as she came through the door. She had a vague idea of what was coming but made an effort to be polite. 'How are you this evening?'

'How do you think I am?'

Anna looked at her. The older woman had a stony look.

'I don't understand,' Anna said.

'You're letting strangers into the building. Do you think that's safe?'

'Strangers?' Anna drew her brows together. 'They may be strangers to you, Mrs Dovner, but they're not to me, otherwise I wouldn't have let them into the house, would I? Besides, it was only one stranger,' she said, meaning Lorraine.

'For now,' Mrs Dovner replied. 'I suppose that young man will be coming in next.'

'Ah, I think I get it,' Anna said suddenly. 'You're talking about the fact that they're African American.'

'You can't bring people like that into the building. You're endangering all the rest of us.'

'"People like that"?' Anna felt herself flush with anger. 'Now I have one more reason to dislike you, Mrs Dovner. You're a racist.'

'Call me whatever you like. The fact remains that I have a right to be safe in my own home.'

'Mrs Dovner,' Anna said, ignoring this last statement, 'you're Jewish, if I'm not mistaken.'

Mrs Dovner looked at her in surprise. 'What has that got to do with anything?'

'I believe you once even told me that relatives of yours died in the Holocaust.'

'Yes, that's right. Why?'

'Then you, of all people, should understand that prejudice is simply evil. Lorraine and Jordan Canady happen to be lovely, decent people,' Anna said, not really sure about Jordan, but that didn't matter now. 'Are you going to judge them simply by the color of their skin, the same way your relatives were judged simply by their religion?'

Mrs Dovner looked at Anna for a long moment, drew in breath as if to speak, and let it out in exasperation. Then she turned and went into her apartment, quietly shutting the door.

With a little smile, Anna started up the stairs to her apartment.

SEVENTEEN

'Anna—' Rob Cahill approached her as her crew assembled on the garage floor. 'Could I talk to you after roll call? There's something I want to tell you.'

'Sure,' she said, and a few minutes later he sat in her office, his tall, muscular body dwarfing the yellow love seat. 'Listen, Rob,' she said before he could begin. 'I know it must be hard for you to do your route alone, but I want you to know I'm working on it and hope to have someone assigned to you within the week.'

He shook his head. 'It's not that. It's something Shari said to me. It probably doesn't mean anything, but I still felt you should know about it. I just remembered it.'

She waited, intrigued.

'It was a little bit after Shari and I started working together, before I...figured out what she was like. We were taking a break and my cell phone rang. It was my little sister in Boston, complaining to me about something our father did. She's always complaining, my sister,' Rob explained. 'I told Randi—that's my sister—she shouldn't be complaining to me; she should be complaining to our father.'

Anna waited, hoping he would reach his point soon.

'Anyway, after I got off the phone, I said something to Shari about how hard it is having a sister. Shari looked at me and said, "I hear ya",' like she had a sister herself, but that's the weird thing. She had told me she had no family. So I said, in a nice way, that I didn't think she really

understood, not having a sister herself, and she looked at
me and smirked. Then she said—I remember it exactly—
"Bell would disagree". I asked her what she meant, but
she wouldn't say anymore; she got up and said we should
get back to work.'

Bell…Anna had already figured out that 'Bell' was
'Arabella.' But Shari's *sister*? *Arabella Farnham*?

'She did say she had no family, right?' Rob said.

'Absolutely. The police had to call her boyfriend to
identify her body.'

He nodded. 'That's what I thought. I figured if Shari
did have family after all, the police would want to contact
them—you know, so they could make funeral arrangements and all. Then again,' he said, slapping his knees and
rising, 'it may not be true. You know how she was. She
said a lot of things. Once you got to know her, you knew
not to believe many of them.'

'True…' Anna said, lost in thought.

'OF COURSE I remember you, Ms Winthrop. You were here
less than a week ago. Why are you calling? Was there
something else you needed to know?'

'Yes,' Anna replied. 'Why didn't you tell me Shari
Baird was your sister?'

The silence that ensued lasted five seconds, which is
long for a silence; Anna knew it from the second hand on
her watch. Finally Arabella Farnham said, 'Are you free
to come over today?'

'I could come at noon.'

'I'll see you then,' Arabella said cordially, but Anna
detected a distinct note of tension in her voice.

As Roberta showed Anna into Arabella's office a few
hours later, the TV star rose and put out her hand, as if she

and Anna were old acquaintances. 'Sit,' she said. 'Can we get you something? Coffee? Tea?'

'No, thank you. I shouldn't be away from the garage for too long.'

'I understand.' Arabella waited for Roberta to leave and close the office door. 'Now, what was it you were saying earlier?'

'That I was wondering why you didn't tell me you and Shari were sisters.'

Arabella's face grew solemn and she looked down, as if deciding how to phrase her thoughts.

Then it was true, Anna thought.

At last Arabella looked up, meeting Anna's gaze. 'Why do you think?' she said.

Anna gave a little shrug. 'Surely not because you were afraid someone would think you had killed her. Forgive me for saying this, but I think you would find it difficult to climb over that courtyard wall, let alone back again.'

Arabella smiled. 'As it happens, I'm quite athletic. But you're absolutely right—I didn't climb over that wall. Nor was I concerned that anyone would accuse me of killing her.'

'They why didn't you tell me?'

'Because if it got out that Shari was my sister, then the truth about my past would get out, too.

'She was blackmailing me, you see. She was an accomplished blackmailer. And to a professional blackmailer, anyone is fair game, even your sister. But let me explain by backing up a bit.

'Shari and I grew up in rural Kentucky, but it wasn't among the emerald pastures and white board fences of Lexington as I've said in interviews. We were what you would call white trash. Until I was fifteen, I lived in a cramped, filthy trailer with Shari, our drug-addicted mother, and our alcoholic father, who was constantly groping us.'

'You were ashamed to let the world know.'

'Yes, and that wasn't even the half of it. But I'm getting off track again.

'My real name is Bella, Bella Baird. My parents always called me Bell. When I was fourteen, our mother died. When I was fifteen, my father tried to rape me. This time the handiest object for fighting him off was a large iron skillet. I bashed him over the head so hard I didn't know if I had killed him. I ran out of that trailer and never went back.'

'Where did you go?' Anna asked.

'To New York,' Arabella said simply. 'On TV and in the movies, girls always went to New York to make good. I started hitch-hiking. I made it as far as West Virginia and was on Route 79, trying to get someone to stop and pick me up, when this guy in a big fancy Cadillac pulled over. I thought he was a real gentleman. And he was, in a way. He asked me if I wanted to make some money— a lot of money—by…doing some things with him.' She laughed. 'Believe me, I hadn't exactly been a nun up to that point. He wasn't asking me to do anything I hadn't already done, except that no one had ever paid me to do it before, let alone paid me what seemed like a fortune.

'I said yes. We went to a motel. He was sweet and kind with me—as I said, a gentleman. True to his word, he paid me. Then he drove me to an Amtrak station and with some of the money he'd given me I bought a ticket to New York.'

Suddenly Arabella's intercom came to life. 'Bell,' Roberta said, 'I've got Regis Philbin on line three.'

'Tell him I'll get back to him,' Arabella said, and looked again at Anna. 'Where was I?'

'You took a train to New York. What did you do when you got here?'

'Guess. I did more of what I'd done for my West Virginia gentleman.'

Anna's eyes bulged. 'You were a *prostitute*?'

Arabella winced. 'I wouldn't use that word, no. What I did was several steps above that. I was a paid escort. My hair was always done, my make-up was impeccable, I wore expensive clothes and jewelry...and I had a killer figure. I fixed up real nice back then. Men—businessmen, usually—would pay my service well to have me on their arm at a cocktail party, a dinner...or in their hotel room. It went well—extremely well—for a good seven years.'

Anna frowned. 'What happened after seven years?'

Arabella's gaze grew cold. 'Shari arrived in town. She was fifteen, the same age I had been when I left home. I had tried to keep my whereabouts a secret from my family. I wanted nothing to do with any of them, nothing to do with anything from my past life.'

'But Shari found you?' Anna asked, and Arabella nodded. 'How?'

'Once in a while I used to send money home, but anonymously. I would wrap a pile of bills in blank paper and mail it home in an envelope with no return address. But one of those times, I made a mistake. I lived in a residential hotel. The piece of "blank" paper I wrapped the bills in was actually a piece of hotel letterhead. I don't know how I missed it, but I did. Now Shari had my address. She kept it for four years until she left home and came to New York to seek me out. Unfortunately, I was still living there, so she found me. That was ten years ago.'

'How did you feel seeing her?'

'I didn't wish the kid any harm, but I barely knew her. I told her honestly that I didn't want any connections to my past life. I gave her money—a lot of money—to get her started and told her never to contact me again.'

'She didn't listen, did she?' Anna said.

'No. Every few weeks she would appear at my hotel and ask for money. I had plenty. And I felt guilty. She was my sister, after all. I gave her what she needed and she would go away.'

'What was she doing? To make a living, I mean?'

'Taking after her big sister. But she wasn't with an escort service. She was a good old-fashioned, honest-to-goodness hooker. She had her own corner and everything. Sometimes when she came to see me she would tell me sob stories about the way her pimp treated her. I would give her a little more money and she would be on her way.

'Then something very unexpected happened to me. One night my escort client was a man named Wes Snyder who said he produced infomercials. He was making one about a new kind of blender and he needed "some decoration", as he put it. In other words, a young woman to look pretty, smile, drink the concoctions the main talent whipped up, and serve some of them to these people who were supposedly from the audience—they were really actors—who sat around this bar that looked like it was in somebody's rec room. He said he couldn't pay much, but what he offered me was more than I made in a week as an escort. Plus, the whole thing would take only a few days. I jumped at the chance.

'I liked Wes, and he liked me. I made another infomercial with him, and this time I made some suggestions on the script and the set. He liked my ideas. He was also falling for me. He asked me to work for him. I said yes; it was time for me to move on from escorting anyway.

'I got more and more relaxed in these infomercials and

let my personality come out…and people liked it. Soon Wes's clients were asking specifically for me in their infomercials.

'After three years of this, CBS asked me to do a low-budget show called *As Seen on TV*. Do you remember it? It was kind of a combination talk show and game show. We had celebrities on and we tried out new products and gadgets. Then the celebrities would choose people from the audience who competed against each other using these products—who could make the best steak in a new skillet, or create the best decorations on a jacket with a rhinestone setter. Then the celebrities voted on the winners.

'It was corny as all get-out, but it was a big hit. After I had done the show for two years, CBS gave me the show I've got now. Now all I had to do was talk to people; no more skillets and rhinestone setters. I jumped at the chance.'

Anna asked, 'Where was Shari all this time?'

'Oh, she would appear, regular as clockwork, and I would give her money and she would go away. We had agreed she would never come to the studio. She was my dirty secret. And my payments to her had slowly turned into blackmail payments. Neither of us ever said that word, but we both knew what was happening. The more famous I got, the more important it was that my past be kept a secret.

'A few months ago, she told me she'd taken a job with the Sanitation Department. I couldn't believe it. I asked her why on earth she would do that. She told me she thought it would give her access to a lot of places she wouldn't be able to reach otherwise. Then I understood. She was also involved with a group that did some kind of urban exploring. I didn't really understand what she told me, but I knew she must be up to no good. On top of that, once or twice she showed up in a cocktail dress. She said she was working as a hostess in some club. She had all kinds of irons in the fire, my little sister.

'One day, not long after I had started on my new show, she came to visit and said she wasn't happy with how much money I had been giving her. She said she knew I was making a lot of money now and she wanted more of it. Tens of thousands more.'

'What did you do?'

'What do you think I did? I gave it to her.'

Arabella was watching Anna, as if to gauge her reaction. Finally Anna said, 'And that was why Shari had your phone number, marked with a picture of a bell. Not because you had once considered her for a show about women who come to New York.'

'That's right. The truth is very simple. She was blackmailing me and called regularly to demand her payments.'

'You must have hated her.'

'Yes, that's exactly the word. She was heartless and cold-blooded and I hated her. But enough to kill her? No. I'm no killer.'

'Neither is the young man the police have arrested for her murder.'

'He works for you, if I recall the news stories correctly.'

'That's right.'

'Which is why you're trying to clear him.'

Anna nodded. 'Would you mind telling me where you were on the morning of April twenty-third?'

'I don't mind at all.' Arabella pushed the intercom button. 'Roberta, would you come in here, please? Bring my calendar.'

Roberta appeared at the door.

'Where was I on the morning of April twenty-third?'

Roberta flipped pages, then looked up. 'That was the

day you didn't feel well. You didn't come in until around two. I know because you had that meeting with Ralph that I had to reschedule.' She waited, smiling.

'All right, thanks, Roberta.'

When the young woman had gone, Arabella turned to Anna. 'I have no alibi, I'm afraid. Am I glad my sister is dead? Absolutely. But as I said, I'm no murderer.'

Anna rose. 'I appreciate your candor.'

Arabella smiled. 'You're not going to start blackmailing me now, are you?' she joked.

'No. What you've told me will never go any farther.'

'I didn't think so. I could tell as soon as I met you. I'm a good judge of character, you know.'

The two women shook hands. Anna saw herself out.

AT THE END of her shift, Anna called Dante at the Marconi Pasta Company. The phone was answered by Lola Wentworth. Anna asked for him.

'Who, may I ask, is calling?'

'Uh…an old friend.'

'This is Anna Winthrop, isn't it?'

Surprised, Anna said nothing.

'You don't have to lie to get through to him,' Lola said. 'You just have to promise me again that you won't tell him I spoke with you.'

'Of course.'

'All right. Hold, please.'

'Anna!' Dante came on the line, as if greeting an old friend. 'How are you?'

She frowned into the receiver. 'I'm fine, thank you.'

'That's good to hear. What can I do for you?'

'I'd like to speak to you again, if you don't mind.'

'I never mind talking with a pretty lady, Anna, but I've told you all there is to tell.'

'No; actually, you haven't.'

'I don't…'

'For example, Avel Petrov.'

'Can you come now?'

'Certainly. I'll be there in ten minutes.'

'How do you know about him?' Dante asked her as she sat down in his office.

'I can't say.'

'Did Shari tell you?'

'No. Why didn't you tell me about him and his club?'

'I didn't think it was relevant.'

'So you just left him completely out of the story.'

Dante's bright smile disappeared. 'What happened was very painful for me. I didn't think it was relevant and I didn't think it was any of your business.'

'Of course it's relevant. It's the real reason Shari never came back. It's the reason you wrote her that note.'

'Sure, I wrote her the note, but Petrov and his club weren't the reason I wanted her back. I loved her.'

'I believe you did. I also believe you would do anything necessary to protect your business interests.'

'Petrov's club was going ahead whether Shari was part of it or not.'

'But you didn't know that. Where were you on the morning of April twenty-third?'

'You sound like Perry Mason.' He punched a button on his phone. 'Lola, where was I on the morning of April twenty-third?'

After a brief silence, Lola's voice came through the speaker. 'You got here late that day, Dante. I think you said you weren't feeling well.'

'Yeah, right,' he said, as if remembering. 'I woke up with a wicked sore throat that morning, felt terrible. I stayed in bed all morning. After lunch I was feeling better, so I came in.'

'Can your wife vouch for the fact that you were home all that morning?'

He gave her a level stare. 'No, I'm afraid she can't. She was out shopping that morning. And even if she could, there's no way I would let you talk to her. So I guess that means I have no alibi—that I crept down that alley, climbed over the wall, and strangled Shari. Oh—and then I took a knife and carved an ankh into her. I almost forgot that part.'

'How do you know about the alley and the courtyard wall?' she asked matter-of-factly. 'No one but the police know about that.'

'Actually,' he said, 'that's not true. I read about it in a news story.'

'Really? Which one?'

'I don't remember.'

They glared at each other as if playing a game of chicken. Finally Anna broke her gaze, rising, and handed him her card. 'If your memory improves, call me.'

EIGHTEEN

THE FOLLOWING DAY, Anna heard shouting outside her office
and went out to find Caitlin and Lorraine arguing, between
them a rolling bucket with a mop standing in it. Lorraine,
her hands on her hips, was leaning forward slightly as she
harangued the younger woman. 'You know something,
princess? I'm sick and tired of doing your work!' Her
words echoed across the cavernous space.

Then came Caitlin's reply: 'And I'm sick and tired of
that big fat chip on your shoulder!'

Anna was about to hurry across the floor to break up
the fight when her cell phone rang. It was Santos.

'Where are you?' she asked. 'It's nearly two o'clock.
Caitlin's leaving any minute. Shouldn't you be outside?'

'I am outside. The limo's already here. I just wanted to
tell you something.'

She waited.

'I got the scoop on Lorraine's husband. Bradley Canady
is doing twenty-five years at Sing Sing for attacking a
woman and nearly killing her.'

'Did you get any details?' Anna asked, her gaze still
fixed on Lorraine and Caitlin.

'He was a janitor at the main post office on Eighth
Avenue. Late one afternoon he grabbed a young female
clerk and dragged her into a closet. He tried to strangle
her, but she managed to kick him hard enough to get free
and escaped.'

'Interesting,' Anna said. Across the garage floor, Caitlin

suddenly checked her watch and walked away from Lorraine. 'Santos, she's heading outside now. You'd better get ready.'

'Right. Thanks. I'll see you later.'

Lorraine had picked up the bucket handle and was wheeling it toward Anna. Approaching, she said, 'I'm sorry about that, Anna. It's just that that girl gets on my last nerve. The spoiled brat thinks she's better than everybody else, that she doesn't have to work like everybody else.'

Anna gave her an understanding smile. 'You'll be pleased to hear that tomorrow is her last day.'

Lorraine's face brightened. 'Good. I'll be by myself—just the way I like it.' She started to walk away, then turned and came back. 'Anna, I want to apologize for my son's behavior on Tuesday night.'

Anna pretended not to understand.

'Jordan was unforgivably rude. I was so embarrassed.'

'Oh, he's just a kid,' Anna said.

But Lorraine shook her head. 'He's twenty-five years old. He should know better. The problem is, since Bradley has been gone, Jordan has been overly protective of me. You know, the man of the house.'

'Surely he doesn't think anyone here would hurt you?'

'No, no, nothing like that. He's embarrassed that all I know how to do is clean, and thinks people take advantage of me. He also thinks people look down on us because we're African American. If you'll forgive me for saying it, he thinks you offered to teach me to read because you pitied me and because you could show me you're better than I am.'

'He certainly has some strong ideas. I hope you know none of that is true.'

Lorraine smiled warmly. 'Of course I know that. I've

told Jordan that. But…' She shook her head and shrugged helplessly. 'It's funny that Caitlin said I've got a chip on my shoulder. I don't think I do, but Jordan definitely does. He's always looking to be offended.'

'Thanks for the apology, Lorraine—though it certainly wasn't necessary. I completely understand. And thanks also for being such a good sport. With Caitlin, I mean.'

'I wish I could have been a better sport. I've been telling myself that she's just a kid—younger than my Jordan— and that I shouldn't take her so seriously, but then she pulls her nonsense and I start to boil.'

'Well, boil no more. As I said, one more day and she's gone,' Anna said, and watched Lorraine drag the bucket away.

JUST BEFORE ANNA LEFT the garage for the day, Gloria called. 'Anna, I won't be at your apartment tonight. I've gone back to Donald.'

'Ping. Pong.'

'What?'

'You're like a ping-pong ball, Gloria. How did he get you back this time?'

'I hardly think that's kind, Anna, calling me a ping-pong ball.'

'You didn't answer my question.'

'He apologized for calling me bossy and closed-minded and asked me to meet him for dinner. We went to Per Se. Donald has connections and got us a fabulous table. It was so romantic.'

'Oh, brother,' Anna murmured.

'What?'

'Nothing. That is good news, Gloria. I'm sorry I called you a ping-pong ball.'

'That's all right. I guess it did look that way. But everything is fine between us now. I'm back home to stay.'

Smiling, Anna put down the phone. Then she left the garage, walking slowly along Forty-Third Street toward home, enjoying New York's distinctive golden dusk.

Halfway between the garage and Eighth Avenue, she spotted the figure of a man standing in the shadows at the entrance to a parking garage. He stood perfectly still, his features indistinguishable; she could tell only that this person was a man, slim and tallish. There was no one else on the street. Uneasy, she crossed to the other side. When she had passed the point at which the man had been standing, she glanced back; he was gone. Turning around further, she saw that he was on her side of the street now, following her, an impassive expression on his face.

He looked familiar but she couldn't say how. When she reached Eighth Avenue, she turned left. She walked a few feet, ducked into the recessed entrance to a shoe repair shop, and waited. Presently he came around the corner, and seeing him this close she remembered who he was: Marco, from Urban Access. When he reached the shop she stepped out in front of him. He jumped, startled. Then he smiled his handsome smile and looked down at her from under heavy lids. 'You got me.'

She gave him a thin smile. 'Marco, isn't it?'

'That's right.'

'Why are you following me?'

He laughed. 'I didn't mean to follow you. I just want to talk to you.'

'Obviously you know where I work, since you were standing about twenty feet away. Why didn't you just come to see me there?'

'This is…sensitive,' he said.

'Well? What is it?'

'Jocelyn asked me to come and speak to you. She wants to know if you've given any more thought to the conversation you and she had in the tunnel on Saturday night.'

'Ah. You mean whether I'm interested in doing that "interesting" activity that Shari and Dennis used to engage in.'

'Yes, I believe that's it,' he said, his sleepy eyes dropping even lower.

'I *have* thought about it, actually, and I've decided against it.'

He frowned. 'Really? That is a shame. We all felt you would be quite good at it.'

'At the "activity", you mean?'

'Mm.'

She shook her head. 'It's just not for me.'

He inclined his head gallantly. 'Fair enough. It certainly isn't for everyone.'

'Of course,' she said, trying to soften her response, 'if I change my mind, I'll be in touch immediately.'

He smirked, moved closer to her. She shifted uncomfortably. 'You're not going to change your mind, Anna,' he said softly. 'You never had any intention of doing...the activity. In fact, you never had any intention of joining UA.'

Fear rippled through her. 'What do you mean? Of course I did. Why else would I have come on that mission in the tunnel?'

He studied her thoughtfully. 'We've got a pretty good idea. You see, we've spoken to Dennis.'

Her stomach did a sickening flip. She said nothing.

'He cleared up a few things for us.'

'Oh?'

'Yeah, like the fact that you were never a friend of his and Shari's. Or the fact that you've been investigating Shari's murder. What's on your mind, Anna? Do you think one of us did it?'

Now it was she who moved closer. 'I wouldn't put it past any of you.'

He looked surprised. 'Hey. We may be a lot of things, but murderers we're not.'

'Really? I think that poor Chinese jeweler would disagree.'

His expression grew icy. He raised his head slightly, assessing her. 'Now listen carefully, Anna. Jocelyn doesn't take kindly to being lied to, especially by people who are trying to pin crimes on her. We had nothing to do with that jeweler's murder, and we had nothing to do with Shari's murder. If you tell anyone we did...well, you'll be very sorry you did.'

She laughed. 'Are you threatening me?'

'No, just giving you fair warning. You see, we know where you work, we know where you live, we know...a lot about you. Come to that, we know a lot about your boyfriend, Santos Reyes, and your sister, Gloria Stone... We know everything. Because that's what we do, remember? Get into places...learn things.'

Fury rose up in her. Suddenly with her left hand she grabbed him by the back of the head and yanked it down so forcefully her face was right in his. 'Now you listen to me, sport. Your team is lucky I haven't had you all arrested already. Now *I'm* warning *you*. If you so much as say boo to anyone in my family—or to me—I will find you and I will hurt you very badly. Do you understand me? Because do you know what I do for a living, Marco? I work with garbage, and I do it every single day. So I know exactly what to do with the likes of you.' Before he knew what was coming, she pulled back the hand not holding his head and slapped his face so hard her hand hurt.

He recoiled, the left side of his face flaming red.

'*Anna?*'

They both spun around. Five feet away stood Santos, in uniform, frowning deeply. 'What's going on?'

'Nothing,' Anna said, and looked at Marco, who shook his head and hurried away.

'Are you sure?' Santos asked, watching Marco's retreating figure.

'I'm sure.'

'Who *was* that guy? Do you know him?'

'Yeah, I know him. He's a member of Urban Access.'

Santos turned quickly to take another look, but Marco had disappeared. 'What was he saying to you? How do you know he's—?' Then, before she could answer, his eyes grew wide. 'Anna, did you—?'

Without moving her head she shifted her eyes to him. 'Ask me no questions and I'll tell you no lies.'

'Why didn't you tell me?'

She met his gaze. 'Guess.'

'Right! I would have been furious—I *am* furious— because these people are dangerous. I told you that.'

'I know. But I found out what I wanted to know and I'm here to tell the tale. So no harm done.'

'Up to now.' He blew out his breath in exasperation. 'All right, what exactly did you find out?'

'How much time do you have?'

'I'll be off duty at six. I'll come get you and we'll go out for a bite. Is Gloria still staying with you?'

'No, she's back with Donald again. Isn't that great?'

He didn't look so sure. 'It would be better if she were still there. Then you wouldn't be alone.'

'Oh, Santos. Don't be so dramatic.'

'Dramatic? Anna, I'm a New York City cop.'

'Which is why I didn't tell you what I was doing. I

didn't want you getting in the way before I was finished with them.' When he looked hurt, she said, 'If I'd told you what I found out about them, you'd have been all over them like white on rice, and it was too soon.'

'True,' he admitted grudgingly, and gave her a kiss before they parted.

That evening, over a Chinese takeout dinner in Anna's kitchen, she brought him completely up to date, told him everything. He took notes. When she was finished, he looked at her and shook his head. 'All of these people are ruthless, Anna. Urban explorers…club owners…You don't want to mess with them.'

'It's a little late for that,' she said brightly.

'The trouble is, none of what you've given me is strong enough to make any arrests. It's all hearsay. We'll keep watching them, catch them in the act. In the meantime, watch your back. You know way too much.'

NINETEEN

At seven the next morning, Anna was at her desk when Santos called her on her cell. 'Anna, I think you'd better come out to the street.'

She went out to the gate, where the usual paparazzi strained against the fence. Several cops stood off to the right; Santos broke away and came over to her. 'You know anything about a catering van?'

She frowned. 'What are you talking about?'

He pointed down the street. 'Caitlin's Rolls is down there, and behind it is a catering van. The driver says he's here to set up the breakfast.'

She shook her head. At that moment the Rolls pulled up to the gate and Caitlin hopped out before her chauffeur had even opened his door. She ran up to Anna. 'Good morning! It's my last day, did you know that?'

'Yes,' Anna said with a smile. 'Congratulations.'

'Thanks,' Caitlin said, beaming, and giggled. 'I appreciate all you've done for me.'

'What have I done?'

'You looked out for me, made sure people treated me right. I was so afraid of how everyone would react to me, but everyone—well, almost everyone—was just wonderful. So I want to say thank you.'

'You just did.'

'No, I want to do something for everyone.'

At that moment the van that Santos had pointed out pulled up behind Caitlin's car. Lettered on the van's side were the words HAMILTON'S CATERING SERVICE. Hamilton's, named for its owner, Caitlin's father, was one of the most exclusive restaurants in Manhattan.

'I don't...' Anna began, puzzled.

'I'm serving breakfast!'

The van's doors slid open and two men in white uniforms jumped out and began pulling out deep aluminum food trays. Another van pulled up behind the first one, and another behind that, and soon phalanxes of servers were hurrying past Anna and Caitlin in both directions. In the center of the garage, a long line of tables was set up, covered in white linen tablecloths, and provided with chafing dishes for the trays of food. A separate table offered coffee and tea.

'I thought about mimosas and screwdrivers,' Caitlin said, 'but I know you're all on duty, so that didn't seem like a good idea.'

Someone called Anna's name and she turned. Allen Schiff stood watching the army of servers as they now set out china, silver, and linen napkins. 'What's going on?'

Anna winced. 'Caitlin is providing breakfast for all of us as a way of saying thank you.'

Allen turned to Caitlin and was about to speak, but as soon as he saw her sweet, eager expression he stopped himself. 'That's very kind,' was all he said.

'Come eat!' Caitlin said, and led the way into the garage, where sanitation workers were already lining up for caviar omelets, raspberry crêpes, and fresh-baked croissants.

From the street a reporter yelled, 'Hey Caitlin, what's up? You throwin' a party?'

She spun around, giggling. 'That's right,' she called back. 'For all my friends!'

Cameras flashed. Automatically Caitlin struck a red-carpet pose, though instead of a couture gown, she wore a T-shirt, jeans, and work boots.

THAT DAY, Caitlin got little work done. On her orders, the caterers didn't depart until well after eleven, so that as many garage workers as possible would have an opportunity to partake of the lavish breakfast.

After lunch, Caitlin knocked on Anna's office door and plunked herself down in the chair beside the desk.

'I should have thought of this a long time ago,' she said. 'I'm hosting a party tonight and I would love it if you and that divine policeman boyfriend of yours could come.'

'That's sweet of you,' Anna said. 'Where will it be?'

'Have you ever been to the Rose? It's a club in Tribeca.'

'I've heard of it,' Anna said, 'but I've never been.'

'Oh, it's heaven. Every month or so I host a party there. Well, "host" is maybe not the right word. I just go in, say a few words. The club pays me outrageously just to show up. Anyway, it's great fun, great music, dancing. Can you come?'

'I'd like to,' Anna said, 'but I'll have to ask Santos. I don't know if he's on duty tonight. If he is, I'll come by myself. What time?'

'I'll be coming out at ten, so be there by then.'

Anna nodded.

Caitlin giggled and clapped her hands together. 'Cool! I'll make sure you're on the list at the door. Listen, thanks for everything, Anna, really. I had no idea work could be so much fun.' Her face grew serious. 'I know my time here has made me a better person.'

'Well, that's wonderful, Caitlin. We've enjoyed having you.' Anna smiled. 'But let's not see you back here anytime soon—if ever.'

With another giggle, Caitlin was gone. At two, when

she emerged from the garage, she blew kisses to all the reporters. Then she climbed into her silver Rolls and it pulled smoothly away from the curb.

'Unbelievable,' Anna said from the sidelines, and turned to see who was standing beside her.

It was Gerry Licari. Still angry, he gave her a blank look before walking silently away.

Santos approached from the street. 'Well, that's that. She's an original, I'll give her that.'

'She added a touch of glamour to the place,' Anna said. 'Speaking of which, she's invited us to a party she's hosting tonight at a club called the Rose.'

'I know that club,' Santos said. 'But she hardly hosts these parties. It's more like she's just there.'

'Yeah, that's what she said. Can you make it?'

'Sure, but late. My shift finishes at eight, then I'll need to shower and change. I could meet you there by nine thirty.'

'Perfect. She's not coming out until ten. Now, what on earth will I wear...'

She worked at her desk until three, and was shutting down her computer when her phone rang.

At first, the only thing she heard was static. Then, very faintly, there came a woman's voice. 'Hello?'

'Who is this?' Anna said loudly.

'Anna'—static—'it's Caitlin!'

'Caitlin, is everything all right?'

'I thought of something...you.'

Anna shook her head. 'Caitlin, we've got a really bad connection. I can't understand you.'

But Caitlin was apparently unwilling to give up. 'Anna,' she said again, '...a cigarette...no one there!'

Anna looked at the phone in frustration. 'A cigarette? No one there?'

'Yes!' came Caitlin's voice, very faintly. 'No one there!' And the line went dead.

Anna immediately called her back; the call went to voice-mail.

She gazed down at her cell phone, shrugged. She would see Caitlin in only a few hours at the club. She could repeat what she had said on the phone then.

At that moment there was a sound in the corridor—footsteps. Anna moved quickly to the doorway to look out. There was no one there.

OUTSIDE THE ROSE, pandemonium ruled. The line of would-be partiers extended all the way around the block on which the club sat, nearly joining itself at the entrance. Bouncers walked the line, working to maintain order and turning away those who were patently unsuitable.

Anna, in a simple short green cocktail dress that matched her eyes, held on to Santos's jacketed arm as they approached the club's front doors, on each side of which a spotlight shot a beam into the Manhattan sky.

'If you think you're on the list, come forward!' a bouncer yelled.

'We're on the list,' Anna said to Santos. 'Caitlin said she would put us on.'

'OK,' Santos said, and they approached the hollering bouncer. 'We're on the list.'

The bouncer took several folded sheets of paper from his inside jacket pocket. 'Names?'

'Anna Winthrop and Santos Reyes.'

The bouncer scanned his list and finally looked up with a smile. 'Guests of Miss Whitelaw. Right this way, please, ma'am, sir, and have a wonderful evening.'

Anna gave Santos an impressed look and they strolled

into the club. Inside, a solid mass of people danced wildly to music so loud and throbbing it shook the floor.

Anna looked at Santos. 'How will we ever get in there? There are so many people we won't be able to move!'

'Easy,' he said. 'We stay on the sidelines. How about a drink?'

'Sure. I'll have a martini.'

'Sounds good; I'll have the same. Back in a jiff.'

While he was gone, she watched the dancing crowd and moved slightly to the music's beat. Suddenly the blast of a siren pierced the air. On a raised platform in the center of the vast room was a giant closed white rosebud. Now it began to open, revealing a tall, thin woman in a black body suit and a wild headdress of sparkling silver and gold that made her look like the personification of the sun. In her hand she held a long sparkly wand, and as she danced and spun and waved it, an endless flow of glitter poured from it, covering the crowd. Everyone screamed with pleasure, a new song began to rock the room, and once again everyone danced.

Suddenly at her side, Santos handed over her drink. 'That's not Caitlin, is it?' he shouted, watching the sun woman.

'No! That's...well, I don't know who that is, but it's not Caitlin. She said she would be out at ten and it's nearly that now.' She took the pick from her drink and slid the fat green olive into her mouth.

'Want mine?' Santos said. Nodding, she took his olive, ate it, and was left holding the two picks. 'Give me those, I'll throw them out,' he said.

'No, wait,' she said, holding them out. 'Look, they're metal, not plastic, and they have a tiny rose at the end. Cute! I want them.'

'All right. Here,' he said, and dropped them into a pocket of his sport coat.

They returned their attention to the festivities. At the stroke of ten the siren blared again, and this time when the white rosebud opened, Caitlin was inside. She wore the tiniest of dresses, all shimmery white; her hair hung wildly around her face. Anna noticed the thin black line of a wireless microphone near her mouth. She held up her arms and cried, 'Hello, Manhattan!'

The crowd roared back in room-rocking unison, 'Hello, Caitlin!'

'Welcome,' she said. 'This is my first appearance since my hard labor'—everyone laughed—'and I'm grateful to all of you for your wonderful support during my difficult time. Before we get under way, there's someone very special I want to thank. I hope she's here. Anna, where are you?' She eagerly scanned the sea of people.

Anna felt herself flush hotly. Santos looked at her in amazement. When Anna had regained her composure, she raised her hand and cried, 'Here!' but her voice was lost in the roar of the crowd.

'Here!' Santos shouted in his deep voice, at the same time pointing down at Anna.

'There she is!' another man cried, and the information was passed along like a ripple to the center of the room, where Caitlin listened and then looked up with a smile. 'She is! Anna, come up here!'

Anna took in the solid mass of people in front of her. She looked up at Santos helplessly, then shrugged and started working her way toward Caitlin.

It was no use. Though everyone she met smiled and urged her forward, people were packed so tightly that at times she could barely inhale. She'd gone only about seven feet when she gave up and squeezed her way back to Santos.

'She can't make it!' a man cried, everyone laughed, and the message rippled its way up to the center.

'That's OK!' Caitlin said. 'I've got a mike; I'll go to her! Which way?'

She was shown the general direction and stepped down from the rosebud platform. 'Hey, handsome,' she purred in a seductive voice to a man as she passed; then, 'Oh, sorry, honey, I didn't know he was taken.' There were roars of laughter.

'You stay right where you are, Anna,' Caitlin said breathlessly, and everyone near Anna looked at her for her reaction. 'I'm almost there!' came Caitlin in a sing-song voice.

Then, for several long moments, there was silence, no commentary from Caitlin. The crowd began to buzz. Santos gave Anna a questioning look.

That was when the scream started. It came from the center of the crowd, the place where Caitlin had been. It was hoarse and shrill and seemed to go on forever. When it finally stopped, a man cried, 'She's bleeding!'

Anna and Santos looked at each other in alarm.

There was another scream. Then a woman cried, 'She's dead!'

Next came the stampede. The solid mass of people began moving inexorably toward the exit; Anna saw shock and fear on the faces that had only moments ago been smiling and laughing. Just in time, she and Santos pressed back against the wall.

'People! People!' a bouncer cried, but no one was listening. Within seconds he was caught up in the crowd himself and carried helplessly toward the doors.

Santos touched Anna's shoulder. 'It's clear enough now,' he said, and jerked his head toward the main room. Now it was possible to move. Like fish swimming upstream, they

dodged the men and women rushing toward them until
they suddenly found themselves breaking through a ring
of people with a space in the center. In the middle of this
space lay Caitlin, half on her side, her arms stretched out
before her, the handle of a knife protruding from her back.

STANDING OUTSIDE the nightclub in the chilly night air, Anna
pulled Santos's sport coat more tightly around her. Beside
her, Santos craned his neck to check the progress of the
police. He turned to her. 'We should go.'

Caitlin Whitelaw was dead. The police had determined
that she had been dead before she hit the floor, the packed
crowd having carried her body along until someone saw
the blood.

Anna and Santos walked several blocks north and
hailed a cab. Inside, they sat like automatons, still unable
to believe what had just happened.

'Why?' Anna said, wiping her eyes.

Santos shrugged helplessly. 'This is New York. Why
do a lot of things happen here?'

But Anna shook her head. 'It has something to do with
that phone call.'

'What phone call?'

'I didn't tell you. Before I left the garage she called me.
We had a terrible connection and I couldn't make out what
she was saying, but I could tell she was trying very hard
to tell me something.'

Santos looked intrigued. 'Did you catch any of it?'

'Not much. Something about a cigarette...'

'A cigarette?'

She nodded. 'And then she said, "No one there".'

They sat in silence, bewildered, as the cab raced up
Hudson Street. Anna began to cry.

When the cab reached Anna's building, Santos walked

her to her door and gave her a hug and a kiss before seeing her safely inside. As the door to the street swung shut, Mrs Dovner's door swung open.

'Don't say a word, Mrs Dovner!' Anna said, still crying. 'Not a word!'

Mrs Dovner popped back inside and the door clicked shut.

As Anna unlocked her apartment door, her phone began to ring. She hurried inside and grabbed it.

'Anna, you're not going to believe this. It's about Caitlin.'

'I know all about it, Gloria.'

'Why are you crying? What's wrong?'

'I was there. Santos and I—we were there at that club.'

'You were? Why?'

'Caitlin invited us to her party.'

'Is it true what they're saying on TV? That the place was so packed that Caitlin's body was carried along like a rag doll?'

'Oh, Gloria, don't say that.'

'I didn't make it up! That's what they're saying on TV.'

'I can't talk now, Gloria, I'm too upset. I'll speak to you later.' Anna replaced the receiver.

She walked to the hall closet to hang up her jacket and then realized it wasn't her jacket but Santos's sport coat. Bless him; he would never have asked for it back.

Reaching up, she pushed some hangers aside. As she grabbed a hanger on the upper rod, a muscular arm shot out and grabbed her by the throat.

TWENTY

WILLY SOTHERN PROPELLED himself from the closet, forcing Anna backwards and slamming her against the opposite wall. Now he had both hands around her neck and his face contorted as he tightened his grip. She clawed at his hands but they were like iron; she tried to dig her fingers into his face but he just shook her off and squeezed even tighter. She began to feel light-headed.

With all the strength she could muster she ground the sharp heel of her shoe into the top of his foot. Crying out in pain, he lifted the foot and shook her free, and as her shoe returned to the floor she lifted the other one and kicked him hard in the shin. Again he cried out, his grip loosening ever so slightly, and in that instant she brought her right knee up hard into his crotch. This time, when he grunted with pain, she broke free and ran headlong into the kitchen, one of her shoes flying off. Madly she yanked open the silverware drawer and reached for a knife but before her hand made contact his arms were around her waist and he spun her around and pushed her back against the counter.

Again his hands were around her throat, squeezing even harder than before. She gasped, her eyes bulging. She clawed at his face again but he barely took any notice, intent on his grip around her neck. She began to see stars. She tried to kick her foot that still had a shoe, but leaning back against the counter this way she was off balance and couldn't put any strength into it.

As the stars grew in number and began to blend, she saw Santos, smiling at her, handsome in his open-necked shirt and jacket…and remembered. Wildly she reached into the pocket of Santos's sport coat and her fingers made contact with the metal olive picks. With what strength she had left she grabbed one of them, brought it out, and drove the sharp point hard into the side of Willy's neck. It went in all the way up to the little metal rose.

His eyes bulged in amazement and he let out a cry of pain. He released his strangling grip. He felt for the offending sword, grimacing as he began to pull it slowly out. Now she was able to straighten. Crazed, she cast her glance about the small room and saw, in the drying rack beside the sink, a cast-iron skillet Gloria had used to make an omelet. She grabbed it, swung her arm out wide, and smashed it with all her might into the side of Willy's head.

He froze, stunned, the fingers that had been pulling the Martini pick quivering slightly.

She smashed him again. This time he went down with a deep groan, and when he was down she smashed him twice more for good measure. When she was certain he was out, she ran for the apartment door, and as she did, the floor shook with a series of rhythmic bangs—Mrs Dovner, complaining about the noise.

On the stairs she whipped out her cell phone and dialed 911. 'Please,' she gasped. 'I've been attacked. Come quickly. He's unconscious, I don't know for how long.' And she gave her address and apartment number.

She ran down the stairs to the front hallway, where Mrs Dovner stood with her hands on her hips, an odd golden turban on her head. 'Missy, do you have any idea what time it is?'

'Go back inside and lock your door, Mrs Dovner,' Anna

ordered breathlessly. 'The police are coming. I—I've been attacked.'

'Attacked!' came Mrs Dovner's voice as Anna went out the front door. 'I told you, didn't I? I told you!' Her voice was drowned out by the wail of a siren as a police cruiser turned on to Forty-Third Street from Ninth Avenue, raced down the block, and jerked to a stop feet from where she stood.

A young cop jumped out. 'Where?' he said.

'Second floor. Apartment two-A. In the kitchen; he was unconscious.'

He gave one nod and bounded into the building, at the same time reaching for his gun.

Another police cruiser screeched to a halt behind the first one. This cop, older than the first, looked at her questioningly. 'Upstairs, second floor, two-A,' she told him. 'He's already gone up.' Before she could say anymore he was inside and on his way up the stairs.

For a few minutes it was eerily quiet, Anna alone in the street. Then, through the glass of the building's front door, she saw the two cops coming down the stairs with Willy between them in handcuffs. Blood ran down his neck and into his shirt where she'd stabbed him. He looked pretty out of it but managed to look at her with his cold eyes before he was shoved into one of the police cruisers.

The younger cop came back to her.

'Are you OK, miss?' When she nodded he said, 'We're gonna need you to come down to the station so we can ask you some questions. Are you up to that?'

'Sure,' she said. 'Let me pull myself together and I'll be there in about half an hour.'

'Right,' he said, and took off.

Upstairs, she burst into tears as she worked to eliminate any traces of Willy's presence in her home. As she worked in the kitchen, it suddenly occurred to her that she had no idea how Willy had gotten in. Not by the door; it had been locked and intact when she arrived home. There were only a few windows in her apartment: two large ones in the living room, opening on to the building's front fire escape and overlooking Forty-Third Street; one in her bedroom at the back of the apartment, opening on to the rear fire escape and overlooking a courtyard; and a small window in her bathroom. Like most New Yorkers, she had long ago had security grates installed on all of them.

Finding nothing amiss with the front windows, she hurried to her bedroom. The window had been forced open and the grate had been pushed right out of the wall; it lay on her bed amid pieces of crumbled plaster.

She called Santos on his cell in case he wasn't home yet. As soon as she heard his voice she burst into fresh tears.

'Anna, what is it?'

'I—I was attacked. There was a man in my apartment. It was that Willy Sothern I told you about.'

'Holy— Are you OK? Did he hurt you?'

'No, not really. I'll probably have some bruising around my neck if there isn't already. I hurt him, though.'

'You did? How?'

'I stabbed him with one of the olive picks from Caitlin's party.' Which reminded her that Caitlin was dead. A deep sadness washed over her. 'Oh, Santos…'

'Anna, stay there. I'm coming over.'

'No. I've got to go to the police station to answer some questions.'

'Fine, I'll meet you there.'

FORTY-FIVE MINUTES later she sat on a bench at the front of the Midtown North station house, waiting until the cops were ready to question her. Santos came through the door, still in his dress slacks and white shirt. He rushed up to her, took her in his arms. 'Are you all right?'

She nodded, resting her head against his hard chest, breathing in the lemony scent of his cologne.

'Let me see what I can find out,' he said as she sat back down, and he disappeared into the back of the station. It was a good fifteen minutes before he reappeared, followed by the second cop who had answered her 911 call.

'This Willy is a tough character,' Santos said.

'Of course he's a tough character,' she said impatiently, 'he's a hit man!'

The cop said, 'He won't say who sent him, if anyone.'

'Either he was sent by Jocelyn Paar—she's the head of Urban Access—or he did this on his own. I know way too much about him.'

'Well, you're safe from him now,' Santos said.

The cop nodded. 'If you'll come with me, there are some things I'd like to ask you.'

The cop, whose name was Clement, sat her down next to his cluttered desk and asked her to tell him exactly what happened from the time she arrived home up until she called 911. Santos leaned against the wall nearby, listening.

'Now,' Clement said when she was through, 'the question is why. Why would this man want to attack you? What did you mean when you said you knew too much about him?'

Reluctantly, she told him the truth—that her quest to find Shari Baird's murderer and clear Tommy Mulligan had led her to these people…that she had infiltrated Urban Access and learned about the relationship among Shari Baird, Dennis Ostrow, and Willy Sothern.

Clement was looking at her disapprovingly. 'I thought you worked for the Sanitation Department.'

'I do,' she said, knowing what was coming.

'Then why are you trying to do police work?'

She took a deep breath. 'I'm not breaking any laws.'

'That's not an answer,' he said patiently. 'The man who killed Ms Baird is safely on Rikers, has been for two weeks. End of story. What do you think you're doing?'

'I'm trying to find the person who *really* did it. Because Tommy didn't. You may not know that, but I do. So what we've got is a difference of opinion, and as I just told you...I'm not breaking any laws.'

Clement shot Santos an angry look, as if this were his fault. Santos looked away.

'All right, then,' Clement said, rising. 'But let me remind you of a few things. First of all, if you continue to consort with these people and you find out about a crime or crimes they've committed but neglect to tell the police about it, you're an accessory. Second, you're willfully putting yourself in danger—as has been demonstrated tonight—and the next time you may not be so fortunate.'

'Thank you,' she said, rising as well. 'I understand.'

Clement gave her a sidelong look. 'You understand, but you intend to go right on doing whatever you want, am I correct?'

She gave him a cool smile. 'Yes, you're correct—I'll do what I need to do to prove Tommy is innocent. And as long as I don't break any laws myself,' she added, 'you can't stop me.'

Clement clamped his mouth shut and looked again at Santos, who shrugged helplessly as if to say, 'What can I do?'

'Get her out of here,' Clement said.

Anna and Santos made it as far as the front desk. 'Hold it,' came a voice behind them. When they turned, detectives Roche and Rinaldi stood in the door to the muster room.

Rinaldi said, 'While you're here, Ms Winthrop, we'd like to speak to you as well.'

Anna looked at Santos, who gave a little shrug.

'This way,' Rinaldi said, and led the way to her desk in back, only a few feet from Clement's.

Glancing in that direction, Anna said, 'I've already spoken—'

'That was about your attack,' Roche said, looking quickly at Rinaldi as if to make sure he'd said the right thing.

Rinaldi nodded. 'This is about Caitlin Whitelaw. Sit down.'

Once again Santos, whom Roche and Rinaldi had ignored thus far, stood against the nearby wall, observing. Anna had taken the seat next to Rinaldi's desk; Rinaldi now sat at the desk and rummaged through some papers for a notebook and pen. Roche stood at the side of the desk opposite Anna.

'I understand you were at this club—the Rose—tonight, is that correct?' Rinaldi asked Anna.

'Yes.'

'I'd like you to tell us what you saw, please.'

Anna cast a quick look in Santos's direction; he nodded his encouragement.

'It was very crowded,' she told the detectives. 'We couldn't even get into the main room. Caitlin came out of the rose—'

'Whoa.' Rinaldi shook her head as if to clear her ears. *'What?'*

From the sidelines, Santos said, 'There was this giant rosebud on a platform in the middle of the room. It opened up and Caitlin was in it.'

'Thank you,' Rinaldi said, 'but I'm speaking with Ms Winthrop right now.'

Anna looked again at Santos. She could tell from his face that he was angry but making an effort to hold his tongue.

'That's right,' she said. 'Caitlin greeted everyone; then she wanted to introduce me to the crowd.'

'Why?' Rinaldi asked, looking baffled.

'To thank me for treating her kindly while she performed her community service at my garage.'

'How sweet,' Rinaldi said, which made Anna want to sock her. 'So how did she introduce you?'

'At first she wanted me to come to her, but it was just too crowded; I couldn't get through. So she came down from the platform and was making her way to me. She was wearing a microphone. All of a sudden she stopped talking. A woman screamed that she saw blood. Then the crowd parted and Caitlin was on the floor in the middle... with a knife in her back.'

Rinaldi nodded. 'Who do you think did it?' she asked matter-of-factly, as if she were asking who Anna thought would win a baseball game.

Anna saw her opportunity. 'Who do I think did it? The same person who killed Shari Baird.'

Rinaldi stared at her, as if she had known what was coming.

'In other words,' Anna went on, 'this person is still out there.'

'Yes, right.' Rinaldi suddenly came to life, her voice mocking. 'Which means Tommy Mulligan is innocent.' Her face grew deadly serious. 'In case you haven't heard it enough times, he is still the only suspect in that murder. As far as we're concerned, the murders of Shari Baird and Caitlin Whitelaw are unrelated. We're speaking to people with whom Caitlin had been in contact leading up to her murder, specifically people she may have clashed with.

That's where you come in. How did she get along with the people over there at your garage?'

'Quite well, actually.'

'I find that difficult to believe. A gorgeous multimillionaire socialite and a bunch of people who—collect garbage? Come on.'

Anna felt herself bristle but worked to keep her cool. 'There were a few minor arguments, but it's true. She was a charming young woman who got along with everyone.'

'A charming young woman!' Rinaldi barked out an ugly laugh. 'Don't you read the tabloids?'

Anna shrugged. 'Be that as it may, everyone liked her, and she seemed to like everyone. She was so grateful to the people at the garage that she treated everyone to a catered breakfast this morning.'

'How lovely,' Rinaldi said, her voice dripping with sarcasm, and Roche laughed silently, his shoulders rising and falling. He reminded Anna of one of the Wicked Witch of the West's flying monkeys in *The Wizard of Oz*. 'You said something about arguments. Tell us about those.'

'*Minor* arguments, I said. They were silly things, really. Another woman who works at the garage was upset one day because she claimed Caitlin wasn't doing her fair share of the work.'

'And who was that?'

'A woman named Lorraine Canady. She's in the Work Experience Program.'

'And how was that argument resolved?'

'I spoke with Caitlin. It wasn't a problem again.' Anna laughed. 'Besides, I hardly think Lorraine, a rather large woman who has trouble walking because of a bad knee, could have slipped into the club, stabbed Caitlin, and escaped undetected.'

'We're really not interested in what you think, Ms Winthrop,' Rinaldi said. 'Now, is there anything else? You said arguments, plural.'

'She clashed with Shari, actually, but I didn't think that counted, since Shari was already dead when Caitlin was killed.'

'You're quite the master of the obvious, aren't you, Ms Winthrop?' Rinaldi cocked her head toward the door. 'You can go.'

Outside on the street, Anna let out a little scream. 'She's insufferable.'

'Yeah,' Santos agreed, 'she's an expert when it comes to clashing with people. Nobody on the force likes her…with the exception of Roche, of course. Word is he's secretly in love with her.'

Anna shuddered. 'A lid for every pot, as they say.' She looked at him. 'Why didn't you defend me when she was so rude to me?'

'She was rude to you the entire time!'

'Exactly! Why didn't you say something?'

'Anna, you know how she is. Talking back only makes her worse. The best approach with her is to let her talk and then get away.'

Anna shook her head. 'I can't believe she's not considering a connection between Shari's and Caitlin's murders.'

'Anna,' Santos said, looking at her. 'Why didn't you tell her about Caitlin's phone call? Had you forgotten about it?'

'Of course not. That's something I'm still working on. I won't have her discounting it and getting in my way before I've even had a chance to figure out what it meant.'

'Right,' Santos said, nodding in mock seriousness. 'In other words, like I've said, you're playing cop.'

'Somebody has to,' she said, and walked ahead of him along the sidewalk.

TWENTY-ONE

THE MURDER OF Caitlin Whitelaw made headlines around the world. How, everyone asked, had her killer stabbed her in the midst of thousands of people, then escaped undetected?

'That's just it,' Santos said, setting down his coffee cup in the booth he and Anna shared at the Akropolis early the following morning. 'There were more than three thousand people packed so tightly into that place that it was impossible to move—you couldn't even get to Caitlin when she called you. It's easy to conceal a knife. All the killer would have had to do is make sure he was near Caitlin when she passed, and slide the knife into her.'

'Santos, stop it!' Anna said, grimacing.

'I'm sorry. You asked me how it could happen.'

She thought for a moment. 'I suppose it was actually very smart. "Hide in plain sight" kind of thing. And he wouldn't even had to have escape, in the normal sense of the word; he could simply have stayed where he was. He would have had to. Isn't there any way for us to know who was there—to know who was near her…?'

As soon as she'd said this, she knew how ridiculous it was.

'Even if we found people who were near Caitlin as she passed, they wouldn't have known who else was nearby. For the most part these people don't know each other. It was total confusion, especially once the murder was discovered. Then it was a stampede.'

Anna nodded, remembering. 'Her murder must have something to do with what she was trying to tell me, Santos, I'm sure of it.'

'Tell me what she said again.'

'Well, what I heard of it was "cigarette" and "no one there". What could that mean?'

'Not a clue,' Santos said, shaking his head. 'And I doubt we'll ever know. Where was she calling from, do you know?'

Now it was her turn to shake her head. They sat in silence.

At last Anna looked up. 'Who's next, Santos?'

He frowned, not understanding.

'First Shari...then poor Caitlin...Willy tries to kill me. Who's next?' Not really expecting an answer, she went on, 'Because this is all related to Shari's murder—you know that as well as I do. Chances are good the same person who killed Shari killed Caitlin. And until we find out who this person is, there's a very good chance he'll kill again.'

Their eyes met.

ANNA SURVEYED her crew, assembled before her for roll call. The mood was somber. After all, only the previous day Caitlin had treated everyone in the garage to a catered gourmet breakfast. Now she was dead. Murdered.

'I need to speak with you about Caitlin,' Anna told them. 'We're all devastated, of course, by her death. Did any of you speak with her yesterday?'

Kelly and Brianna both raised their hands. Anna addressed them. 'Did she say anything unusual to you?' They shook their heads. 'Did she seem agitated about anything?'

'Like what?' Brianna said with a puzzled expression.

'Anything. Did she happen to say anything about a cigarette, or about someone not being there?'

'Not being where?' Fred Fox asked, his blue eyes bright.

Anna shook her head. 'I don't know.'

Now everyone looked completely baffled.

'She was happy,' Kelly said, her eyes red. 'She thanked us for being so nice to her while she worked here at the garage.'

'Yeah,' Brianna said. 'And she invited us to that party. I couldn't go because my brother is in town.'

'And I couldn't, either,' Kelly said, 'because I had a date.'

'Anna,' Art Lederer said, 'why are you asking us that—about a cigarette and no one being there, I mean?'

'Caitlin called me late yesterday afternoon. She was on her cell phone and we had a very bad connection, but she wanted to tell me something—something she had just thought of. Those were the only words I could make out before we lost the connection. I called her back but I got her voicemail. I figured I would see her at the party and she could tell me then what was on her mind.'

Everyone was silent.

'Anna,' Pierre Bontecou said, raising a forefinger to get her attention. 'If she didn't say anything to Kelly and Brianna, and she didn't say anything to you before she left, then whatever it was she was trying to tell you must have occurred to her later, probably a little before she called you, right?'

'Right.'

'Then you need to speak to people who were with her then, find out where she was.'

She nodded, smiling. 'That's exactly what I intend to do.'

Back in her office, she began this process by calling the office of Caitlin's father, Hamilton Whitelaw. She had to speak to at least four secretaries and assistants before Whitelaw's *personal* assistant, a young man who identified himself as Preston Smith, got on the line. 'Ms Winthrop, this is the worst possible time for you to call. I'm sure I don't have to tell you that Mr and Mrs Whitelaw are devastated...'

'I know that, Mr Smith, but it's Caitlin's death I'm calling about. If I could just speak to Mr Whitelaw briefly.'

'I'll see,' Smith said, and Anna was put on hold. After a few minutes Smith came back on. 'I'm putting you through. Hold, please.'

'Yes?' came Whitelaw's growl of a voice.

'Mr Whitelaw, first let me say how terribly sorry I am—'

'What do you want?'

'As you know, Mr Whitelaw, I supervised Caitlin's community service at the Sanitation garage.'

'Yes, yes, I know who you are. I met you. Get to the point.'

'Caitlin called me late yesterday afternoon and tried to tell me something.'

'What?'

'Wait, hear me out. She sounded upset.'

'So what did she tell you?' Whitelaw demanded impatiently.

'That's just it. We had a bad connection and I could only make out a few words.'

'Which were?'

'Something about a cigarette and someone not being there.'

There was silence on the line.

'Listen, miss, I don't know what kind of game you think you're playing, but you've got some nerve calling and bothering me with this nonsense, today of all times. Don't you dare call me again. The Commissioner is a personal friend of mine. If you bother me or anyone I know again, I'll have you fired.'

The line went dead. Undaunted, Anna immediately redialed Whitelaw's office and again worked her way through the maze of assistants until she had Preston Smith on the line again.

'Ms Winthrop, didn't Mr Whitelaw just tell you not to call again?'

'Mr Smith,' she said, ignoring his question, which she figured was rhetorical anyway, 'help me out and you'll never hear from me again.'

A deep sigh. 'What is it you want?'

'Caitlin called me yesterday afternoon at three o'clock. She was upset. She tried to tell me something—something I'm convinced is important…something I think relates to her murder.'

'What was it?'

'The connection was bad, but I made out something about a cigarette and then something about someone not being there. First of all, do you have any idea what she could have been talking about?'

'Not the slightest. She did smoke…'

'Where would she have been when she called me? Do you have any idea?'

'Oh, really,' he said impatiently. 'Caitlin is—was an adult with her own staff and a busy schedule. I haven't the foggiest idea where she would have been. She could have been anywhere!'

'Her own staff?' she said.

'Of course. She was a business person, just like her father.'

'Can you tell me how to reach her office?'

'Absolutely,' Smith said, and immediately rattled off a phone number. 'Bother them. And please don't call here again.'

CAITLIN'S ASSISTANT was a woman named Honoria Shreiver. 'Ms Winthrop, can you truly be so insensitive as to bother us today, of all days? Really.'

Again Anna explained that it was because of Caitlin's death that she was calling.

'And how is that?'

Once again she explained Caitlin's urgent, cryptic phone call. 'So I'm looking for someone else she might have said these things to.'

'Isn't this something the police should be looking into?'

'I've told them about it,' she lied. 'They don't feel it leads anywhere. I'm convinced it does.'

'I see,' Shreiver said in a hostile tone. 'Around three, you said? Caitlin was at Parisienne. It's a boutique she loved on Madison at Sixtieth Street. That's where she would have been calling you from.'

THE WINDOW OF Parisienne displayed three mannequins dressed in black-and-white shirt dresses; on the floor sat three pairs of shoes and three handbags.

Inside, Anna found herself immersed in white: white walls, white beaded curtains, a white cantilevered stair-case to an upper room. Glancing up, she could see that this upper room had been done entirely in black.

A young woman approached her. She was tall and wil-lowy, with boy-short ginger-colored hair. 'How are you today?' she asked, discreetly looking Anna up and down.

Anna, who had changed for this visit into expensive black slacks and an equally expensive pale-pink sleeveless silk top, wondered how this woman would have reacted if she had worn her Sanitation uniform.

'Very well, thank you,' Anna said. 'I wonder if you can help me.'

The woman smiled. 'That's what I'm here for. Are you looking for something in particular?'

'Actually, I'm not here to buy anything. It's about Caitlin Whitelaw.'

The woman's face took on an expression of sadness mixed with confusion. 'I don't…'

'My name is Anna Winthrop. Yesterday afternoon at three o'clock Caitlin called me on her cell phone and tried to tell me something—something important—but the connection was so bad that I could barely make out what she was saying. I never got to ask her what it was, but as I said, I could tell it was important to her. She sounded agitated, upset. She was at this store when she called me. I thought maybe she had told someone here what was on her mind.'

'I was here,' the woman said. 'I'm Ellen Guest. Now let's see…Caitlin got here around a quarter past two.'

Then she had most likely come here directly from the garage, Anna thought.

Ellen went on, 'She was looking for a dress for—that party. At first, when she got here, she was in a great mood. She joked that she had just been sprung, like she had been in jail. I knew she meant her community service at that garbage depot or whatever it is. There was another woman here, also trying things on, and she and I laughed when Caitlin said that.

'She tried on a lot of dresses. That was nothing new.' Ellen laughed. 'I swear she liked trying things on more than buying them. Sometimes she was here all afternoon. What time did you say she called you?'

'Three o'clock.'

'You know,' Ellen said, turning to Anna, 'something interesting did happen around then. The other woman I said was here when Caitlin was—she's an older woman by the name of Regina Helmond. Regina's a long-time customer of ours. She's a doll, but she's always complaining; that's just Regina! For instance, she'll tell you she's not feeling well, or that she threw out her back, or that she's starving on her new diet—that kind of thing. Well, yesterday she told us she had recently quit smoking.' She laughed. 'It had only been two days, but she said she was "absolutely dying." She's very dramatic.

'Well, at one point, both Regina and Caitlin were in the dressing rooms, trying things on.' Ellen indicated two adjacent booths with shuttered doors at the back of the shop. 'Even in the dressing room, Regina was moaning and groaning that she was dying for a cigarette. After a while she came out of the dressing room, and just as she did, a cigarette went flying from Caitlin's dressing room over the wall into Regina's. Caitlin was giggling. She must have been puzzled when Regina didn't respond, because she said, "Aren't you going to say thank you?"

'I said, "Caitlin, there's no one there". Caitlin popped her head out of her dressing room, realized what had happened, and we all laughed. Regina even pretended to rush back into the booth for the cigarette Caitlin had thrown her. We do have such fun here sometimes.

'At any rate, that's when the interesting thing happened. Caitlin had gone back into her dressing room to finish trying things on. Suddenly she popped her head out again. She wasn't smiling anymore. Her face was all serious. She said to me, "What did you say?" I was confused and shook my head, and she said, "You said, 'There's no one there'."

'In record time she was out of that booth, fishing in her purse for her cell phone. She was muttering to herself, saying, "I see it now. How could I not have seen it? It could only be that way".'

Anna's heartbeat quickened. 'Did she tell you what she meant?'

Ellen gave her an apologetic look. 'I'm afraid not. She started dialing a number on her cell phone—I guess she was calling you—and at that moment Regina came up to the counter with two dresses she wanted and I got involved with that.'

'In other words, you didn't hear what she was saying to me.'

'I'm afraid not.'

'What happened then?'

'I finished up with Regina and she left the shop. When I looked over at Caitlin, she was turning this way and that to try to get a better reception on her phone—you know, the way people sometimes do. I guess she was trying to call you back. But this time she closed the phone and said, "No service". She looked so upset. I offered her our phone, but she said, "No, that's all right. I'll see her tonight". Then she left, and she hadn't bought a thing. That's how I knew she was really distraught. That had never happened before.'

TWENTY-TWO

From the corner of the Palm Court in the Plaza Hotel, Anna and Gloria watched well-heeled guests come and go. Anna leaned back in her high-backed blue velvet chair and gazed at the famous laylight, its stained-glass vines and flowers curling around the central ribbed dome. Just out of sight, behind a nearby palm tree, a woman in a jewel-blue gown played a harp.

'Magnificent, isn't it?' Gloria said, and gazed happily around. She looked back at Anna. 'Why do you look so sour?'

'Because I'm not sure why I'm here,' Anna answered truthfully.

'You're here,' Gloria said, 'because Donald thought this would be a nice way for us to celebrate getting back together...the new us.'

'And where do I fit in?'

'I told you. He wants to thank you for taking such good care of me.'

Anna frowned suspiciously. She doubted that. More likely, he wanted to win his way into Anna's good graces, since Anna knew first-hand of his infidelities. 'Whatever,' she said, adjusting the scarf she had worn around her neck to hide the evidence of Willy Sothern's attack.

'Thanks a lot, Anna,' Gloria said sarcastically. 'I really appreciate the support. Can't you just sit there and smile? I mean, it's not like I'm asking you to do something horrible. I think you can suffer through high tea at the Palm Court.' She gave a little gasp. 'Here he comes. Smile.'

Anna smiled. Donald walked toward them. He was smiling, too. He wore a tan vested suit that showed off his athletic physique to full advantage. Though Anna wasn't particularly fond of Donald, she had to admit, as she had many times before, that he was the most handsome man in the room, with his thick, wavy blond hair, dreamy pale-blue eyes, chiseled features, cleft chin, and dazzling smile. Too bad he was such a drip.

'Anna,' he said, and bent to kiss her cheek.

'How are you, Donald?' she asked.

'I'm well, Anna, thank you,' he said, and took Gloria in his arms and kissed her deeply.

A show just for me, Anna thought.

'Darling, isn't it beautiful here?' Gloria said to Donald.

'That's why I chose it,' he said brightly. 'Nothing but the best for my two girls.'

Oh, brother. Anna could think of nothing to say. Already she was bored out of her gourd. Perhaps she would have a headache soon.

A waiter appeared as if from nowhere. 'Good afternoon. Are we having tea today?'

'Absolutely,' Donald said, 'the best you've got,' and he looked at Gloria and Anna and grinned.

'The one-hundred-dollar menu?' the waiter asked in a lower voice.

Donald nodded and the waiter went away.

'A hundred dollars?' Gloria faltered, eyes wide. 'Donald…'

'Each, Gloria,' Anna said. 'A hundred each.'

'Oh, my,' Gloria said, as if this were far too extravagant, and inwardly Anna laughed. As if money had ever been an issue for any of the Winthrop children. Nor was it an issue for Donald, one of Manhattan's more successful plastic surgeons.

'Anna,' Donald said, and when she turned to him he wore a sober expression. 'I wanted to tell you how sorry I am about that woman who was killed at your garage... and then this poor Whitelaw girl. You must be quite upset.'

'Yes, I am, Donald. Thank you.'

The waiter arrived with their first course. When he had gone, Gloria reached for a brioche covered with lobster salad and fresh asparagus. 'Yum.'

'That one is especially delicious,' Donald said.

Gloria looked at him. 'I thought you said you'd never been here before.'

'No, darling,' he said lightly, 'I said *you and I* had never been here before. If I remember correctly, I told you I'd been here once with the president of the hospital.'

'Oh,' Gloria said, and shrugged, for once knowing when to quit.

Anna reached for a chocolate pot de crème. 'Speaking of the hospital,' she said, taking a spoonful of the rich, creamy custard, 'how's business, Donald?'

'Quite good, actually.'

'And it's about to get a little bit better,' Gloria said, looking as if she had a secret. 'Right, honey?'

He smiled and held out his hand in a gesture that said, 'Tell her if you like.'

Gloria turned to Anna. 'Donald's giving me a wonderful getting-back-together present.'

'Oh?'

Gloria nodded. 'A new face!'

Anna looked at her in alarm.

'Now, Gloria,' Donald said, 'that's not entirely accurate. In fact, when I'm finished, no one will think you've got a new face. They'll ask if you've done something different with your hair, or they'll say you look…refreshed!'

Anna frowned. 'I thought it was considered unethical to perform surgery on a relative.'

'That's just a matter of opinion,' Donald said, waving the idea away. 'If it's all right with Gloria and it's all right with me, there's no problem.'

'What are you going to do, exactly?' Anna asked him.

'Oh, just a little fine-tuning,' Donald said, clearly reluctant to discuss it in detail.

'I'll tell you,' Gloria said. She put her hands to each side of her face and pulled the skin tightly. 'See this tight new jaw line?' she said through her squeezed mouth. 'That's what I'm going to have after my suture suspension. Along with that, I'll have a neck lift—'

'Not exactly,' Donald interrupted. 'You're right, we are going to do a suture suspension. We're also going to do some liposuction to the neck area, a temporal lift, and a full-face chemical peel. Oh—we're also going to remove the buccal fat pads.'

Anna looked at Gloria. '*Why?* You're twenty-eight years old.'

'You'd be amazed at how many young people are having cosmetic surgery these days,' Donald said. 'Especially in Hollywood.'

'This isn't Hollywood,' Anna said, ignoring Donald. 'Why, Gloria?'

'To look better, of course! There's always room for improvement, Anna. I'm not so vain that I think I'm perfect. Besides,' Gloria went on, 'I'm the wife of one of Manhattan's most respected plastic surgeons. How would it seem if I didn't look my best? Doctors have to showcase their work!'

Anna had no answer to that. She reached for a pink-frosted éclair decorated with edible gold. A real headache was coming on.

LATE THAT NIGHT, Anna was awakened from a sound sleep by the ringing of her cell phone. Groggily she opened it and said hello.

A hysterical squeaky female voice burst from the phone; Anna held it away from her ear. 'Who is this?'

'I told you, it's Taffy! Taffy Grant!'

'What's wrong?'

Taffy was crying. 'I should never have helped you. I should never have let you into my apartment.'

'Why? What's happened?'

'Come over and see!' Taffy shouted, and the phone went dead.

Anna quickly dressed. Outside, she hailed a cab and within minutes was at Taffy's apartment building. Taffy buzzed her up. When Anna got to her floor, Taffy's door was ajar.

Anna knocked gently. 'Yeah,' came Taffy's voice from inside. 'Come on in.'

The apartment looked as if a cyclone had hit—furniture toppled; the TV pushed on to the floor, its screen smashed. All of the drawers in the small kitchen had been yanked out and dumped; likewise, the contents of the cabinets had been swept to the floor, which was a sea of silverware and broken china and glass.

The bathroom and two bedrooms had fared no better.

'Tell me what happened,' Anna said to Taffy, who still sat on the couch, crying.

'There was a knock on the door. I opened it—I know I shouldn't have—and this guy burst in. I think he looked familiar but I'm not sure. I see a lot of guys. He said his

name was Petrov and that he was looking for something.
He seemed really angry. He pushed me aside and started
tearing the place apart.'

'What was he looking for?'

'He wouldn't say. Anna, why did you send him here?'

'I didn't send him here! Why did you think I had?'

'Because you looked around Shari's room, too—I don't
know. I guess it doesn't make much sense. I'm so upset.'

'Did he find whatever he was looking for?'

'I don't think so. He seemed just as angry when he left.'

'Did he say anything else?'

'No, just his name. I screamed at him that I was going to
call the police, and do you know what he did? He grabbed
my cell phone, threw it on the floor, and crushed it under
his foot. Then I ran to the regular phone and he tore the
whole thing out of the wall. I had to call you from my
neighbor's apartment.'

'Call the police. Tell them his name is Avel Petrov and
that he's got a peep show club or whatever you call it on
West Forty-First Street called Paradise.'

'Then you do know him!' Taffy cried.

'No, only his name and that he owns that club. Have
you ever heard of it before?'

'Sure, but I don't know this Petrov guy.'

'All right. Call the police and tell them what I just told
you.'

As Anna made her way to the elevator, she could still
hear Taffy crying.

Ten minutes later she was on West Forty-First Street,
gazing at the sparkling, flashing entrance of Paradise,
'a gentleman's club', according to a sign above the door.

A man dressed all in black stepped out from behind a
column near the door. 'Can I help you?' He looked her up
and down. I must look a mess, she thought.

'I'm looking for Mr Petrov.'

The man stepped back. 'And why is that?'

'I want to talk to him.'

'Well, obviously. About what, specifically?'

She had to speak to him before the cops got there. She decided to try the truth. 'Shari Baird.'

'What about her?' He put his hands on his hips.

'Look, friend,' she said, and mimicked his stance. 'He can talk to me or he can talk to the cops. You just tell him someone's here to speak to him about Shari. I think he'll see me.'

Mention of the police—not exactly a lie, since they were no doubt on their way—seemed to impress him. With his gaze fixed on Anna, he got out his cell phone and pressed a button. 'Yeah, there's a woman here to see you,' he said in a low voice. He asked Anna, 'What's your name?'

'Anna Winthrop.'

He repeated her name into the phone. 'She say's it's about Shari.' He listened, then said to Anna, 'What about her?'

Anna held her ground, saying nothing.

'She'll only tell you, boss...Got it.' He closed the phone. 'Go all the way to the back, through the double doors, door at the end of the corridor.'

Paradise made the Marconi Pasta Company look like a tired old rat hole. The main room was vast and mirrored, with rows of massive chandeliers spaced across the ceiling. To the left stood rows and rows of video booths; to the right, a large display of pornographic videos and DVDs. Beyond this display, farther to the right, an elegant double staircase curved up to a second floor, where a sign that read DELIGHTS OF PARADISE stood on an easel near red velvet curtains.

Men wandered in and out of the video booths, browsed the merchandise. Two men started up the stairway toward the show.

'Hey,' came a woman's voice to Anna's left. There, bigger than life, stood a showgirl—a smooth-skinned Amazon in a gold lamé bikini costume so brief it was barely there; a high feathered headdress; and a matching flourish of feathers atop her shapely rear end. Anna thought she looked like some kind of pornographic turkey.

'Hey,' Anna said back.

'You like girls?' the woman asked. 'We could have some fun when I'm through with the show.'

'Thanks, but I'm here to see Mr Petrov.'

'Oh,' the woman said, disappointed. 'Through there.'

There was an unmarked door at the end of the corridor at the back of the club. Anna knocked on it and a male voice called out, 'Come.'

She opened the door. Behind a sleek glass desk sat a handsome man who looked around thirty. His hair was shaved so close that he was nearly bald. His features were regular except for his nose, which was too large for his face but actually accounted for his distinctive looks. 'Who are you?' He had a light Russian accent.

She didn't have much time. 'I'm a friend of Shari's. What were you looking for in her apartment?'

'None of your business. Get out of here.'

'Tell me or I'll call the police.'

He laughed. 'Call the police? Why? You can't prove I was there.' He checked his watch. 'I have to help with the show.' He stood. 'If you must know, I have every right to search Shari's room. She had an interest in this club. I needed to see if she had any papers relating to that. What business is this of yours?'

'I'm trying to find out who killed her.'

'We know who it was—' he began, but she cut him off.

'No, it wasn't him.'

'And who do you think it was—me?'

'Maybe.'

'And why would I kill Shari?'

'Maybe because once you'd gotten all of her trade secrets out of her, you didn't need her anymore and didn't want to have to share your profits.'

He came out from behind his desk and paused near her at the door. He laughed derisively. 'That's ridiculous. I loved Shari. We were going to get married.'

'Oh, really? And where did Dennis Ostrow fit in?'

'Who?'

It was her turn to laugh. 'Guess you didn't get *all* the secrets.'

Looking troubled by what she said, he went past her and strode toward the club's main room.

As Anna emerged into the street, a police car pulled to a stop in front of the club.

MONDAY MORNING, Anna switched on the TV as she got ready for work. It seemed every station was still covering Caitlin's murder; 'Death of a Party Girl' was the title of one of the shows. Anna switched off the TV, taking up the previous day's newspaper instead.

Here, too, was more coverage of Caitlin's murder— nearly the entire first page, in fact. Anna scanned it and was about to throw it aside when something caught her eye. The author of a sidebar put forth the possibility that Caitlin had been murdered by the Ankh Killer. After all, the author reasoned, Caitlin had been at Midtown Central 13 garage when Shari Baird was killed, and Shari may have been a victim of the Ankh Killer.

It was tenuous at best, fuzzy logic. She threw the paper aside and sat quietly thinking...

From the end table she grabbed a pad of paper, a pen, and a recent issue of *Time* magazine that she had saved because it covered the Ankh Killer's victims through Paulette Edwards. Anna began to jot down thoughts.

Ankh Killer Victims
Lauri Shepard 27 Single
Carmela Santiago 38 Engaged
Crista Sherrod 33 Single
Paulette Edwards 27 Divorced
Shari Baird (?) 25 Single
Ruth Wolf 67 Married
Caitlin Whitelaw (?) 21 Single

She had added the question marks after Shari and Caitlin's names to indicate doubt as to whether they had been victims of the Ankh Killer. For several moments she scrutinized her list. There was no pattern that she could discern.

Frowning, she looked again at the article in *Time*. Then she amended her list.

Lauri Shepard 27 Single Firefighter
Carmela Santiago 38 Engaged Zoo worker
Crista Sherrod 33 Single Interpreter
Paulette Edwards 27 Divorced Nail salon owner
Shari Baird (?) 25 Single Sanitation worker
Ruth Wolf 67 Married Museum docent
Caitlin Whitelaw (?) 21 Single Socialite

Still no apparent pattern. Perhaps there *was* no pattern. An idea occurred to her. She remembered Santos saying once that serial killers often killed according to a schedule. She looked again at the magazine and added more information to her list.

Jan. 26 Lauri Shepard 27 Single Firefighter
Feb. 26 Carmela Santiago 38 Engaged Zoo worker
March 26 Crista Sherrod 33 Single Interpreter
April 17 Paulette Edwards 27 Divorced Nail salon owner
April 23 Shari Baird (?) 25 Single Sanitation worker
April 25 Ruth Wolf 67 Married Museum docent
May 8 Caitlin Whitelaw (?) 21 Single Socialite

Interesting, Anna thought. Lauri, Carmela, Crista, and Ruth had all been killed on either the twenty-fifth or the twenty-sixth of the month. Was this meaningful?

Getting an idea, she picked up the phone and dialed her parents' home. They were inveterate early risers. Her mother answered.

'Anna, darling, this is a nice surprise. I guess this means you're still alive.'

'Very funny, Mother.'

'I'm sorry, dear, that wasn't funny at all, was it? I guess it's my fear talking.'

'Mother, don't be so dramatic. Is Daddy there?'

'Yes, hold on, dear.'

After a moment, Jeff Winthrop came on the line. 'Anna! How's my favorite girl?'

'I'm fine, Daddy.' Anna smiled. His favorite girl was whichever one of the three he happened to be speaking to. 'I want to ask you something.'

'Of course.'

'Do you remember years ago you took all of us to the

Metropolitan Museum of Art to see a special exhibit about ancient Egypt?'

'Yes, of course. It had been brought over from the Egyptian Museum in Cairo. It was a traveling show.'

'Right. And this man met us there and told us things about the exhibit as we walked around.'

'Ah, yes, of course. That was my old school chum Henry Burton. Why do you ask?'

'I was wondering if I might speak to him.'

'Speak to him? Why, dear?'

'I…want to ask him some questions about the Ankh Killer.'

'The Ankh Killer! What would he know about that? He's an Egyptologist, not a detective.'

'I know that, Daddy,' she said patiently, hoping he wouldn't ask her any more questions. 'Can you please put me in touch with him?'

'Certainly. Your mother and I bumped into him about a year ago at a charity dinner. He still lives on the Upper West Side. I'll give you his number.'

She took it down, thanked him, and hurriedly left for work.

TWENTY-THREE

DR HENRY BURTON lived in a majestic old brownstone on Riverside Drive at 104th Street. As Anna climbed the steps at exactly noon, the front door opened.

He was much as she remembered him—smallish, of medium height, balding, a sweet face. He reached out and took her hand. 'You were a little girl when I last saw you.'

'Yes,' she said, smiling. 'Nine years old. I appreciate your seeing me.'

He waved it away. 'Anything for Jeff Winthrop. How's he doing, by the way? And your lovely mother?'

'They're both fine, thank you.'

'Good, good. Come into my study. I hope you like coffee.'

His study was on the first floor and had a large window that looked out on to the sidewalk. Though his large desk was clear except for a computer and a phone, clutter covered every possible surface in the rest of the room, from the hieroglyphic prints and antique maps on the walls to the statuettes and pieces of chipped pottery that lined the mantel of the large fireplace to Anna's left.

'Now,' he said, his hands clasped as he leaned forward, 'how can I help you, Anna?'

'I'm sure you're familiar with the Ankh Killer.'

He frowned. 'Of course. Horrible, just horrible.'

'And you're probably aware that a woman was found murdered in the Sanitation garage where I'm a supervisor, and that the killer had carved an ankh into her chest.'

'I did read that, yes. But if I'm not mistaken, the police weren't convinced that this was the work of the Ankh Killer.'

'That's what I'm trying to get at,' she said. 'You see, I was thinking that if we could find some sort of pattern that the Ankh Killer follows, that might give us an answer as to whether he committed the murder in my garage.'

A housekeeper entered the room bearing a coffee tray, which she set down on Burton's desk.

'Thank you, Martha,' he said, and she smiled at them both and left.

'What sort of pattern?' Burton asked.

'I don't know; that's what I'm looking for.' She took her list from her pocket and laid it on his desk so that he could read it. 'This is what I've come up with so far.'

Brows lowered, he studied the list. Almost immediately he looked up at her. 'You believe that poor Whitelaw girl could have been murdered by the Ankh Killer? Why?'

She shook her head. 'I don't know…she was doing community service in my garage when Shari Baird was killed. If the Ankh Killer murdered Shari, and Caitlin saw him, maybe he murdered her, too. I know, it's far-fetched.'

He studied the list again. 'You know,' he said, looking up again, 'I never noticed these dates.'

'Right,' she said. 'Four out of the seven murders—or out of six, if you don't count Caitlin—were committed on either the twenty-fifth or the twenty-sixth of the month.'

'I think you've got something here,' he said, and more animated now, he turned in his chair to a bookcase built into the wall beside his desk. He scanned the line of tall volumes, then pulled one out, laid it on his desk, and began turning pages. 'Ah,' he said, 'I was right.

'Let me give you a little background,' he said. 'The ancient Egyptians used both a lunar and a solar calendar. In the lunar calendar, each lunar month was named after an Egyptian god, goddess, or major festival. Here,' he said, turning the book around so Anna could see it, 'look at the page for this year, 2009, and then look at the entry for the second month.'

Anna found it.

January 26, 2009, to February 24, 2009
Rekh Neds—Sacred to the Little Fire Goddess

She felt a chill run through her. 'Lauri Shepard was killed on January twenty-sixth. She was a firefighter.'

Burton looked at Anna's list. 'Carmela Santiago, February twenty-fifth.'

Anna read the next entry.

February 25, 2009, to March 25, 2009
Renwett—Sacred to the Snake Goddess

'The Snake Goddess,' she said, looking up. 'Carmela worked at the Bronx Zoo.'

'More specifically,' he said, consulting the magazine again, 'she worked in the reptile house. How about the next month?'

'It's called...I can't pronounce it, but it's spelled H-n-s-w. It begins on March twenty-sixth...'

'The day Crista Sherrod was murdered,' he said. 'What god is it connected to?'

'It says, "Sacred to the Falcon-Headed Moon God".' She knit her brows. 'Crista was an interpreter at the UN. I don't see a connection there.'

'Hold on.' Burton rummaged through a stack of magazines on the floor beside his desk. Finding the one he was looking for, he flipped pages and then held it up for

Anna to see. In the corner of the page was a photograph of Crista Sherrod, holding one arm aloft. On her raised hand she wore a leather falconer's glove, and on the glove sat a falcon. 'There's our connection,' he said. 'Now, what about April?'

She looked again. 'The next lunar month is called Hnt-htj and is sacred to the Wolf God.'

'Ruth Wolf,' they said in unison.

Anna nodded. 'She was killed on April twenty-fifth, the day that month begins.'

'Which means,' Burton said, 'your two other April victims—Paulette Edwards and Shari Baird—are extras; they don't fit.'

Anna said, 'This helps confirm what I've thought all along—that Shari was not murdered by the Ankh Killer. Now we know Paulette wasn't, either.'

'Which means you've got a copycat on your hands...a copycat who isn't aware of the date pattern.'

Anna nodded thoughtfully, taking this in. 'What about Caitlin?' she said, and found the next entry. 'The month called Ipt Hmt begins on May twenty-fourth—interesting: not the twenty-fifth or twenty-sixth—and is sacred to the God with Hands and Arms Concealed.' She frowned. 'Maybe the connection is to the killer's hands and arms being concealed in the crowd?'

Again Burton wrinkled his nose. 'A stretch, I think.'

'Which means,' Anna said, 'that if we are correct, Caitlin is not the Ankh Killer's May victim...that the Ankh Killer will murder again on May twenty-fourth...and that somehow his victim will be connected to the God with Hands and Arms Concealed.'

'That's two weeks from today,' Burton said, and their gazes met.

'Why this pattern?' Anna said. 'What is significant about the beginning of a lunar month?'

Dr Burton leaned back in his chair. 'To the ancient Egyptians the new moon meant new life, rebirth, renewal, rejuvenation. This would fit with the carving of the ankh, in the sense that this man believes that by taking life he is giving himself new life.

'Moon worship, of course, goes back thousands of years, but today it is an underground religion. My guess is that the Ankh Killer is somehow connected to this group, which has taken the ankh as its symbol because it represents eternal life, a link between humans and the gods. However, I believe this killer has perverted the group's beliefs for his own purposes—made himself a god, if you will. As the forensic psychologists have been saying on television, the killer's reasons for perverting these beliefs no doubt go back to something in his own life—abuse, mental illness, a lifelong sense of failure or ordinariness... perhaps all of the above.'

Anna placed the book back on Burton's desk. Though her heart went out to this maniac's victims, she was interested in the Ankh Killer more for who he hadn't killed than who he had. She rose.

Dr Burton rose with her. 'The police need to know about this theory of ours, Anna. If we're correct, and the Ankh Killer isn't caught in time, he will very likely take a new victim on May twenty-fourth. The God with Hands and Arms Concealed...

'As for your investigation, I think it's safe to say Caitlin Whitelaw was not a victim of this man. Neither, as we've said, were Paulette Edwards and Shari Baird, though there is a strong possibility they were both killed by the same person. If I were you, I would look for any similarities between these two specific murders. Figuring out who killed

Paulette could lead to who killed Shari...and that would clear your young man.'

She looked at him in surprise. 'You're talking as if he's innocent without a doubt.' When he nodded matter-of-factly, she asked, 'Why?'

'Because that's what you believe.' He gave her a kind smile. 'I don't know you very well, Anna, but I can tell you're a very good judge of character.'

She returned his smile.

'Now,' he said, 'is there anything else I can do for Jeff Winthrop's charming daughter?'

She looked at him sharply; she'd had an idea. 'Actually,' she said, 'there is something...'

DETECTIVES RINALDI and Roche were not nearly as receptive as Dr Burton had been. In fact, they were downright hostile. Across her desk heaped with papers, Rinaldi gave Anna an exasperated look. 'This is the second time we've had this kind of trouble with you.'

Leaning against a nearby wall, Santos looked over in surprise. So did Detective Roche, who stood next to Santos.

'*What* kind of trouble?' Anna asked levelly.

'You playing cop.'

'Listen,' Anna said, her patience having run out, 'less than a year ago I "played cop" and caught a murderer. You have a short memory.'

'No, I don't,' Rinaldi said, leaning forward on her arms.

'I see,' Anna said. 'Then you don't want me to play cop even though I've been successful?'

'Right. We would have achieved the same results you did, if you had left us alone to do our job. Now you're at it again, but this time you've got some cockamamie theory about…gods with no arms and legs!'

'The God with Hands and Arms Concealed,' Anna corrected her.

'Whatever!' Rinaldi cried angrily, and stood. 'Get out of my sight.'

Santos stepped forward. 'Don't you speak to her that way. She's trying to help you.'

Rinaldi spun on him. 'You mind your own business, too! What are you? A beat cop! We're homicide detectives. Let us do our job.'

'I would,' Santos said, taking Anna by the arm and leading her out, 'if you knew how!'

At this, Roche started angrily after Santos, but Rinaldi stopped him. 'Let him go. He's probably got some moon god to arrest!'

Anna and Santos could hear them cackling even as they went out the front door of the station house on to the street.

'Idiots,' Anna muttered.

Santos nodded. 'They give the police a bad name.'

'How do these two survive?'

He shrugged. 'They're obnoxious but usually successful. That's all that matters.'

They walked a little down West Fifty-Fourth Street. 'Santos,' Anna said, turning to him, 'I want you to help me. I need to know if there are any similarities between Paulette's and Shari's murders. Can you find out for me?'

'Playing cop again?' he teased, then grew serious. 'I'll see what I can do.'

'ACCORDING TO the Medical Examiner's office,' Santos said when he called Anna at the garage a short time later, 'Paulette and Shari were both strangled by a right-handed person, which I realize doesn't help much. Paulette had skin under her fingernails. They ran the DNA but there was no match. Shari had very short nails, no doubt due to her job, so there was no DNA there to check. Not surprisingly, the ankh carvings were also both made by a right-handed person. But there was more than that. On both of the ankhs, the vertical stroke was roughly the same length as the horizontal stroke, which is incorrect; the vertical stroke should be longer.'

'Interesting. What about Lauri, Carmela, Crista, and Ruth?'

'They were all strangled by a *left*-handed person, and their ankhs were carved—all correctly—by a *left*-handed person.'

'I've been meaning to ask you,' she said. 'Do the police know if anything was taken from Shari after she was killed?'

'You mean the way Paulette's ring was taken? As far as I know, no. She had a pack of cigarettes in one pocket. In another she had a wallet, but everything appeared to be intact. According to her boyfriend, she didn't wear jewelry when she worked—no rings or necklaces. Nothing was taken from any of the other victims, either—except for Paulette, of course.'

Anna thanked him and rang off.

There was a knock on her door. Hal Redmond stood in her doorway. 'Anna, there's some guy to see you. He won't give his name, but he says you know him. He's got a Russian accent.'

Anna's eyes grew wide. 'I'll come out.'

Avel Petrov was waiting for her just inside the gate. He wore a well-tailored navy three-button suit, a crisp white shirt, and a tie. When he saw her, he smiled charmingly. 'Anna!'

'You can cut the act, Petrov. What do you want?'

'I want to talk to you.'

'About what?'

'About Shari.'

'What about Shari?'

He looked furtively around. Satisfied that no one was within earshot, he said, 'I wasn't completely forthcoming about her. Can we go someplace to talk?'

'Sure, someplace public. How about Madison Square Garden?'

He laughed charmingly. 'I'm not that bad, am I?'

'I don't know; are you?'

Standing near the door to the break room stairs, Hal called out, 'Is everything all right, Anna?'

'Yes, I'm fine,' she called back. Hal nodded and walked away. She turned back to Petrov. 'There's a bar near here that I like.'

'Sounds perfect.'

They walked to Hurley's and took a quiet table in the back. 'I appreciate your seeing me,' he said.

'I told you, you can quit the gentleman act. Gentlemen don't trash people's apartments.'

'Perhaps if I told you the whole story, you wouldn't judge me so harshly.'

She gave him a dubious look. 'OK, shoot. Tell me the whole story.'

A waitress took their drink order. When she had gone, Petrov turned his handsome face to Anna. 'I first met Shari at a party given by one of my…colleagues.'

'Oh, right, you're with the Russian mob,' Anna said matter-of-factly as the waitress brought their drinks. He looked at Anna in shock. When he looked up to see if the waitress had overheard, her face was completely impassive, as if she had heard but couldn't care less. This was, after all, New York.

'Is something wrong?' Anna asked when the waitress had gone.

'How dare you say such a thing to me! That's entirely untrue.'

She gave him a pitying smile. 'Isn't that what you people always say?'

Again he looked at her in surprise.

'Go on,' she said. 'You met Shari at a party.'

'Yes. It was quite an elegant party and I thought she was extremely beautiful. She was with Dante Marconi.'

She nodded. 'Makes sense.'

'Not to Shari. Halfway through the party she came up to me at a moment when I was alone and asked if she could speak with me privately. I agreed and we went to another room. She said she wanted to go into business with me. She said that since the Disneyfication of Times Square and Forty-Second Street, there were only a handful of places like Marconi's left, so…Marconi's, being the largest, had that business cornered, even though it was a dump.

'She said she had heard I had access to money. She wanted to form a partnership with me. I would provide the money and she would provide the know-how. She would show me everything that had worked for Dante, plus she had a lot of ideas of her own. She said her plan couldn't fail. She even talked about the possibility of opening other establishments like it in the future, both in New York and in other cities.'

'What kind of business were you in before Paradise?' Anna asked.

'I have owned a number of other gentlemen's clubs over the years, but never any on this scale. Shari started telling me some of her ideas for a new club. I was extremely impressed. I told her I would think about it and get back to her. She told me that was fine but that I'd better not take too long, because if I wasn't interested, she would find someone who was.'

'Obviously, you told her you were interested.'

'Yes…but I also told her I didn't want any trouble with Dante. He's got some powerful connections of his own and I didn't want to be on his bad side. So I suggested that Shari and I pretend to meet at Marconi's; I would be one of her customers. Then I would make believe I was falling for her, and then Shari would leave Marconi's and Dante to be with me. Only then would we reveal that we had decided to start a new club. I didn't want Dante to know we had started planning it while Shari was still working for him—that she was basically selling him out.'

'Then Shari wasn't in love with you?'

'No,' he said with a laugh. 'Nor I with her. It was purely business. Especially for Shari.'

'What do you mean?'

'Let me continue. She and I went right to work. I found the space, we began renovating…before we knew it, we were hiring staff. Everything went better than I had ever imagined it would.'

'Then what was the problem?'

'The problem,' he said, 'was that Shari was actually in the employ of a very powerful mob figure here in New York. She was his girlfriend, in fact.'

'But I thought you were in the mob.'

'I told you to stop saying that. I'll be straight with you, Anna. I may not always play by the book, but I am not in the Russian mob or any other mob, for that matter. That's a myth Shari perpetuated. I'm just a businessman.

'Shari's boyfriend, on the other hand, is a known mob

figure. His name is Aldo "The Eye" Giordano. Have you ever heard of him?'

'Yes, I have, actually,' she replied, 'though I'm not sure in what context.'

'You can Google him when you get home. If there's something illegal going on in Manhattan, he's involved in it. What I hadn't known was that Giordano and Shari had been having an affair for over a year. She was acting as a sort of triple agent. Dante thought she was his girlfriend, but she had gone to Marconi's simply to collect his secrets. She had come to me offering me those secrets, so that I would build a club. In truth, the person she was working for was Giordano.

'Once our club was finished, he was ready to make his move. A week after Paradise opened, two of his men grabbed me as I left by the back door. They drove me to the Meadowlands in New Jersey. They let me live…just barely. They made it clear they owned me now. They were taking over the club; I would now work for them. They needed my expertise, they said. What Giordano had done was let me do the heavy lifting and then sweep in and take over.'

'But that's outrageous!' Anna said. 'Did you go to the police?'

He took a sip of his drink. 'As I said, I'm not in the mob; however, I don't always play by the rules. The police are not exactly…sympathetic to me. It would have done no good. All it would have done is gotten me killed by Giordano.

'So now there I am, running the club I built but no longer own. I can't even leave.'

'Why not?'

'Because Giordano will kill me if I leave. Leaving is the first step toward turning on him, he says. He pays me well, I'll give him that, but I am...how do you say it, a bird in a gilded cage.'

'When you found out what Shari had done, did you confront her?'

'No. I never had a chance. From that time on I never saw her without Giordano. Even if I had confronted her, what good would it have done? She would have run straight to him...and I would be dead.'

Anna considered what he had told her. 'How horrible. The only answer for you is to simply disappear.'

'You're right, and don't think I haven't thought of it. But if and when I do it, I had better do it right, because it seems Aldo "The Eye" Giordano is well named; he has eyes everywhere. You never know who they are...as I found out with the lovely Shari.'

'Why did you trash her apartment?'

'Just after Giordano's goons "convinced" me to work for him, Shari called me. She wanted to make sure I had "settled in" to the new arrangement. She revealed that when we were together, she had recorded hours and hours of conversations we had had—conversations in which she had led me to say horrible things about Giordano. She told me on the phone that if I ever got restless and thought about changing "the situation", I should remember that she had these tapes and would be only too happy to play them for Giordano.

'Yesterday I was reading some articles about Shari's murder and found some references to where she had been living at the time she was killed. I did some further investigating, found her actual address, and went there looking for the tapes.'

'Did you find them?'

He shook his head. 'I should have known better than to

think she would have kept them there. Who knows where she hid them?'

'If they even exist.'

He nodded. 'I thought of that, too. But I can't take that chance. So that's what I was doing at Shari's apartment. I was like a madman. I can't blame Taffy for calling the police.'

'What did you tell them?'

'That Shari and I had had an affair and that she had some things of mine. They believed it—it wasn't entirely untrue. I promised to pay for any damages. That was OK with Taffy, so the cops let me off.

'Now tell me…' Petrov said. 'How on earth did Shari come to work for the Sanitation Department?'

'It doesn't seem to make sense, does it? At least not at first glance. Let's just say Shari had an idea that working for Sanitation would give her access to more than just garbage.'

He nodded knowingly. 'I don't know exactly what you mean, but I get the drift. I should have known.' He downed the rest of his drink and set down the glass. 'I wouldn't wish murder on anyone, but I have absolutely no sympathy for Shari. If anyone ever asked to be murdered, she did.'

'But who do you think did it?' she asked.

'Wasn't it this man, Mulligan?'

'No, definitely not.'

'Then it could be anyone. Probably half of Manhattan wanted her dead.'

ANNA TOOK THE SUBWAY to Eighty-Sixth and Lexington and walked three blocks west toward Fifth Avenue. Soon the Metropolitan Museum of Art's imposing neoclassical façade came into view. In the center of a step about a third of the way up sat Libby, gazing down at her cell phone, busily texting. She looked up as Anna climbed the stairs toward her. 'Oh, hey.'

'Hey. Thanks for meeting me.'

'Sure.' Libby looked puzzled. 'You never said why you wanted me to meet you here,' she said as they ascended toward the museum's entrance.

'There's someone I want you to meet,' Anna said. 'Have you ever been here before?'

'Once when I was really little. I don't remember it.'

Anna led a wide-eyed Libby through the ancient Egyptian art collection to the reconstructed Nubian temple called the Temple of Dendur. Beside its looming sandstone gate, in a white seersucker suit and bow tie, stood Henry Burton.

'Anna,' he said, smiling, and took her hand. Anna introduced Libby. 'A pleasure,' he said. 'Come.'

Libby continued to look bewildered as he led them through a door marked EMPLOYEES ONLY, down a corridor, and into a large, airy studio. Two long conference tables covered with butcher paper ran the length of the room, and at these tables, squirming restlessly, sat two dozen children around the age of eight.

A plump, cheerful-looking woman with curly brown hair hurried over to them. 'Welcome!' she said.

Henry introduced her to Anna and Libby as Danielle Braverman. 'She's in charge of our new children's arts and crafts program,' he explained.

Danielle nodded and turned to Libby. 'I can't thank you enough.'

Henry put up a hand. 'I'm afraid we're getting a little ahead of ourselves. I haven't asked Libby yet.'

'Asked me what?' Libby asked.

Henry turned to Danielle, who said to Libby, 'This is something new we're trying here at the museum—an arts and crafts class for the smaller children. They're going to be making things based on objects in the Egyptian collection. Today is the first day—we're making simple clay pots. The problem is that we got a much larger response than we expected. I don't want to turn any of the children away, but I can't do it all myself. Can you help me?'

Libby turned and looked up and down the tables of children—some hitting each other, others wiggling and laughing, two picking their nose. She laughed. 'Sure, I'll help.'

'Oh, thank goodness,' Danielle breathed. 'Come on, I'll show you where we keep the supplies. We'd better get the class started before they revolt.'

Libby hurried after Danielle, having forgotten about Anna and Henry.

'Thanks,' Anna said softly to the Egyptologist, who responded with a nod and a wink.

TWENTY-FOUR

NOT LONG AFTER Anna arrived back at the garage, Gloria called. 'I've been meaning to speak to you.' She sounded angry.

'About what?'

'About your behavior at the Plaza yesterday.'

'What about my behavior?'

'Anna, you're supposed to be supportive of me. You looked utterly bored and you were your usual sarcastic self with Donald.'

Anna supposed she was right. 'I'm sorry, Gloria. I should have behaved better, or just not come.'

'Well,' Gloria simpered, 'he's being very good to me and you should be pleased about that.'

'Oh, I'm pleased. I just don't think you need to have your face completely reconstructed at the age of twenty-eight.'

'We told you, my face will not be "reconstructed". It will be tightened and smoothed...refreshed.'

'You don't *need* tightening, smoothing, and refreshing.'

'That's not for you to say. You're making me angry again. I'm hanging up.' The line went dead. Shaking her head, Anna grabbed a half-finished bottle of spring water from the corner of her desk, unscrewed the cap, and took a swig. Gloria was impossible.

When she looked up, Gerry Licari was standing just outside her office, waving a white handkerchief. 'Truce?' he said meekly.

She laughed. 'Truce. Come on in, Gerry.'

He sat in the chair beside her desk. 'I've just realized what a jerk I've been.'

'You just realized it?' she said with a smile.

'I'm sorry, Anna. I overreacted. It's just that when you called Vera, I panicked.'

'I understand.'

'Actually,' he said, smiling, 'she told me she secretly thought it was kind of cool to be considered a murder suspect. How is it all going, by the way?'

She shrugged; she would tell him nothing.

'You don't have any leads?' he asked.

'No,' she replied, smiling but watching him carefully. He rose. 'Friends?'

'Always,' she said. When he put out his hand she shook it firmly, at the same time letting out a great yawn.

'Hey,' Gerry quipped, 'that reminds me of Vera on Saturday night!'

'I'm so sorry,' she said, covering her mouth in embarrassment. 'I don't know what's come over me. I'm suddenly so tired.'

'Go home. Get some rest.'

'Will do,' she said, and watched him as he went back out to the corridor toward his office. A few minutes later, he popped his head in and wished her a good night.

''Night,' she said, and yawned again.

He was right. She needed to go home and take a break from all this.

Her cell phone rang. It was Santos. 'Are we still on for tonight?'

'Tonight?'

'Anna, are you all right? You sound weird.'

'I'm just really tired. Forgive me, but I think I need to just stay home tonight.'

'Sure.' He sounded disappointed. 'If you change your mind and want some company, just give me a call.'

'OK,' she said, and as she closed her phone she was overcome by a wave of dizziness. 'So tired,' she said, and folded her arms and put her head down. She would have a quick nap and then make her way home…

She dreamed she was wrapped tightly in cotton wool and couldn't breathe through it. When she struggled to take in air, the cotton wool suffocated her and it smelled so very bad, like garbage. Then in her dream there was a terrible rumbling noise, as if made by the air as it tried to pass through the cotton wool…

She couldn't open her eyes but somehow, deep behind her dream, she knew she must, and she tried…tried…and got them open. She was in a dark place, surrounded by foul-smelling garbage; she would know that smell anywhere. The rumbling sound was here in her waking world, too, and as it continued, the garbage in which she lay tightened around her, encasing her…

I am in a garbage truck!

She tried to scream but nothing came out; her throat was so very dry. With all her might she tried again, and this time some sound came out—hoarse, but sound nevertheless. The garbage tightened around her, pressing into her, something sharp poking into the small of her back. She screamed again.

'Kelly, wait!' she heard from beyond the dark garbage. 'Stop it!'

The rumbling stopped.

'Back it up!'

The rumbling began again and the garbage receded. She could move more freely now. Soon the garbage was loose enough that it toppled down in front of her and she found herself looking into the horrified face of Brianna.

'Oh my—Kelly! Anna's in here!'

'What?'

Then both women were leaning into the truck, taking her by the arms and helping her out.

'Anna, who did this to you?' Kelly asked.

'I don't know,' Anna replied, and the garage began to swim. 'I…I'm fine…' And then the floor came up to meet her and she fell into Kelly's arms.

SHE OPENED HER EYES and saw Santos's face. She leaned forward suddenly and kissed him on the lips.

'Well!' he said happily. 'I guess you're feeling better.'

She was in a hospital bed, an IV in her arm. Beyond the window lay the darkening Manhattan skyline. 'What happened?'

'You were drugged, for starters. What did you drink yesterday afternoon?'

She searched her memory, shook her head. 'I don't—No, wait. I had a bottle of spring water.'

'Where?'

'On my desk.'

'For how long?'

She considered. 'All afternoon. I was drinking from it slowly.'

He nodded. 'Well, at some point when you weren't in your office, someone went in and slipped you a Mickey. The doctor thinks it was a sleeping syrup, probably chloral hydrate. That's why you were so tired when I called you. You passed out. Then whoever drugged you got you into the hopper of one of the collection trucks. It was the one parked nearest your office, so whoever did it wouldn't have had to move you far. Fortunately, Kelly and Brianna had the two-to-ten shift; otherwise you could have been in there all night.'

'I don't understand. If this person wanted me dead, why didn't he just come into my office and kill me? Why put me in the garbage truck?'

'Why do you think? Maybe because he hates you, didn't want you to die as easily as that—wanted you to die...like garbage. Or maybe he's showing us how smart he is—he can drug you and put you in the back of one of your own trucks without anyone noticing.'

'But how could he have gotten in? You can't just come through the front gate...except when socialites are arriving,' she joked, remembering how Dennis Ostrow had sailed in unchallenged on his motorcycle.

Santos said, 'Don't you remember your theory about the stack of boxes in the courtyard? Last time I looked, they were still there—you really should have them removed. Or who says this person would have had to get in? Maybe he was *already* in.'

She looked at him thoughtfully.

'Knock knock. Anybody home?'

They both turned. In the doorway stood George Mulligan, leaning on his cane. He walked slowly into the room. In his free hand he carried a bouquet of flowers, which he handed to Anna.

'Thank you, George. How did you know I was here?'

'I went to see you at the garage. Someone there said you were in the hospital.'

'I see. George, I'd like you to meet my boyfriend, Santos Reyes.'

The two men shook hands.

'You're a lucky man,' George told Santos.

Santos smiled. 'Yes, I am. All I have to do is keep her alive.'

'Ah, yes,' George said, nodding, and turned to Anna. 'I think,' he said quietly, 'it's time to stop.'

She frowned in bewilderment. 'Stop what?'

'Stop the investigation. That's why I went to see you at the garage. Though I appreciate your efforts, Anna— more than you'll ever know—I can't ask you to do this anymore, especially if you're ill.'

'I'm not ill,' she told him. 'At least, not anymore. Some-one drugged me yesterday afternoon and put me in a gar-bage truck. I nearly got compacted last night.'

He gaped at her in horror. 'Exactly my point, then. I was going to say you should stop because we weren't get-ting anywhere. Now I see that's not true. You've gotten close—dangerously close.'

And he doesn't even know about Willy attacking me. 'Which is why I can't stop now,' she said. 'Whoever killed Shari did this to me, and chances are good he works in the garage.' She shook her head. 'Tommy didn't do it and I won't leave him in that terrible place.'

George searched his pocket for a handkerchief and dabbed his eyes. 'Bless you. He sends you his best, by the way.'

'How is he?'

'Not well. It's a horrible, tough place. You would think jail would be safe, but it's the opposite. It's harder to sur-vive in there than on the outside. Colleen visited him for the first time yesterday and it went surprisingly well. But they miss each other terribly…and wonder if they will ever be married.'

'Of course they will. Tell them both to keep the faith,' she said. 'We're still on the case. And now,' she said, lift-ing her intubated arm, 'let's get a nurse in here to unhook me. I need to get out of here and change. We're having dinner at your brother's house tonight, Santos, in case you've forgotten.'

HECTOR ANSWERED the door in a cobbler style apron, a wooden spoon in his hand. 'Anna,' he said, and gave her a kiss on the cheek; then he gave his brother a one-armed hug. 'Thanks for coming. I'm not much of a cook, but what I lack in talent, I make up for in enthusiasm.'

Anna and Santos laughed.

'How about a glass of wine?' Hector asked them both. They both asked for white, and Hector hurried off to the kitchen.

'Is Libby here?' Anna asked Santos.

'I don't know,' he said. 'Let's go see.'

He led her down the apartment's narrow corridor and knocked on a door to the left.

'Enter!' came Libby's voice.

Santos opened the door and stepped back. A twin bed stood against the left wall. In the far right corner, Libby stood behind an easel, a palette in one hand, a long brush in the other. On a desk between the easel and the door she had set up a still life—apples, oranges, and grapes on an artfully draped white tablecloth.

'Hey, Anna. Hey, Uncle Santos,' she said, and dabbed at the canvas propped up on the easel.

'What's going on, Lib?' Santos asked.

She looked up from her work and smiled. 'Anna, remember what you said after the movie about getting past the bad stuff to get to the good stuff?'

Anna nodded.

'Well, I thought to myself, if I get the bad stuff done, why can't I have some of the good stuff now? So...*voilà!* There's the coolest art supply store on Seventieth Street.'

Hector appeared in the doorway with two glasses of white wine. 'Lib, honey, are you joining us for dinner?'

'Would you mind if I didn't, Dad? I'm in the middle

of a difficult part of my painting and I really don't want to stop.'

'That's fine,' Hector told her, and Anna and Santos followed him silently out of the room.

THE NEXT DAY, Anna rested. She had considered cancelling Lorraine's reading lesson that evening but had then thought better of it, not wanting to disappoint her.

The buzzer rang a couple of minutes after seven. Looking out her front window, Anna saw Jordan Canady's forest-green SUV taking off up the street.

When Lorraine arrived at the top of the hall stairs, limping slightly because of her bad knee, she was carrying a plate covered with aluminum foil. 'Pecan chocolate chip cookies,' she said, preceding Anna into the apartment. 'For us to enjoy with our tea.'

'How thoughtful,' Anna said, and set down the plate on the kitchen counter.

Lorraine turned to her, her face concerned. 'I heard you were sick yesterday. Is that why you weren't at work?' Anna nodded. 'Are you OK?'

'Oh, I'm fine,' Anna said, waving away her concern. 'Now let's get started. I've got a wonderful book for us to read this week.'

They sat together at the dining table. Anna handed Lorraine this week's book, and as Lorraine took it, Anna noticed a bracelet on the older woman's wrist—a shimmering twist of silver, violet, and gray seed beads.

'That's beautiful,' Anna said.

'Oh, thank you! I made it.'

'Really?'

'Mm-hm. It's crocheted beads, real popular now. I sell them; haven't I ever mentioned that?'

'No, I had no idea.'

Lorraine nodded. 'It's a way to make a little money on the side. I wear one of my creations every day—though not at the garage, of course.' She laughed. 'I always say, you've got to display your work, be an advertisement for what you do!' She opened the book to the first page. 'This one looks really fun, Anna.'

But Anna wasn't listening. Snatches of conversations, bits of information, floated around in her mind…and then fell into place like the pieces in a child's sliding tile puzzle.

Doctors need to showcase their work…

You've got to display your work, be an advertisement for what you do!

Paulette Edwards owned a nail salon…had long, elaborately painted nails…Those nails…

Before Anna even knew what she was doing, she turned to Lorraine and said, 'It was Paulette who scratched Jordan's face.'

Lorraine looked at her in bafflement. 'I beg your pardon?'

Like an automaton, Anna said, 'Jordan strangled Paulette.'

Now Lorraine's face grew hard and cold. Suddenly, with surprising agility, she jumped up from her chair, knocking it over, and scrambled for the kitchen. She began yanking open drawers, their contents flying; then she spun around and in her hand was one of Anna's large carving knives.

'Why couldn't you have left it alone?' she screamed, brandishing the knife, as a thumping sound came from beneath the floor. She took no notice. 'Why couldn't you have minded your own business? Jordan is all I have left. There is no way I'm going to lose him the way I lost Bradley.'

She smiled shrewdly, her eyes narrowing. 'That white

boy is going to take the blame for what I did—he can rot in prison, for all I care. As for you…I thought I'd gotten rid of you yesterday like the piece of garbage you are, but you seem to live a charmed life. Not anymore.' She advanced on Anna, knife-first. 'Don't you dare move or I'll cut your throat right here.' Her gaze fixed on Anna, she pulled a cell phone out of her pocket and pressed a button. 'I need you,' she said; 'she knows. Where are you?…Well, get up here, now.' She flipped the phone shut and dropped it back into her pocket. 'He's not far,' she told Anna.

They stood like that, motionless, for several minutes, during which Anna considered trying to kick the knife out of Lorraine's hand, but Lorraine was standing too close. She also considered kicking Lorraine, but even in pain the older woman would need only to push the knife forward a foot or two into Anna's throat.

A few feet from where they stood, the buzzer sounded. With her free hand Lorraine reached to the intercom and pressed the button, holding it down for several moments. Then there were footsteps on the stairs outside the apartment, followed by a soft knock on the door.

'You're going to let him in,' Lorraine said. 'Move.'

Anna walked toward the door, Lorraine and the huge knife behind her. As soon as she had thrown the last of the locks, Jordan pushed his way in, his face set in a cold expression. 'What do we do?' he asked his mother, and shot a glance at Anna.

'We're going to show her what we did to Paulette,' Lorraine said. 'Take this,' she ordered, handing him the knife. 'I'm going first. You walk behind her. Was there anyone downstairs?'

He shook his head. Where was Mrs Dovner when you needed her? Anna thought.

'Good,' Lorraine said. 'Let's go.'

They left the apartment and moved together down the stairs, Lorraine in front, Anna close behind her, and Jordan close behind Anna, the tip of the knife only inches from her back. At one point Lorraine nearly tripped on the stairs, which brought Anna up short and the tip of the knife pierced the skin of her back. She let out a gasp of pain.

Lorraine spun around. 'You keep your big mouth shut,' she whispered hoarsely, and continued downward to the vestibule. There, Lorraine hurried to the front door and looked out its window. 'There's nobody coming,' she said. 'Let's go.'

They marched her out the front door, down the steps, and into Jordan's SUV. Lorraine sat in the back with Anna. She had taken the knife from Jordan and now held it to Anna's neck.

Jordan drove to a quiet block on West Forty-Ninth Street. 'Park here,' Lorraine instructed him, and he took the first available space and killed the engine. 'Now get out and come around,' Lorraine said. 'Open her door.'

He did as he was told. 'Wait,' he told Anna before she could step out of the car, and he looked in both directions. When he was satisfied no people or cars were coming, he said, 'All right, get out slowly. Mom, keep the knife on her. We gotta go quickly.'

He led them about twenty yards along the sidewalk and then into a wide alley. Near the front of the alley sat a large Dumpster. Far at the back, against one of the buildings that formed the alley, was a complex of fire escapes, a ladder reaching nearly to the ground.

'Behind the Dumpster,' Lorraine ordered.

Back here, Anna had no trouble understanding how Jordan could have strangled Paulette without anyone on the street noticing. The Dumpster was a virtual wall, its sides only a few feet from the alley's walls.

'Hold her up against the Dumpster,' Lorraine told Jordan, who spun Anna around, grabbed her wrists, and held them over her head.

Lorraine handed the knife to Jordan and advanced slowly on Anna.

She's going to strangle me.

In a sudden movement, Lorraine grabbed the front of Anna's shirt and ripped it open, buttons flying. 'You thought I was going to strangle you first,' Lorraine said with a laugh, as if she'd read Anna's mind. 'No such luck. Like I told you, we're going to show you what we did to Paulette.'

She grabbed the knife back from Jordan and came toward Anna, aiming the point at the exposed flesh of Anna's chest. Jordan chuckled, his eyes aflame. 'Oh yeah...'

Lorraine stuck the tip of the knife into Anna. Searing pain shot through her and she tried to cry out, but Lorraine had clamped her hand hard over Anna's mouth.

'That's one line,' Lorraine said, and brought her face up close to Anna's. 'What do you think so far?'

'All right, drop it!'

The man's voice had come from the right; Anna turned her head slightly and saw a police officer standing near the wall, gun drawn. 'I said, drop the knife,' he said, and Lorraine let it drop; it fell to the pavement with a clang. 'All right, now back away from her, both of you.'

Before Lorraine and Jordan had stepped back more than a few feet, two other officers appeared from the other side of the Dumpster and grabbed them, pulling their hands behind their backs and handcuffing them.

'Are you all right?' the first officer asked Anna; then he saw the blood. 'Guess not.' He called to someone at the street. 'Get a bus!' Then he took her gently by the arm and began to steer her toward the sidewalk. 'It's a good thing we got here when we did,' he said.

'But how did you know?' she asked him.

In answer, he pointed toward their right. There, standing on the sidewalk in her housecoat and pink fluffy slippers, was Mrs Dovner. Leaning on her cane, she made her way slowly over.

'This lady called us,' the officer explained.

Mrs Dovner nodded. 'I heard noise in the hall and opened my door a crack to see who it was.'

Nosy as ever, Anna thought.

'I saw him'—she indicated Jordan, who was being pushed into one of the cruisers parked at the curb— 'holding a knife to your back. So I called the police, told them to look for the dark-green SUV. I gave the police the license plate number.'

'Thank you, Mrs Dovner,' Anna said.

Mrs Dovner shrugged; then the corners of her mouth lifted in a tiny smile. 'I told you those people were trouble.'

TWENTY-FIVE

AT A BACK BOOTH at Sammy's Coffee Corner, Anna smiled across the table at Santos as she took his hand. With her other hand she delicately touched the thick bandage taped to her chest.

'Are you ready to fill me in?' he said.

She nodded. Jordan Canady had confessed to everything, and this confession had enabled Anna to fill in the gaps in her story.

'I'll start with the murder of Paulette Edwards,' she said, and took a deep breath. 'On the night of April seventeenth, she closed up her nail salon and walked along West Forty-Ninth Street toward home. As Jordan said in his confession, he had felt an urge to kill a woman for some time. He had noticed Paulette on the street more than a week earlier and had watched her each evening since, waiting for the right time. On this night, as she approached the alley where he was hiding, Jordan saw that at this particular moment the block was otherwise deserted. The right time had come. Just as Paulette passed, he darted out of the alley and grabbed her.

'They struggled, Paulette scratching Jordan's face. But she was no match for the strong young man. He strangled her. He took a valuable ring from her finger. Then he dumped her body in a Dumpster at the entrance to the alley.

'The next morning, Lorraine noticed the ring on Jordan's dresser. She confronted him. Eventually he admitted what he'd done.

'Lorraine was terrified. Not that Jordan had committed murder, but that there was a possibility she would lose him as she had lost her husband, Bradley, who as we know is serving a twenty-five-year sentence at Sing Sing for assault. Like father, like son. Lorraine wasn't about to lose her son, and she would do anything necessary to make sure she didn't.

'She had to make sure nothing connected Jordan to the murder. She had an idea. She made him take her to the Dumpster where he had left Paulette's body. Fortunately for them, it was still there. They had brought a step stool with them. While Jordan stood watch, Lorraine climbed into the Dumpster and carved an ankh into Paulette's chest to make her murder look like the work of the Ankh Killer.

'But there was one problem—a big one. Someone saw Jordan kill Paulette: Shari Baird. She was at the back of the alley, checking out the place where Tommy had told her she would be able to break into a building without being detected because of the shielding Dumpster. She followed Jordan home.

'A few days later, after Jordan and Lorraine thought they were in the clear, Shari approached Jordan on the street near his apartment. She told him she had seen him strangle Paulette and that if he didn't want her to tell the police, he would have to pay her. He agreed to meet her again, then hurried home and told his mother about Shari's blackmail. To Lorraine, the solution was simple: get rid of Shari.

'Jordan met Shari and gave her a small initial payment, promising more money soon. Then it was he who followed her...all the way to Manhattan Central Thirteen garage. He told Lorraine that was where Shari worked.

'Lorraine was already in the city's Work Exchange Program, cleaning in other Sanitation garages. She urged her crew chief to send her to Manhattan Central Thirteen, explaining that because it was closer to where she lived, walking there would be easier on her bad knee. He agreed, and Lorraine reported for work at my garage. Now all she had to do was wait for the right moment...

'It came on the morning of April twenty-third, when Lorraine saw Shari go out to the courtyard for a smoke. No one else had seen Shari go out there. Lorraine would go out for a smoke, too.

'But there was a problem: Lorraine was out of cigarettes. She went in search of someone to ask, and came upon Caitlin near the door to the break room stairs. Lorraine knew Caitlin smoked. But Caitlin, who was still angry at Lorraine for complaining that she was doing all of Caitlin's work, refused to give her a cigarette. Not wanting to miss her opportunity, Lorraine hurried out to the courtyard anyway.

'Shari, of course, had no idea Lorraine was Jordan's mother. Lorraine approached Shari, asking her for a cigarette and a light. Shari gave her a cigarette and lit it for her. In the next instant Lorraine had her hands around Shari's throat, strangling her.

'Rather than simply leaving Shari's body where it lay, Lorraine hid it under one of the large, empty wooden crates stacked against the courtyard wall. Lorraine wasn't finished with Shari yet. As with Paulette Edwards, she had had an idea. She would find another safe moment to return. She left the courtyard and re-entered the garage. Just inside the door, she stubbed out her cigarette and returned to her cleaning.

'She found another safe moment a short time later. Hurrying back out to the courtyard, she dragged Shari's body out from under the crate, tore open her shirt, and carved an ankh into her chest. Like the ankh she had carved into Paulette, this one wasn't quite right, the vertical stroke the same size as the horizontal one, rather than longer as it should have been. After Lorraine had carved the mark into Shari's flesh, she hurried back into the garage.

'That night, Lorraine told Jordan that carving the ankh into Shari's body had been a stroke of genius. Another ankh killing would make what she and Jordan had done to Paulette's body all the more credible.

'A short time after Lorraine had carved the ankh into Shari and returned to the garage, Tommy went out to the courtyard for his appointment with Shari. Finding her dead—murdered—he panicked. He and Shari had been seen arguing. He had been overheard threatening to kill her. He knew he would be blamed. He ran back into the garage, passing Brianna, who was on her way out to the courtyard for a cigarette. Brianna found Shari dead and screamed for help. Tommy, in the meantime, changed his clothes and fled. He got on a subway headed north. That's where the police found and arrested him.'

Santos frowned. 'But what did Caitlin have to do with all of this? I don't see…'

'Wait,' Anna said. 'I'm not finished yet.' She took a sip of coffee and thoughtfully set down her cup.

'Let's back up a bit, to when Lorraine first saw Shari go out to the courtyard. Lorraine asked Caitlin for a cigarette. Caitlin turned her down. Lorraine went out to the courtyard anyway.

'What Lorraine didn't know was that after refusing her a cigarette, Caitlin sat down to rest at a place in the garage *that had a view of the courtyard door.* She saw Lorraine come back in from the courtyard *and put out a cigarette.* How, Caitlin wondered, had Lorraine gotten a cigarette, when she had just said she was out of them and asked Caitlin for one?'

Santos raised his index finger. 'Couldn't Lorraine have asked for a cigarette even if she had some of her own? People have been known to do that.'

'I've thought of that. Caitlin would have thought that was unlikely. After all, she and Lorraine had been fighting lately; Lorraine had nothing but contempt for this young woman who she considered a spoiled, lazy brat who didn't do her share of work. Lorraine would have spoken to Caitlin no more than necessary. Also, Lorraine's considerable pride would have prevented her from asking for a cigarette unless she absolutely had to.

'So Caitlin was puzzled, curious. When Lorraine was gone, Caitlin slipped out to the courtyard to see who had given Lorraine the cigarette...but no one was there, of course, since Lorraine had hidden Shari's body under the crate. This discrepancy would continue to trouble Caitlin...

'In the meantime, Lorraine kept an eye on me as I tried to clear Tommy of Shari's murder. Lorraine couldn't believe her luck when I offered to teach her to read. Now she could keep an even closer eye on me, right in my own home.

'It took two weeks for Caitlin to realize the meaning of what she had seen in the garage. It came to her, of all places, at the Parisienne boutique, where she had gone after leaving the garage. When a woman in the dressing room next to Caitlin's moaned that she was dying for a cigarette, Caitlin playfully tossed one over the wall. When the woman didn't react, Caitlin came out of the dressing room and was told that the woman *wasn't there*.

'Cigarette...*wasn't there*...

'Suddenly Caitlin knew. Agitated, she grabbed her cell phone and called me at the garage. What she said was: "She had a cigarette, but no one was there!" But as Ellen Guest at the boutique later told me, the shop is in a "dead zone" and our phone connection was poor.'

Anna looked down sadly. 'I repeated what I could make out—*Cigarette...No one there*—and thereby sealed Caitlin's fate. What I didn't know was that Lorraine was outside my office, about to start cleaning the floor of the corridor. She overheard me. *She* knew immediately what Caitlin was trying to tell me. Now someone else had to die. I heard a sound outside my office and went to see who it was, but there was no one there; Lorraine had quickly slipped away.

'Lorraine rushed home to Jordan and told him what she had heard. Caitlin must be eliminated—the quicker the better, to reduce her chances of reaching me. Once again, Lorraine had an idea. Jordan would attend Caitlin's party at the Rose that evening. Jordan is an exceedingly handsome young man and dresses well. Lorraine made sure he was dressed expensively that night and that he arrived early to get a place near the head of the line outside the club. Fortunately for Lorraine and Jordan—unfortunately for Caitlin—the bouncers allowed him in. Jordan had a knife concealed in the inside of his sport coat.

'The club, as you recall, was packed so tightly with people—more than three thousand of them—that it was literally impossible to move. Jordan positioned himself near the platform in the center of the club, knowing Caitlin was likely to come down at some point. And she did, when she tried to reach me to introduce me to the crowd.

'It was a simple matter for Jordan to press himself up against Caitlin and slide the knife into her. Poor Caitlin was dead almost immediately, but her body was carried along for a moment by the solid mass of people...until someone saw the blood, the crowd parted, and Caitlin's body fell to the floor, the knife protruding from her back.'

Anna shook her head, her eyes moist. 'So much death... So many clues...'

'How, exactly, did you put it all together?' Santos asked.

'It was during Lorraine's reading lesson last night. When I admired a bracelet she was wearing, she told me she made and sold them, and that she wore one of her creations whenever possible, because *you've got to display your work, be an advertisement for what you do.* I remembered that Gloria had said something similar when she told me Donald was going to do some work on her face: *Doctors have to showcase their work!*

'That made me think of Paulette Edwards. She had owned a nail salon. In her photographs, you could see her long, elaborately painted nails. They were *her* advertisement. Thinking of nails made me think of something that had been bothering me, though perhaps not completely consciously. When Jordan picked up his mother at my apartment after her first reading lesson, he had a cat in a carrier in the back of his SUV. That explained the scratch on his face. But something about that troubled me. Now I knew what it was: Jordan's scratch was dark, not fresh. The cat could not have made it that day. The whole vet story was a means of explaining the mark on Jordan's face—the mark Paulette Edwards had made as she struggled for her life...

'As I said, everything came together as I sat with Lorraine. The truth so stunned me that before I knew it, I was speaking my realization aloud. Now I had to die, too.

'Snoopy Mrs Dovner, true to form, saw Lorraine and Jordan march me out of my building at knifepoint and called the police.' She laughed. 'I guess it's fair to say Mrs Dovner saved my life.'

Santos winked at her. 'We'll have to make sure she knows that.'

Anna smiled. 'Don't you dare.'

TWENTY-SIX

IN HIS RENTED basement room on West Thirty-Seventh Street, the Ankh Killer put down his newspaper, his face set grimly. Now he knew who the copycats were; they had been caught. Lorraine Canady, who had actually carved the ankhs into Paulette Edwards and Shari Baird, was being held on Rikers Island in one of the women's facilities. It would be difficult to get to her—not impossible, but difficult. Her son, Jordan, on the other hand, would be easy to reach. He would be the first to pay for what he and his mother had done.

The Ankh Killer knew Rikers Island well. He had spent a lot of time there over the years. Several of the guards had been sympathetic to his plight, doing him favors, bringing him special items like food, cigarettes, drugs. There weren't many guards like that, but when you found one, he was worth his weight in gold. All it took was money, and the Ankh Killer had plenty of that.

He could think of no reason why one of these guards wouldn't do him one more favor...

With his right hand he stroked Bastet, purring on the sofa beside him. With his left hand he picked up the phone.

AT 8:37 A.M., THE ANKH KILLER sat on the shuttle bus to Rikers Island. Beside him sat a heavy Hispanic woman who cried during the entire ride. At least whoever you're visiting today will still be alive when you leave, thought the Ankh Killer.

Looking out his window, he saw the familiar bill-board near the entrance to the bridge. CITY OF NEW YORK—CORRECTION DEPARTMENT, RIKERS ISLAND—THE BOLDEST CORRECTION OFFICERS IN THE WORLD. He smiled.

Inside the Control Building, he didn't see his friend at first. Then he appeared, sober-faced, standing behind two other guards. He and the Ankh Killer made eye contact. His friend gave an almost imperceptible nod.

After security, everyone made for the buses that would take them to their inmates' buildings. The Ankh Killer left the crowd and slipped into the men's room. He took the middle stall and waited.

Nearly ten minutes later he heard the men's room door open, heard footsteps. The door of the stall to his left opened and closed and he saw a pair of shiny black shoes. Then a soft parcel wrapped in a plastic shopping bag was pushed toward him under the wall. Opening it, he smiled at the hat and the fresh, clean uniform, which he hung for the moment on the hook on the door of the stall. Then came the knife; it slid toward him and did a little spin. He placed it carefully on top of the toilet paper dispenser for now. Then came the small roll of plastic tape. Finally came the length of rope; he placed it on top of the knife.

He pushed the empty plastic bag back under the wall. The hand that grabbed it then grabbed his hand and shook it warmly. The Ankh Killer squeezed back. What would the world be without friends?

He left the men's room first, as they had agreed. Back in the hectic hallway, he walked briskly, no one taking any notice of one more prison guard...

Nor did anyone think twice as he entered the long, low Eric M. Taylor Center, passed the front desk, and made his way toward the dormitory-style inmate housing.

He found Jordan Canady cleaning in one of the shower

rooms. The young man was on his knees in a corner, quietly scrubbing away. The Ankh Killer approached him. 'How's it going, son?'

Jordan looked at the Ankh Killer's shiny black shoes, then returned his attention to his cleaning. 'It would go a lot faster if you'd leave me alone,' he muttered.

'Get up.'

Now Jordan looked up at him. 'Huh?'

'I said get up.'

Slowly Jordan stood, then positioned himself directly in front of the Ankh Killer, an insolent expression on his handsome face.

'This way,' the Ankh Killer said, and indicated a row of toilet stalls facing the showers.

Looking puzzled, Jordan walked ahead of the Ankh Killer and stopped in front of the stalls, unsure what to do. The Ankh Killer opened the door of one of the middle stalls and motioned for Jordan to go in.

'Oh, now you want me to clean toilets?' Jordan shook his head as if to say, 'What kind of place is this?' Then he walked slowly into the stall. 'I'm gonna need a brush.'

'I have what you need,' the Ankh Killer said, and looking quickly right and left to make sure no one was around, he followed Jordan into the stall. Once inside the cramped space he moved quickly, shutting and locking the door.

Jordan spun around. 'What the——?'

'Turn around.'

'What?'

'Turn around!' the Ankh Killer repeated, keeping his voice low.

Reluctantly, Jordan turned to face the toilet. Immediately the Ankh Killer grabbed the younger man's arms and yanked them hard behind him. Jordan let out a yelp of pain.

'Be quiet,' the Ankh Killer said, holding Jordan's wrists together with one hand and getting the rope from his pocket with the other. He tied Jordan's wrists tightly together.

'Turn around again,' the Ankh Killer ordered, and when Jordan didn't obey, he spun him hard around. 'Do you know who I am?' he demanded through clenched teeth, his face inches from Jordan's.

'Yeah, you're a crazy person,' Jordan said, and drew in breath to cry out for help.

He never got to finish the breath. The Ankh Killer smacked a length of tape across his mouth, sealing it completely shut. Jordan's eyes bulged as he struggled to breathe through his nose. But that would do no good, because in the next instant the Ankh Killer's strong hands were at his neck, squeezing hard. Jordan made a guttural noise, his chest heaving as he tried desperately to draw air through his constricted throat.

'No,' the Ankh Killer said, maintaining his stranglehold. 'I'm the man you stole from. *I* didn't kill Paulette and Shari—you and your fat mother did. How dare you copy me...make a mockery of my sacrifices?' He shook Jordan's neck. 'You didn't even do it right, not even close.' He released his grip. Jordan's chest wheezed as he frantically drew in air through his nose. As he did, the Ankh Killer grabbed the front of his gray jump-suit and with a strong sharp motion tore it down the middle.

'Here,' the Ankh Killer said, bringing the knife close to Jordan's smooth, muscular chest. 'Let me show you how it's done.'

Jordan struggled and moaned, his eyes wild. The Ankh Killer stuck the knife into the center of his chest and bore down, cutting deeply. Blood spurted from the incision. Jordan tried to kick out his foot, but the space was cramped

and the Ankh Killer was pushing him backwards so that
he landed on the toilet. As the Ankh Killer moved closer,
Jordan leaned back, trying to escape the blade. But there
was nowhere to go.

The Ankh Killer now made the horizontal stroke; fresh
blood sluiced down. From behind the tape came Jordan's
muffled scream.

'Almost done,' the Ankh Killer said, smiling, and with
a sudden movement of his wrist he gouged out the circle
of the ankh. Then, as Jordan's eyes rolled backward in response to the exquisite pain, the Ankh Killer pocketed the
knife and returned his hands to Jordan's throat. 'Oh—one
more thing,' he said softly. 'You have to die now.'

Now he squeezed even tighter than before. Jordan's
chest heaved as he struggled…and then at last he visibly
relaxed, his last smothered cry fading away. As the life
ebbed from him, the Ankh Killer watched his eyes.

'Yes,' said the Ankh Killer, inhaling deeply. 'Yes. The
life that leaves you flows into me… From you to me… Yes.'

Twenty minutes later, the Ankh Killer was on the
shuttle heading back over the bridge to Queens. Turning
slightly in his seat, he shot a glance back at Rikers Island
and smiled a slow, satisfied smile.

'To ANNA!' Tommy said, raising his champagne glass. On
his left, his fiancée, pretty Colleen, wiped tears from her
eyes and raised her glass. On Tommy's other side, George
Mulligan, eyes equally moist, held his glass in Anna's
direction and mouthed the words, 'Thank you.'

Afterward, Colleen came up to Anna. 'I don't know
how to thank you.'

'There's no need,' Anna said, and the two women embraced.

'Come, talk to me,' Colleen said, and they sat on a sofa

on a quieter side of George and Tommy Mulligan's living room. 'I want to ask you something.'

Anna smiled, nodded.

'What was Shari like?'

Anna frowned, not understanding.

Colleen said, 'I mean, was she the heartless monster everyone's making her out to be?'

'An unequivocal yes to that. Why?'

Colleen wrinkled her brows and gazed down into the bubbles of her champagne. 'This may not make any sense to you. I know Tommy was unfaithful to me, and I'll never talk about it again. But I'll think about it. And when I do, I'd like to think Shari was such a manipulative monster that Tommy—well, that he wasn't really himself when he...when they...'

'I know what you're saying. You want the comfort of knowing that she had cast such a spell over him that he didn't really have any choice.'

Colleen smiled. 'Exactly...Is that true, Anna?' she asked, hope in her eyes.

Anna looked at her frankly. 'Actually, it is. Shari cast her spell over a lot of people. But it was a bad spell. She was beautiful and enticing. She was also completely amoral; you don't come across people like that very often.'

Santos and George came over to where the two women were sitting.

'I had no idea this boyfriend of yours was such a whizz in the kitchen,' George said, looking at Santos. 'He's promised to teach me how to make *lechón asado*.'

Colleen grinned. 'We can serve it at the wedding!'

As if on cue, Tommy joined the group. 'Serve what?' he asked, smiling.

'Cuban roast pork,' Anna told him.

'Deal,' Tommy said, and in the next moment his eyes

filled with tears that overflowed and ran down his cheeks. 'I'm sorry,' he said, embarrassed, and wiped his eyes with a napkin.

George put his arm around his son's shoulder and squeezed him tight. 'Tears of happiness are always welcome.'

'To tears of happiness!' Anna said, raising her glass. To her surprise, everyone in the room joined in the toast. When she lowered her glass, she realized she was crying, too.

LATER, ANNA AND SANTOS said their goodbyes and caught a cab outside.

'I found myself tearing up in there,' Santos said as they headed downtown.

Anna smiled and snuggled up against him. 'Softie.'

'Oh, by the way,' he said, remembering. 'I got a call during the party. I've got some information to pass along to you.'

She raised her brows enquiringly.

'Dennis Ostrow has been arrested as an accessory to the murder of Lok Huang. Half a million dollars' worth of diamonds have been found hidden under the floor of his rented room.

'They've also arrested Jocelyn Paar and her crew—two women and two men. They were caught breaking into the back of a curio shop in the Wing Fat Shopping Arcade in Chinatown.'

Anna nodded in satisfaction.

Santos's cell phone began to ring; he pulled it from his jacket pocket, opened it, and listened. After a few moments he said, 'All right, thanks for letting me know,' and snapped the phone shut. He looked at Anna. 'Jordan Canady was just found murdered at Rikers.'

She sat up. 'What?'

He nodded. 'Apparently someone got into the prison—they don't know how yet—and killed Jordan in the men's room where he was cleaning.'

'How was he killed?'

'Strangled…and there was an ankh carved into his chest. One other thing, too. It's strange…'

She looked at him.

'He was found with his arms pulled tightly behind his back and his hands tied together.'

'What's today's date?' Anna asked suddenly.

'What?'

'The date.'

He frowned. 'It's May twenty-fourth. Why?'

She nodded slowly, her eyes unfocused. 'The God with Hands and Arms Concealed…' she murmured softly.

Santos hadn't heard her. 'I suppose it's justice,' he said.

But Anna shook her head. 'Evil justice,' she said, and peered out into the bright sparkling Manhattan night, knowing the Ankh Killer was still out there.

* * * * *

REQUEST YOUR FREE BOOKS!

2 FREE NOVELS
PLUS 2 FREE GIFTS!

WORLDWIDE LIBRARY®
Your Partner in Crime